W9-BTH-704

HELL'S HIGHWAY

by
Gerri Hill

Bella
BOOKS

2011

Bella Books, Inc.
P.O. Box 10543
Tallahassee, FL 32302

Printed in the United States of America on acid-free paper
First published 2011

Editor: Anna Chinappi
Cover Designer: Judy Fellows

ISBN 13: 978-1-59493-260-1

PUBLISHER'S NOTE

Other Bella Books by Gerri Hill

CHAPTER ONE

"Will you hold still? I swear you're worse than a child."

Cameron winced as Andrea pulled out another stitch. "Need I remind you that you are neither a doctor nor a nurse," she said.

Andrea looked up, giving her an incredulous look. "You have more scars than I can count and a penchant for jumping off cliffs and you're complaining about my nursing skills?"

"It hurts."

"Big baby," Andrea murmured as she cut through another one.

"And two cliffs do not make a *penchant*," she countered. "Besides, this one was not my fault."

"No? Sticking with the rattlesnake story, are you?"

"I'm telling you, it was seven feet long, easy."

Andrea smiled, then leaned closer and kissed her. "Then I'm glad you jumped. I'm just thankful there wasn't a nasty cactus at the bottom like in Sedona." She patted her arm. "All done. Let's see if we can go a month without having to do this again."

Cameron looked at the wound on her arm, now healed. It wasn't much of a cut and if Andrea hadn't been around, she knew she wouldn't have even bothered with a doctor. But Andrea was around and ten stitches later, they were on their way. That was nine days ago as they'd left the canyons of Utah and headed for the cooler climate of Colorado while they waited for their next assignment.

She watched with a sense of contentment as Andrea scooped up Lola and kissed her before putting the purring black kitten on Cameron's lap. She wasn't certain how much longer she could refer to her as a kitten—she was growing so fast. She ran her fingers through the soft fur, reflecting on the last six weeks since they'd left Sedona. It still amazed her how easily she and Andrea had eased into their new life together.

They worked well as a team. That was obvious from the Patrick Doe case in Sedona. Murdock had given her the okay to add Andrea to their team despite his reservations, and their partnership continued to flourish. But it was their personal life, here in the motor home, which surprised her. They were able to separate the two whenever they were in the company of others. It was unspoken, yet they slipped into their professional roles without many disagreements. But once back here, they reverted back to Cameron and Andrea, friends and lovers still learning to coexist in this tiny space they shared with one spoiled cat.

"How soon before Murdock sends us out on another case?" Andrea asked as she started on their dinner.

"Hard to say. One time I went three weeks. Why?"

"I really need to get back to Sedona and do something with my stuff. Not that there's much, but I do need more clothes."

Cameron eyed the faded jeans she wore, her gaze lingering. Something about the sway of Andrea's hips had mesmerized her from the beginning. She looked up guiltily as Andrea cleared her throat.

"You're checking out my ass? Seriously Cameron?"

Cameron felt her face blush and she laughed. "What? I can't do that anymore?"

Andrea's expression softened and she walked over, leaning down to kiss her gently. She pulled away with a smile, then brushed the hair on Cameron's forehead affectionately.

"You can check out my ass any time you want. I love you, you know."

Cameron nodded. "Me too."

Andrea's gaze held hers for a moment longer, then she returned to the kitchen. Cameron's mind flashed back to earlier that afternoon when they'd come back from a short hike, only to find themselves in bed, satisfying the sexual need that had taken hold of them while they were out. Innocent touches, a brush of a hand, lingering glances, finally a kiss—all igniting the fire that seemed to always linger just below the surface. Cameron had to stop herself from taking Andrea right there next to the tree she had her pinned against. Andrea wouldn't have minded, she knew, as her hands had already crept under Cameron's shirt with a purpose. Andrea's eyes had been filled with heated desire as Cameron pulled away from her, nearly dragging her back to the motor home for their afternoon tryst.

Her musings came to an end as a soft beeping on the console told her Murdock was calling. She slipped on her headphones before answering.

"Cameron Ross," she said.

"Please hold," came the pleasantly animated voice of the automated secretary Murdock now used.

"Of course," she said, half expecting the computer to answer her.

"Cameron? Not interrupting anything, I hope."

"Now Murdock, what in the world would you possibly be interrupting?"

"Oh, Cameron," he said with a quiet laugh. "I know we did a rush job on getting Sullivan her credentials, but her file finally crossed my desk."

"And?"

"And I'm assuming you took the photo that was submitted?"

"Yeah. And?" she asked, glancing at Andrea who was pretending not to listen to the conversation.

"And you're going to tell me this is strictly a *professional* arrangement?"

"Of course, Murdock. I know the rules for that sort of thing. You think I'd buck that?" She grinned at Andrea who had stopped pretending not to listen and now had turned around and leaned on the counter, blatantly watching her.

"I'm not even going to answer that, Cameron. Let's do a video conference. It's time I met her face to face. Besides, I've got some news. Five minutes."

The call ended and Cameron removed her headset, a shy smile directed at Andrea. "Video conference. He wants to officially meet you."

"Are we in trouble?"

"No. Rules are rules and he knows I break most of them. I'm sure he's just curious, that's all." She flipped open her laptop, logging in quickly. "Five minutes," she said.

"I'll hold off on dinner then. I was just going to do a quick veggie burger and fries."

Cameron wrinkled up her nose. "We could order pizza."

Andrea made a face at her. "I draw the line at three times a week. Besides, I think we're a little out of reach of pizza delivery. Thank God," she added.

It was an ongoing battle with them—Cameron trying to see how many times a week she could get her beloved pizza and Andrea trying to get her to eat a little more variety. Before she could offer a retort, two quick beeps signaled that Murdock had logged in to their session. She smiled as his face came into focus.

"Hi Murdock, you're looking well."

"Thank you, Cameron. As are you."

Cameron held Lola in her lap. "You've met Lola, of course," she said, stroking the kitten's fur.

"Yes, your little tiger. How about I meet your new partner?"

Cameron motioned for Andrea to join her on the loveseat. "Andrea, come meet the boss."

Andrea smiled easily. "Special Agent Murdock, a pleasure to finally meet you."

"Deputy Sullivan," he said with a nod. "Or should I say *Agent* Sullivan. Welcome to the team."

"Thank you."

"I must commend you. I had nothing but compliments from the authorities at Canyonlands. Even in regard to Ross here. That's a first. I'll credit you with keeping her in line."

"I have found she's mostly all bark and no bite," Andrea said.

"Must you two discuss me as if I'm not here?" Cameron asked, feigning annoyance.

"Well, Special Agent Ross, it's just rare that I send you on an assignment and I don't receive a dozen complaints about you. Mostly from our own team," he added with a smile.

Her eyebrows shot up. "*Special* Agent Ross?"

"Yes. Our group finally warrants recognition, it seems. They've bumped up our status to that of real agents." His smile turned into a smirk. "We have more clout than they do and we finally get equal billing. And I have a title change as well. Director of Operations."

"A director, huh?"

He nodded. "They had to come up with something. That's the only thing that's changing. Andrea is technically on probation, so her title won't change for six months. And I'll have you know I had to pull some strings just for that. They apparently weren't impressed by her LAPD training." He looked directly at Andrea. "No offense."

"None taken."

"Are you finding the arrangements satisfactory? I'm sure it's a little cramped in there for the two of you." His eyes drifted to Cameron's lap. "And a cat."

"We've managed fine," Andrea said, with just a hint of a smile. "If we didn't get along so well, it might make it difficult."

"Yes, well, it was a rather rushed job. And a surprise. Ross was never one for partners. I was shocked she requested one now."

Cameron felt a hot blush light up her face as Andrea turned

suspicious eyes on her. She had told Andrea that Murdock was the one who insisted she take a partner, not the other way around.

"Really? Well that explains why she's so bossy then," Andrea said, her eyes questioning.

Cameron cleared her throat. "Have we had enough chit-chat? I assume you have an assignment," she said.

"Unfortunately, yes. Where are you? Still in Utah?"

"We're in southern Colorado," she said. "Just outside of Durango."

"I'll need you to head west," he said. "Two weeks ago a headless body was found twelve miles east of Barstow, California, along I-40," he said matter-of-factly. "Unidentified female, naked. She was wrapped in a brown plastic tarp and dumped in the desert. A motorist stopped with a flat tire found her."

"And the motorist has been cleared?"

"Thoroughly. Yesterday, a second body was found. This one just outside the boundary of Joshua Tree National Monument. Same as the first. Naked. No head."

"Okay, help me with my geography. I'm assuming they're close together?"

"Joshua Tree hits I-10 on its southern border," Andrea supplied. "But the northern part would be closer to I-40. They're both in the Mojave Desert, although Joshua Tree creeps into a southern desert—Colorado Desert, I believe."

"I forgot you're from LA, of course," Murdock said. "You're more familiar with that area than I am. The second body was found along I-10 near what they call the Cactus City rest area—near Indio—which I'm told is a major stopping point for travelers," he said. "So the two sites aren't that close."

"So another serial killer," Cameron said. "Great."

"I don't know if either of you are familiar with the FBI's investigation of the Highway Serial Killings. They have a huge database that I've given both of you access to. The concentration is mainly along I-40, east of Oklahoma City. The database covers every body found dumped along an interstate highway. There are well over four hundred, if that gives you any idea," he said.

"So multiple killers, obviously," Andrea said.

"Yes. There could be dozens. But the two bodies found in

the desert are obviously linked. It'll give you a chance to play with your algorithms again, Cameron."

"Long-haul truckers?" Cameron asked. "That would seem obvious. They almost exclusively use the interstates."

"Most likely."

"Don't most trucks have GPS tracking now so their companies can keep up with them?" Andrea asked.

Murdock nodded. "Yes. However, there are thousands of companies and getting access to their records would require subpoenas if they weren't willing to volunteer the information. Not to mention the small companies which don't have GPS tracking. And then there are individual owners of trucks who contract out. It's an endless search."

"So the database is for information only?"

"They've been able to link some murders and they've arrested a few. Very few. I'll email you the links and you can take a look yourself."

"Okay. So who do we contact?"

"Riverside County Sheriff's Department is investigating the one in Cactus City. They have a substation and a coroner in Indio who did the autopsy. San Bernardino County Sheriff's Department is looking into the one found near Barstow. The county coroner did the post. I'll email you both files."

"And both victims are unidentified?" Cameron asked.

"Yes. One age eighteen to twenty-two. The other, twenty-five to thirty."

"Both departments know we're coming?"

"Yes. And from what I understand, they are both happy to hand it over to you. It's a cold case as far as they are concerned."

"So we have no resources?"

"I'm afraid you won't have the sheriff's department at your beck and call like you did in Sedona, no," he said. "For the investigation, we're on our own. They'll assist, of course, with backup if necessary. But both of these are very large counties, not only in population but also square miles. They're stretched thin. The bodies were found in remote, unpopulated areas in the desert. They've done a check through Missing Persons but without a face, it's pretty useless. Frankly, there's not much to go on."

"And you naturally thought of me," Cameron said. "Thanks, Murdock."

"Well, I figured you were getting bored since you wrapped up the Canyonlands case so fast. By the way, I talked to your guy Jason at Quantico. He said to give him a call if you needed to do some searching in the database. He worked on the design of it. He said you can incorporate what you use now for your algorithms with it."

"That's what he said, huh?"

Murdock grinned. "No. He spewed off some technical mumbo jumbo crap but that's what I deduced from it."

Cameron nodded. "Are we on our own with the motor home too? Or do you have someplace in mind where we can park her?"

"I'm sorry but I don't. There's federal land all over out there, but everything is so remote, I have no idea where you'll want to be. When you find a spot, let me know. I can make arrangements for you, even in protected areas."

"Okay, Murdock. We'll head out in the morning."

He nodded. "One more thing. Reynolds is putting together his own team. He's taken Jack from Collie's old unit, the others are new. I've got him on standby for this one."

"Come on, Murdock. You know I don't—"

"You don't have a choice, Special Agent Ross," he said. "If these young women end up being locals, you're not exactly the one we want talking to the media."

Cameron rolled her eyes. "You're sending a whole team in to handle the media? That's about all they did in Phoenix, they should be good at it."

"Reynolds *is* good at it. Besides, I'm hoping this will be low profile. Unidentified victims won't have family members demanding answers. Reynolds and his team need something to get their feet wet with."

"Surely you don't expect *me* to handle that?"

"For some odd reason, Reynolds took a liking to you, despite the complaints he had about you. That's a first. I thought I'd take advantage of it."

"I don't want some newbie of a team following me around," she said. "I work alone."

"Then why did you insist you needed a partner?"

Cameron glanced sheepishly at Andrea, then back to Murdock. "Okay. Fine," she conceded.

Murdock laughed. "Like I said, Reynolds is on standby. I haven't deployed them yet. I'll wait for your first report before deciding what to do, but I need to get them some action."

"Okay," she said with a nod, knowing that was Murdock's way of saying Reynolds would be joining them in a few days.

"Welcome to the team, Andrea. Try to keep her in line. Safe travels."

He signed off before either of them could reply as was his habit. Cameron closed the laptop, embarrassed now to be alone with Andrea. Murdock had completely blown her cover.

"Anything you want to explain?"

Cameron shook her head. "I think Murdock pretty much covered it, don't you?" She stood, running her fingers nervously through her hair, trying to find the words to explain why she'd lied.

"So you thought you needed an excuse for me to come with you?"

"Didn't I? If I'd told you I didn't want to leave Sedona without you, would you have just given up your job and come with me?"

"I'm not sure. When you found me crying in the bathroom I was asking myself how I could just let you walk out of my life so easily." She shrugged. "I don't know what I would have done. I only know I was hurting because you were leaving."

"Well, this was all I could think of. I wanted you with me, but I knew you needed a purpose. Joining the team seemed to make sense. We work well together."

"Yes. And Murdock went along with it?"

Cameron took Andrea's hands and pulled her to her feet. "His team is ex-military but I convinced him your training in LAPD was sufficient." She squeezed tightly against Andrea's fingers. "I'm sorry I lied, Andi. But I just couldn't leave without you."

Andrea tilted her head, eyebrow cocked. "I pulled my weapon on my captain. Does he know that?"

"Yes, of course. Who do you think put together the files on you?"

She shook her head with a smile. "The thing that got me fired with LAPD probably helped get me hired with the FBI. Amazing."

Cameron hesitated. "Are you angry? I mean, about the whole thing."

"Of course not," Andrea said. "Truth is, I think it's sweet."

"Sweet, huh? Well, it seems kinda silly now. I mean, I should have just told you how I felt and we could have talked about it."

"But?"

"But I was afraid you'd turn me down," she admitted honestly. "This way, if you said no, it was about the job and not about us."

Andrea was studying her, and Cameron did her best not to shift uneasily under her gaze. It had seemed like a good idea at the time. Now, she was feeling a bit vulnerable over the whole thing.

Andrea's gaze softened and she moved closer, linking her hands behind Cameron's neck. She kissed her softly, then moved her mouth to her ear. "I love you," she whispered before pulling away. "The thought of you and Lola walking out of my life was killing me. So I'm glad you asked Murdock to let you have a partner. And I'm even happier that I'm that partner."

Cameron closed her eyes and held Andrea tightly, feeling the completeness she always felt with her. She'd thought—after Laurie died—that her chances of finding some happiness in her life were gone. But Andrea filled her, heart and soul. She'd only been half a person before Andrea. Andrea was the part that had been missing. She'd recovered after Laurie. That's because, while she loved Laurie, it was never like this. She didn't feel it deep in her soul like this. If anything happened to Andrea, she didn't think she'd survive.

And that scared her to death.

CHAPTER TWO

Andrea moved quietly through the tall trees, along the same trail she and Cameron had taken yesterday. Dawn was already chasing the shadows away, and she noted how much her morning routine had changed since she'd met Cameron. In Sedona, she always had such a deep-seated compulsion to race along the trail, getting to her rock slab before dawn, as if she had somehow failed if she wasn't there in time to greet the sunrise, to meet the new day head on. She knew that was a necessity then, that was how she survived mentally, emotionally. That was how she lessened the guilt that she carried.

All that changed when Cameron came into her life. She still felt like she needed this time alone—and Cameron encouraged it, in fact—but she wasn't as compelled to find a spot for her early morning Tai-Chi sessions and reflections as she had been in the past. It was no longer a necessity to survive. She found she needed it now, if for nothing else, than to enjoy the solitude and to take time to give thanks for the peace in her life. It gave her a time to look inside herself and recognize the changes there.

Today she climbed along the trail, the high altitude making her breathing labored and she stumbled over a rock, catching herself on a limb. She paused, looking for the spot they'd found yesterday, a side trail that would take her to an open space and provide a view of the mountains...and the sunrise.

She tried not to feel guilty that she wasn't back at the rig helping Cameron get ready to move. She had planned to help this morning, but Cameron had said she could do it just as easily and had nearly pushed her out the door with a quick kiss and a "please be careful." Andrea couldn't help the smile that came to her face. Cameron would never admit it, but she suspected Cameron needed her alone time as much as Andrea did. She usually took a run in the evenings while Andrea started dinner, much like Andrea took her morning hikes while Cameron took care of breakfast. It was a practice that had now become habit, which seemed to suit both of them.

She pushed on, finding the break in the trees after ducking under a low-hanging pine. While certainly beautiful here, she did miss the unobstructed views and the red glowing sunrises of Sedona, the earth flaming in color around her as she raised her arms to the new day, her skin bathed in the reddish hues. She closed her eyes, picturing one of the hundreds of sunrises she'd seen, not surprised by the clarity of it in her mind's eye.

She took a deep breath, not minding the tall Ponderosa pines blocking her view. In fact, the sweet aroma added to the stillness of the morning as it came alive with chirping birds and chattering squirrels. Finally, those sounds receded to the background as she shifted into form, her practiced movements coming without thought and she glided through her routine, her focus turned inward as her slow, even breathing chased all thoughts from her mind.

CHAPTER THREE

"Christ, this is in the middle of nowhere," Cameron said as she peered through the windshield at the endless Mojave Desert—sand, cactus and a smattering of creosote bushes stretching out for miles in every direction, the hulking shape of distant mountains the only bump on the horizon. "Who the hell lives out here?"

"Desert dwellers," Andrea said. "Some people love this."

"Where the hell are we going to park the rig?"

"I vote for Joshua Tree. I've been there a few times hiking. They have good campgrounds, both in the northern section and southern."

"If we camp close to where the body was found—in the southern section—that's a hell of a long way from Barstow," Cameron said.

Andrea had spent some time in the desert when she lived in LA, but it wasn't until after the ambush that she ventured as far out as Joshua Tree and the Salton Sea. She knew they could find camping—and water—in the National Park, but yes, it was a long way from their first body.

"How about this," she suggested. "Go to Barstow first. Find the local police who Murdock said would show us the site. Then visit the county coroner and go over the autopsy report. We can just park for the night somewhere."

"And then go to Joshua Tree?"

"Yes. I don't think we'll be able to sit in one place like you did in Sedona," she said.

"Okay," Cameron agreed. "Find the email with the name of the police chief who we're to contact. Give him a call and let him know we're about an hour from Barstow."

Andrea nodded, moving Lola off of her so she could open her laptop. The kitten hopped down and moved to the back of the rig, finding her favorite spot on the loveseat. Andrea turned her attention back to her email, her gaze going to Cameron occasionally.

Something was up with Cameron and she wasn't quite sure what it was. She could tell it was a relief for Cameron to leave Canyonlands. Once they were away from people and alone again, she was back to her old self. But now, since Murdock's call, she'd reverted back to being a bit distant from her. It was as if each mile that brought them closer to Barstow increased her apprehension. She wanted to find out what was going on in that beautiful head of hers but she didn't want to push. She knew Cameron's past affected her, knew of the protective shield she put up around her.

But that shield had dropped in Sedona. It surprised her now that Cameron was trying to put it back in place.

"This is it?" Cameron asked, hands on her hips as she stared down at the spot he pointed out.

Andrea's gaze followed Cameron's, seeing nothing but rocks

and sand. The heat of the midday sun baking the already crisp desert—the temperature was still stifling, even for September. Andrea was used to the desert around Sedona where September finally brought a relief from the summer heat.

"Yep, this is it."

"Crime scene tape?"

"Took it down a week ago," the officer said as he spit a line of tobacco juice a couple of feet away from Cameron's boot.

Andrea saw the expression on Cameron's face, and she quickly stepped forward before Cameron took the man's head off.

"Officer Burke, the crime scene investigators went over the area though, right?" she asked, watching as he packed his wad of tobacco tighter in his lower lip.

"Oh, yeah. After they took the body—what was left of it—they took a bunch of pictures and some soil samples or something." He spit again. "Wasn't nothing here. No blood, nothing." He shrugged. "Bet you a hundred bucks she was just a fender lizard," he said.

Cameron's eyebrows shot up. "Fender lizard?"

"Hooker. That's what the truckers call them. They hang around truck stops, go knocking on the cabs at night."

"Soliciting?"

"Yep. My brother is a trucker. He says sometimes those girls won't take no for an answer." He spit away from Cameron this time as his eyes raked over both of them. "You two really FBI?"

"Really," Andrea said as his eyes lingered on her chest. She had ditched her shirt earlier and was left in only a tight white T-shirt. She glanced at Cameron, wondering if she had more questions for him but she shook her head as she turned her back to them, her gaze moving across the desert. "Well, Officer Burke, thank you for showing us the spot. We'll find our way back."

"If you need something else, just swing by the station." He tipped his hat politely at them, then spit one more time before leaving them.

"Déjà vu," Cameron murmured as his car pulled away. "Dumped body and no evidence."

"Yeah. Eerily familiar," she said as she wiped the sweat that threatened to roll down her cheek. "At least in Sedona, we had trails."

Cameron took the now familiar GPS gadget from her shoulder pack and marked their location, then glanced at Andrea. Andrea dutifully pulled up the notes on her cell phone where she'd jotted the location from the report Murdock had emailed them. She showed it to Cameron who nodded.

"This is the place."

"Did you doubt him?"

"Didn't you?" Cameron asked as she walked a circle, her eyes scanning the desert floor.

Andrea waited patiently. She'd been through this routine with Cameron in Sedona and knew she just wanted to be thorough.

"Why behead them?"

Andrea wondered if this was a test or if Cameron simply wanted her opinion. "To prevent identification would be the logical answer," Andrea said. "But he left the fingers so he's not concerned with fingerprints."

Cameron nodded. "So then why?"

"Trophy?"

Cameron smiled and nodded. "Some serial killers keep trinkets, an article of clothing, a picture, something of each victim so that they can go back and relive the kill."

"Keeping the head is a bit extreme. Not to mention the smell and decomposition."

"Yeah. If he's a trucker, he's not keeping the heads in the truck with him. He'd have to have a place somewhere, somewhere remote."

"If he's beheading them, he'd also have to have someplace to carry out his crime in private. You're not going to do something like that in a truck either."

"So maybe it's not a trucker."

"A local?"

Cameron shrugged.

"Maybe he's not keeping the heads," Andrea said. "Maybe he dumps them someplace else."

"Why go to the trouble of cutting off the head if you're just going to dump it?"

"Well, we learned from Patrick Doe that serial killers like to toy with the police. Maybe that's all he's doing."

"And maybe he's keeping them as trophies," Cameron said. "Let's go visit the coroner."

CHAPTER FOUR

The county coroner was located in Apple Valley, about thirty-five miles from Barstow. Instead of leaving the rig in Barstow and driving the truck, Cameron wanted to be closer to Joshua Tree so they pulled into the small city in the motor home, towing the truck behind them. Andrea sat back and watched as Cameron handled the rig with expert ease, maneuvering through traffic as the GPS guided them to the coroner's office. Parking, however, did not prove as simple.

"I hate cities," Cameron murmured as she circled through the parking lot and back to the street.

"Park illegally? We have government plates," Andrea suggested.

"Murdock hates when I do that," Cameron said with a smirk. "Sounds like a plan."

"You enjoy pushing his buttons, don't you?"

"What? You mean now that Collie is out of the picture?"

Andrea noted that Cameron rarely mentioned Collie's name since his murder. Even though she claimed their love-hate relationship was mostly hate, Andrea suspected Cameron missed Collie more than she let on. Of course, Collie just added to a long list of comrades and team members who Cameron had lost over the years.

"Was Murdock always in charge? I mean, did he recruit you?"

"He's ex-military too. They formed two units to begin with. He was going to lead one of them, but the guy heading the operation dropped dead of a heart attack at fifty-two. They pulled Murdock in to take over and only raised his level as high as Special Agent. We have more clearance and leeway than your typical agents, but they wanted to keep us on the back burner," Cameron explained.

"Are there still two units? You only mentioned Collie's team. Now Reynolds's."

"He's got another team that stays pretty much on the East Coast. I've never worked with them." She pulled the rig to a stop along a curb plastered with no parking signs. "Will this do?"

Andrea grinned. "Yes. Perfect."

"Great. And we'll be sure to tell Murdock it was your idea when we get a ticket."

"Dr. Agnew?"

"Yes, yes. And you are?"

"FBI. Ross and Sullivan." Cameron showed him her FBI badge as did Andrea. Dr. Agnew appeared to be in his eighties with a head full of thick, white hair. She found it hard to believe he was still practicing.

"FBI?" He looked them over head to toe, both dressed in jeans and boots, although Andrea had put her shirt back on, covering the tight T-shirt. "Are you sure?"

Cameron arched an eyebrow. "Yeah, quite sure. Are you sure you're Dr. Agnew?"

Andrea stepped forward and held out her hand to him which he shook vigorously. "Special Agent Ross and I are here about an autopsy you did a few weeks ago."

"I've done a lot of autopsies, missy. You'll have to be more specific."

"Headless female found east of Barstow," Cameron supplied.

"Oh. That one. Yes. I remember. Jane Doe 23, I believe."

"Twenty-three? That many?" Andrea asked.

"Some years more, some less. The desert can be brutal if you're not prepared. Of course, the desert didn't take them all," he said as they followed him into an office. "Gunshot, knife wounds, strangulation. The occasional car accident," he continued as he motioned to the visitor's chairs. "Some will get identified over the course of the year so we're not really left with that many truly unidentified bodies. May I ask why the FBI is interested in this one?"

"Serial killer," Cameron said.

"Not in this county," he said with a shake of his white head. "I would have surely heard of another victim matching this one if it was in one of the other districts." He scratched his head. "Although I recall something similar seven, eight, maybe even ten years ago now. We seemed to have had a rash of headless victims. That's not something you forget."

"The one we're referring to is recent. Riverside County," Andrea said. "Near the southern border of Joshua Tree. Just last week."

"Oh? That would be Dr. Copeland's area then. Indio?"

"Yes."

"I'm surprised I wasn't consulted. But he's good. A little on the young side, but competent."

Cameron hid her smile. Young to this man would be someone in their sixties. Instead, she leaned forward. "Can we see the file, please?"

Dr. Agnew looked from one to the other. "FBI and all, I'd have thought you'd already hacked our computer and taken a look."

"There is certain protocol to follow," Cameron said, glancing at Andrea, hoping for a little help. She was ready to get the file and get out of there.

"Dr. Agnew, if the file is electronic, a copy would be helpful. You can just email it and we'll be out of your hair," Andrea said.

He smiled at her, the kind of smile a grandfather might give a young child who'd asked a silly question.

"The official copy is on the computer. They insist on it. My copy, however, is kept locked in the file cabinet. As it should be."

"And the two copies are different?" Cameron guessed.

"Well, one of the secretaries takes my notes and puts together the file for the computer." He gave them a sly smile as he took his glasses off. "I don't trust those damn computers. You never know who all is out there in the World Wide Web." He put his glasses back on before continuing. "Not sure I trust the whole process really—a secretary, most likely without a college education, is writing up something as important as an autopsy report. No sir. Probably doesn't even spell half the words right."

Cameron sighed and grabbed the bridge of her nose. "Andi," she said quietly. "Do something."

Andrea cleared her throat. "Dr. Agnew, if we could take a look at your hard copy, then perhaps compare it to the electronic version, that would be helpful. Maybe even make a copy of your file. We want to be thorough," she said with a smile.

He nodded. "You can have a copy of mine, sure. But you'll have to get one of the secretaries to get you the one off of the computer."

"Great, not a problem," Andrea said as she glanced at Cameron.

"Do you remember if she had any tattoos or piercings?" Cameron asked.

"That'll be in my notes. I don't recall," he said as he sorted through his keys.

"And she was Caucasian?"

"Yes," he said, opening one of the file cabinets and thumbing through what appeared to be color-coded files. "Here it is. Yes, Jane Doe 23." He handed it to Andrea. "The head was removed post-mortem," he said. "Sexual trauma, as noted. This one was odd in that she had a strange mixture of drugs in her system."

"How so?"

"High dose of phenobarbital, which is used to euthanize animals. Sleep aid. And cocaine, if I recall."

"Cause of death?"

"There were no obvious injuries to the body that would have caused death. She had ligature marks on her wrists and feet, indicating she was bound. The amount of phenobarbital in her system, well, based on her weight, I would assume it was enough to kill, although I'm not positive. Obviously, it's used in animals that weigh far less than a human."

"You list cause of death as drug overdose," Andrea said as she skimmed the file.

"Yes."

"But you're saying the phenobarbital wasn't enough to kill her?" Cameron said.

"With the mixture of drugs she had in her system, who knows?"

Cameron's eyes narrowed. "So you're saying you settled on drug overdose because there was no conclusive cause of death?"

"What are you implying, Agent Ross?"

"Did she die of a drug overdose, did she die from phenobarbital or is it inconclusive?"

"Does it really make a difference? I've listed it as a homicide. Her head was missing."

"Of course it makes a difference," Cameron said loudly. "A defense attorney would have you for lunch with this."

"Young lady, I have been through my share of defense attorneys, thank you very much. They don't scare me."

"Dr. Agnew, if we do have a suspect who lives long enough to go to court, we'll need to prove COD. Beyond a shadow of a doubt," she added.

"Excuse me," Andrea interrupted as she read through the file. "Two small burn marks at the base of her neck, above the shoulder." She raised her eyebrow. "Stun gun? Taser?"

"I don't recall." He held his hand out. "Let me see that."

Andrea glanced at her, giving her a slight smile. Cameron returned it. How could she not? The situation was bordering on comical.

"Yes. They were beginning to scab over, but yes, a Taser could have made those marks." He grinned. "So too could a vampire."

"Oh dear God," Cameron murmured.

"I'm kidding, of course," Dr. Agnew said with a chuckle. "Let's go with stun gun. That would be easier to prove to your defense attorney," he added as he smirked at Cameron.

"A Taser usually doesn't leave a mark," Andrea said. "Unless it was administered at very close range. What is your opinion?"

"Judging by the size of the wound, I would say it was a repeated action at very close range, yes." He glanced at Cameron. "The stun gun, not the vampire."

Cameron sighed as she'd had enough of this conversation with the peculiar Dr. Agnew. She stood, urging Andrea to do the same.

"May I have a copy?" Andrea said, motioning to the file he now held.

"Of course. Let's go out front, and I'll have one of the ladies copy that for you. If you want them to email you the other file, they can do that too." He grinned. "Or so I'm told."

They followed him back out the way they'd come. Cameron bumped Andrea's shoulder playfully and leaned closer.

"You want to take the vampire angle? That could be fun."

"Hush," Andrea whispered as she elbowed Cameron away from her. Their eyes met for a moment and Cameron saw matching amusement in Andrea's. She smiled affectionately at her before again slipping into her professional role.

CHAPTER FIVE

It was well after six when they drove into Indio and the temperature had yet to dip below the century mark. She could see the heat waves radiating off of the pavement and Andrea glanced at Cameron, wondering where they would park for the night. She'd called Dr. Copeland earlier and they were scheduled to meet him at nine in the morning. He was kind enough to email them his report so they'd have a chance to compare it to Dr. Agnew's.

"City park?" Andrea suggested.

"We could always find an RV resort with full hookups," Cameron said. "Running the AC nonstop will drain our solar batteries in a hurry."

Andrea touched the console screen, loving that she had Internet and a browser at her fingertips. "I'll find one."

Cameron sighed. "I miss Sedona."

"Yeah? Sonny Winfield had you spoiled?"

"It was a great place to park, wasn't it? A few junipers, some oaks. Great view."

"And temperatures below a hundred," Andrea added. "This is brutal."

"Yeah. And I don't foresee this being a quick and tidy case."

"Okay, here's one. The Thorny Cactus RV Park," she said. "Sounds sleazy."

"Check the price. That will let you know whether it's a local joint with a lot of permanent residents or not."

"What am I looking for?"

"Monthly rates at least seven hundred. That'll be a real resort."

"Then we'll skip The Thorny Cactus. They only want two-fifty." She went back to her search, finding another. "Mojave Luxury Resort. Eight-twenty-five a month."

"That's more like it."

"Pool. That sounds great, doesn't it?"

"Do you have a suit?"

"No. Do you?"

Cameron shook her head. "Skinny-dip?"

"Sure. We can add getting arrested to Murdock's list of rules we've broken today."

"We didn't get a ticket," Cameron reminded her.

"Only because the meter maid was lying in the street from the electric shock she got."

Cameron grinned. "It was funny, wasn't it?"

Andrea laughed. "Yeah, it was. You were quite helpful. She'd just gotten knocked on her ass from the shock, and she was still able to flirt with you."

"She wasn't flirting."

"The piece of paper she handed you wasn't her phone number?" The onboard GPS kicked in, silently directing them to the resort. Andrea had muted Clair's voice the first day. "Looks like four blocks to the north and you'll turn right," she said.

"Okay. And she only gave me her phone number in case we needed help with something."

"Sure she did."

Cameron gave her a cocky smile. "Well, what was I supposed to do? Ignore her?"

"Of course not. Drop-dead gorgeous meter maids don't come along every day." Even though they were teasing, Andrea still felt a tiny bit of jealousy and she hated it. Truth was, Cameron wasn't really flirting, she was simply helping the woman to her feet and offering apologies. The woman—who *was* drop-dead gorgeous—had batted her eyes and had nearly ended up drooling on Cameron's feet. Andrea stared at Cameron now, her beautiful smooth tan face, the unruly sandy blond hair, which was in need of a trim, the smile playing on her lips. No, she couldn't blame the woman for fawning over her. Back in Sedona, Andrea had resisted Cameron for a whole week before falling for her charms.

"You're staring," Cameron accused. "What are you thinking?"

"None of your business. Turn here," she said.

"You could put Clair on so you wouldn't have to monitor it."

Andrea laughed. "Your affair with Clair is over, remember. I'll be your GPS voice. It looks like it's about five, six blocks down."

"Andi," Cameron said quietly.

"Hmm?" Andrea met her eyes, already knowing what Cameron's question would be.

"Can we have pizza for dinner?"

"Seriously?"

"Please? I've seen signs. Local joints, the chains. It's been like a week since we've had it."

"It's been four days." Then she laughed. "No. It's been two. You grabbed a couple of slices when we stopped for fuel in Flagstaff."

"That hardly counts."

"Your obsession with pizza is bordering on, well, an obsession," she said. She also knew they would indeed have pizza for dinner. Pizza and sweet red wine. Normally they'd talk. Cameron telling her stories from her military days, Andrea sharing events when working for LAPD. She could talk freely now about her team, about Erin and Mark, without the guilt suffocating her. Tonight, though, they'd talk about the case and they would most likely go over Dr. Copeland's file so they'd be prepared in the morning. And she wanted to take a better look at the database on the highway killings. Now that she had FBI credentials, she wouldn't be as limited. Cameron also said she wanted to give Jason at Quantico a call so she could understand how to use the algorithms with this new case. So yes, pizza would be in order.

"I currently only have one obsession," Cameron said, interrupting her thoughts as she wiggled her eyebrows teasingly, causing Andrea to smile. "Now this looks like a resort," Cameron murmured as she turned into the complex. "And look. A pizza place right across the road."

"How convenient is that?"

"Why do I always feel so stupid after talking to Jason?" she asked as she reached for a piece of pizza.

"I think computer geeks enjoy doing that to us common folks," Andrea said. "But did you learn anything?"

"Oh, hell, he logged in remotely and is tweaking it because he was afraid I'd jack it up." She held her pizza up. "This is pretty good for a local joint."

Andrea only flicked her eyes at her, causing Cameron to laugh. Their good-natured battle over pizza was mostly for show. Andrea was quickly becoming a connoisseur.

Cameron took the recliner, mimicking Andrea's position on the loveseat with a laptop balanced on her legs. Minus one cat, of course, as Lola was busy begging from Andrea.

"Anything jump out at you on the autopsy report?" she asked.

Andrea shook her head. "They read surprisingly the same, except for the tox reports. Both had sexual trauma. Both had phenobarbital, but Dr. Copeland's doesn't mention any other drugs."

"So no sleep aid or cocaine," she said. "That indicates the first girl was a user."

Andrea nodded. "The concentration of phenobarbital was a lot higher on Dr. Copeland's girl. He listed that as cause of death."

"The other—Jane Doe 23—already had drugs in her system. Maybe it didn't take as much," she suggested.

"True. But would he have known that? Wouldn't he already have had a syringe set up?"

"Maybe he's really cruel. Maybe he administers it drip by drip, slowly, so they know what's coming."

"Or maybe the dose he administered to Jane Doe 23 was the norm. Maybe it wasn't enough for the second victim, and he had to give her a second shot."

"Logical, I suppose, if this is his first experimentation with it," Cameron conceded. "Not nearly as cruel as mine though."

"And I suppose we are looking for cruel and nasty since we don't have heads." She tilted her head thoughtfully. "We also need to consider the vet angle."

"You mean a rogue veterinarian murdering women?"

Andrea smiled. "Well, I was really just thinking of one whose clinic was broken into and had drugs stolen." She shrugged. "Of course, we can go with your rogue vet if you'd like."

"Again, yours is more logical. And probable," she said. "I'll email Murdock and ask him to run a check." She watched as Andrea's eyes scrolled across her screen. "Are you still looking over the reports?"

"No. I'm actually in the database. It's really fascinating." She looked up. "Murdock was right. Most of it is concentrated in the east but California has its share as well. Some of this information goes back thirty years."

"Headless victims?"

"Yes, some. Also heads found but no bodies to match. Torso minus the legs. Legs and arms found, no other body parts." She shook her head. "People are crazy."

"Indeed."

Andrea's brow drew together as her eyes still scanned the screen. "Listen to this," she said, glancing up quickly. "Eight years ago a headless body was found between Barstow and

Needles, on I-40. She was ID'd by fingerprints. A prostitute. Connie Bernstein, age twenty-four."

"Fender lizard, as our very helpful cop from Barstow calls them," Cameron said.

"Yeah. But that's not all. Over a two-month period, four bodies in all were found, same as this. Two on I-40, one on I-10 and one on I-15, between Barstow and Vegas. Two were ID'd, two remain unidentified." She shook her head before Cameron could ask. "No, none in the same location as our two. The one on I-15 was much closer to Vegas."

"Same MO? Wrapped in a tarp?"

"No. Wrapped in sheets. No mention of phenobarbital though. The other girl who was identified was also a prostitute. She worked out of Las Vegas. Connie Bernstein worked a truck stop outside of Needles."

"Four bodies. Why did he stop? Serial killers don't stop."

"Maybe he goes underground for a while like Patrick did."

"For eight years? Doubtful."

"So maybe he couldn't kill," Andrea said. "There's only one place that can prevent you from it."

"Prison."

"Yes. Maybe he was convicted of another crime, was locked up for eight years—"

"And is now out and carrying on his killing."

"Yeah." Andrea set her laptop aside. "Plausible?"

"Sure it is. Just don't know if it helps us."

"Why not? We find inmates who went in eight years ago and were just released, say, in the last six months."

"Released from where? In this area? In California? In Arizona? Nevada? You're talking thousands, Andi."

Andrea leaned back with a sigh, nodding when Cameron offered her more wine. "With all of our forensics and technology available today, how can we possibly have a crime scene without any evidence? I mean, a fingerprint smudge on the plastic at least. But no. Nothing. No fibers, no hair."

"Our second victim has tattoos," Cameron said. "Maybe that'll help with an ID."

"Haven't they already run that through Missing Persons?"

"Yes. I was thinking maybe we could show it around. Maybe some of the busy truck stops."

"So you like my eight-year-hiatus theory? That he's back and going after hookers again?"

"Well, the MO is not exactly the same. We have plastic now, not a sheet. And phenobarbital wasn't used either. But it's someplace to start."

"You know, if we think it's a hooker, I could always go undercover. Hit some of the trucker hangouts."

Cameron was surprised by the sudden panic she felt in her gut and she shook her head. "No way."

"Why not? We might get lucky."

Cameron stood, nearly pacing now as she envisioned Andrea dressed up like a hooker, trying to lure their serial killer to her. She met Andrea's gaze head-on. "No. Absolutely not."

She wondered what look she had on her face as Andrea studied her quietly. Finally one eyebrow shot up.

"You want to talk?"

The words were spoken softly, and Cameron was afraid by what Andrea meant by them. Talk? Talk about the case? Or *talk*? She looked away, trying to buy time.

"Cameron, sweetheart, what's going on?"

"Nothing. I thought we were talking," she said, hoping to appease her. The look in Andrea's eyes told her she had not.

"Cameron, something's going on with you. I can see it, so don't tell me nothing is wrong."

Cameron took a deep breath, trying to keep her expression as normal as possible, even managing a smile. "Really, I'm fine. Just trying to focus on the case." They both knew she was lying, but Andrea's next question surprised her.

"Do you love me, Cameron?"

Again, she felt like someone had punched her in the gut. "God, yes. Why would you ask?"

"Why don't you ever tell me?"

"I tell you," she said. "I tell you all the time."

But Andrea shook her head. "No, you don't. You say 'me too.' But you never say the words. In fact, I don't think you've said those three words since we left Sedona."

Cameron felt her chest tighten, and at that moment she wanted to be anywhere other than stuck inside the motor home having this conversation. She must have had a look of panic on her face, and she guessed Andrea thought she was about to bolt from the rig. Andrea got up and took her hands, her smile as reassuring as if she were talking to a frightened child.

"Cameron, I don't mean to imply that you don't love me. I know you do. I see it when you look at me. I feel it when you touch me, when we make love."

"Then what's wrong?" Cameron asked weakly.

"Tell me why you won't say the words."

Their eyes held for a long moment, then Cameron finally let out a defeated breath, realizing how childish she must seem to Andrea. She cleared her throat and reached over for her wineglass.

"I haven't had great luck with people I've loved," she said before taking a sip. "I've lost so many."

"So you think if you lost me, it wouldn't hurt as much because you didn't say the words?"

"No, Andi, that's not it." Cameron turned away, embarrassed now, but Andrea pulled her back around.

"Tell me."

"Everyone I've loved is gone. My parents, my brother. Laurie. Partners, teams." She ran her fingers through her hair. "Hell, even people I didn't love. Like Collie," she said. "I thought, well, if I don't say it out loud, then maybe," she shrugged and tried to smile. "Maybe the fates won't know and you'll be spared," she finished in a whisper.

She expected Andrea to laugh at her foolishness but was surprised to see the threat of tears in her eyes.

"Trying to fool the fates, huh?"

"I know it's silly, Andi. But I feel so strongly about us, about you. I feel like, finally, I have a family. You and Lola. This rig feels like home now. If something happened to you, I couldn't survive. Not this time. I...I couldn't go on."

"You're the strongest person I know, Cameron. You've been through so much. You would—"

"No. I don't think so. I couldn't take losing you."

Andrea looked like she was about to protest again but she said nothing. Instead she gave Cameron a gentle smile and squeezed her hand as she motioned toward the kitchen.

"I'll clean up from dinner."

"Andi, wait. I—"

"I know, sweetheart. Me too."

CHAPTER SIX

Leaving Dr. Copeland's office, Andrea studied Cameron as they headed back to the truck, wondering at her sullen mood this morning. She assumed it was either from the lingering effects of their conversation last night or Murdock's earlier call informing them that Reynolds and his team were on their way. She guessed it was the latter, especially since they'd ended the night making love with wild abandon, Cameron finally giving voice to her feelings. She was so tough and in control when in her professional mask, yet sometimes—when they were alone— Cameron displayed a vulnerability that made Andrea's heart break. It was a side of her that she'd only let Andrea see once in Sedona, the night Collie was killed. Andrea had seen years' worth of grief cross her face that night as Cameron tried to run from it.

Last night, too, as Cameron had made love to her, Andrea knew she was trying to tell her without words what she was feeling. Andrea had stopped her, rolling them over and pinning Cameron to the bed with a hard kiss.

"I love you. And I know you love me," she said. "You don't have to convince me."

"I just—" Cameron's eyes held hers fiercely and Andrea didn't dare look away. "I love you," she whispered, as if still clinging to the hope that the fates would not hear. "Everything feels right in my world now. You make everything feel so right, Andi. I don't want to lose this."

She didn't ask Cameron to say the words again. As she'd told her, she didn't need to hear them to know. But as Cameron made love to her, those words slipped out time and again, as if Cameron were freeing herself from the bounds she'd placed.

She'd been nearly shy this morning, avoiding any conversation of the hours they'd spent pleasuring each other. Too many hours, Andrea thought as she fought back a yawn.

"Tired?" Cameron asked unexpectedly.

"Yes." Then Andrea playfully bumped her shoulder. "But I'd do it all over again."

Cameron laughed and her dark mood seemed to dissipate. "Dr. Copeland wasn't any more helpful than the vampire doctor."

Andrea smiled at Cameron's reference to Dr. Agnew. "Were you expecting him to hand you a suspect?"

"Well, you did when I landed in Sedona," Cameron reminded her.

"I think you were the only one who believed me." Andrea held up her phone, showing Cameron the pictures of the tattoo she'd taken. "This might help us ID her. The lion is unusual." Andrea paused. "Or did you want Reynolds and his team to do the truck stops?"

Cameron snorted. "I don't want Reynolds or his guys anywhere near this case. God, what the hell is Murdock thinking?"

Andrea hid her smile at Cameron's outburst. She'd been expecting it all morning.

"I mean, he could have at least waited for us to give him some feedback or something," Cameron continued. "What the hell is Reynolds going to do? We have no leads, no evidence. We don't even know where to start with this one and Murdock is sending in a whole goddamn *team*?"

"Covering both I-40 and I-10, there are probably a lot of truck stops," she said. "It wouldn't hurt to have extra bodies doing the legwork."

Cameron stopped abruptly. "You do realize that if we have company on this one, we have to be very careful."

Andrea stared at her questioningly. "Careful?"

"Yeah. Us. You and me," she said, motioning between them. "What we did last night is not allowed," she said, her lips twitching in a smile before she started walking again.

"Oh. Well, I know it's frowned upon," she said. "And you told Murdock we weren't—"

"Murdock knows I'm lying," Cameron said. "He's willing to ignore it as long as no one calls him on it."

"So when Reynolds gets here, we have to pretend that we have a business relationship only?"

"Yes."

"Oh, come on. We live in a motor home that has one bed. Who's going to believe we're not lovers?"

"They don't have to believe it. We just can't give them anything to go to Murdock with. Like, oh, 'the two dykes can't keep their hands off each other'."

Andrea grinned. "Well, that much is true."

Cameron stopped again. "Last night was fantastic," she said, her voice low. "I'm sorry I got so weird about—"

"Don't be, Cameron. But you can't protect me to the point that I can't do my job. The profession we're in...there are risks, we both know that. We've both *seen* that."

"You're right. I know." Cameron's gaze lingered, as if she wanted to say something else, then she smiled. "So, sheriff's department next?"

"Yeah. Let me call them." She was already looking for the notes she'd put in her phone earlier. "Deputy Morales," she said. "He's listed as the one to contact." She eyed Cameron, her face damp with perspiration. "You want to do it from the truck with the AC running?"

Cameron wiped her brow and nodded. "I'm not really the desert type," she said.

"No? You fared pretty well in Sedona," Andrea said as she listened as the call went through.

"You can't compare Sedona to the Mojave Desert," Cameron said. "At least we had trees there." She opened the door for Andrea and winked. "Let's hope our next investigation takes us to a beach somewhere."

Andrea laughed, then slipped back into her professional mode as the phone was answered.

"Yes, this is Agent Sullivan, FBI," she said, still not comfortable with her new title. "I would like to speak with Deputy Morales, please. Is he at the station?"

"No, he's on patrol. What is this in reference to?"

"The unidentified female, found out at"—Andrea glanced again at her notes—"Cactus City rest area," she said. "Special Agent Ross and I are assigned to the case. Is there someone else I can speak with?"

"Yeah, hang on. Let me see if the chief deputy is available."

Andrea glanced at Cameron. "Morales is on patrol. She's going to get someone else."

"Ask if they can email us the coordinates for the site. We don't really need an escort out there," Cameron said.

Andrea nodded as a male voice came on the line.

"I'm Chief Deputy Grace. What can I help the FBI with?"

"Yes, thank you. Agent Sullivan here. I'm calling about the unidentified female, found out at the Cactus City rest area," she said. "I'd like—"

"The headless woman?"

"That's the one," she said, flicking her eyes to Cameron.

"Yeah, we got word you would be involved in this one. I don't have much to tell you, Agent Sullivan. The report is barely a page long. Of course, I can pass on the coroner's report. That's not a lot of help either."

"We've already spoken to Dr. Copeland and have a copy of

his post. I understand forensics came up empty. I'm assuming you're aware of the victim that was found outside Barstow?"

"Oh, sure. Headless bodies being found tend to make the news," he said. "We just don't have any leads. Hell, we don't have any evidence. San Bernardino County doesn't either."

"I understand. Is it possible for you to email us the report? We'd also like to take a look at the dump site."

"Sure. I can have a deputy run you out there."

"If you have GPS coordinates, we can find it," she said, smiling at Cameron.

"Yeah, they're in the report." He paused. "So you guys are going to totally work the case?"

"It's been assigned to us, yes."

"We'd like to be kept in the loop, Agent Sullivan. Especially if the victim turns out to be a local."

"Of course," she said. "Understood."

"Hang on a second," he said quickly and she could hear mumbled voices as he covered the mouthpiece.

She glanced at Cameron who stared at her questioningly. "Someone interrupted him," she explained.

"Sorry, Agent Sullivan, but you'll probably be interested in this. Just got a call...a bicyclist down near Blythe reported a body near the road. Headless."

"Blythe? I'm not familiar with it," she said, trying to picture a map in her head, but Cameron was already using the onboard computer, pulling up a map on the console.

"It's on I-10, at the Arizona border. The bicyclist estimated it was about ten miles west of Blythe. We have deputies en route. It's outside of the city limits but the Blythe PD will be the first at the scene. Highway patrol as well."

"We'd like to be involved, of course," she said.

"Yes, but this is our call until we determine if it's linked to the other victim."

"I think it's safe to assume that, don't you?"

"No offense, Agent Sullivan, but this is our jurisdiction. You may observe only. If the ME confirms the same killer, then we'll gladly step aside and let you work it as a serial. Until then, it's our case."

"Understood," she said. "We'll head toward Blythe now."

"Deputy Morales will be on the scene. I'll make sure he gives you a complete briefing."

"Thank you. I appreciate it. We'll be in touch." She nodded at Cameron, who started the truck, knowing the conversation had come to an end.

"Good job," Cameron said as she pulled away. "You have much better diplomacy than I do."

"Maybe it's because I remember all too well how it felt to have the FBI come in and take over," she said.

"Me?"

"No, not you. You were actually very nice about the whole thing, other than the two files you had on me," she said with a smile. "I mean when I was in LA. They were normally a bunch of pricks."

Cameron laughed out loud. "Yes, I can name several who fit in that category," she said. "So? What's up? Body?"

"Yes. Blythe is on I-10 at the Arizona border." Andrea looked at the map on the console. "Looks like it's over an hour's drive. We've been told to stand back until the ME confirms the link."

"He can dictate all he wants but my badge trumps his," Cameron said with a rakish grin. "As if having a rash of headless victims isn't linked to the same killer. Maybe you should shadow their crime scene, make sure they don't miss anything."

"I appreciate your vote of confidence in me, sweetheart, but my forensic training was years ago, as you well know. I doubt I could offer anything to them."

Cameron sighed. "I guess I need to call Reynolds and see where his team is. They were flying to Palm Springs. He wanted to make that their base."

"Palm Springs?"

"Yeah. Apparently Collie taught him well. He shot down my suggestion of the Holiday Inn in Indio," Cameron said. "We'll meet tonight at their hotel to go over everything. Now that we have a third victim, we might have more of a pattern."

"Do you still want to check out the dump site?"

"We'll see how much time we have. I'd like to, yes."

She nodded, knowing Cameron wasn't expecting to find

anything at the rest area, but she suspected it gave her a sense of the killing—a sense of the killer—to see where the body was dumped. She'd recognized that need in Cameron when they were in Sedona. The dump sites were nothing but disturbed rocks yet Cameron would study each one, methodically writing in her tablet what she saw and sometimes what she thought she saw. Andrea had no problem giving Cameron that time.

"You think it's silly that I want to see the sites?"

"Of course not," Andrea said, surprised that Cameron had guessed the direction of her thoughts. "It's what we do."

CHAPTER SEVEN

Cameron gritted her teeth as she watched as many as fifteen people traipsing near the spot where their victim lay. "Goddamn idiots," she murmured, already reaching for her FBI credentials.

"Cameron," Andrea warned. "We need to work with these guys. Don't piss them off first thing."

"Excuse me," she said loudly, ignoring Andrea's words as she held up her badge. "Excuse me," she said again. "Who's Morales?"

A middle-aged man separated himself from the others, his sheriff's uniform drenched in sweat. "I'm Morales."

"Special Agent Ross, Agent Sullivan," she said, glancing at Andrea.

"Yes, I've been expecting you. Please note that this is still our—"

"Have the crime scene investigators finished?"

"No. They just started," he said, pointing to two men who hovered over the body.

"Then why the hell are all these people contaminating the scene?"

"No one's touched the body," he said, "although the bicyclist opened the tarp. Blythe PD was first on the scene."

"Can you please ask everyone to back away? Jesus, have they had training? Don't they watch TV?"

Andrea stepped forward with a stern look at her. Cameron closed her mouth, but her gaze never wavered from Morales.

"Deputy Morales," Andrea said, her voice calm. "I'm a former sheriff's deputy myself. The FBI is always a little...pushy," she said, glancing at Cameron. "We know you have jurisdiction until the ME verifies the link. But just between us out here in the field, that's pretty clear-cut, don't you think? I mean, you were at the Cactus City scene, weren't you?"

"Yeah." He looked toward the body, the brown tarp having been removed. "It's the same," he nodded. "No doubt in my mind. But my orders are—"

"I understand. We're not trying to jump the gun," Andrea said. "We just don't want to leave anything to chance. Like contaminating the crime scene," she said, glancing at the group of officers still watching the crime scene investigators.

"You're right. I'm sorry. I should have secured it better. We've got highway patrol, Blythe PD, us," he said. "Everyone wants a piece. Now you." He stepped away, addressing the collection of officers. "Guys, let's back up. Let CSI do their thing," he said. "The FBI is going to oversee this one."

He glanced at them and Cameron nodded her thanks as the officers dispersed. "You're amazing," Cameron said quietly. "Thank you."

Andrea smiled at her. "Do they watch TV? Really, Cameron? That's what you came up with?"

"Sorry. It just popped out." She headed to the body. "Let's go take a look." At Andrea's hesitation, she stopped. "What?"

"We just asked them to move back so they wouldn't contaminate the scene. Why, then, are we allowed near the body if they're not?"

Cameron bit her lip, wanting to play her FBI trump card, knowing she could do anything she damn well pleased. She knew how to examine a scene without tainting it. But once again, Andrea's logic won out. "I hate when you do that."

"What? Contradict you?"

"No. Logically tell me that I'm a conceited, arrogant bully." She watched Andrea try to hide her smile as Deputy Morales came over.

"I called it in. I told them it was the same killer. They still want to wait for the ME to confirm but he did say you could bring in your own forensic team, if you'd like."

Cameron shook her head. "Our *team*," she said, glancing at Andrea, "is en route to Palm Springs now, but we'll leave the forensics to your guys."

"If it's like the last one, there won't be anything. Tarp appeared to be brand new, right out of the bag. Nothing special about it. One you could pick up at any sporting goods store," he said. "Body was clean. You've read the report so you know there was sexual trauma but no fluids found. I did a quick glance at this body and—"

"Morales?"

He looked over at the forensic guy who had called for him. "Excuse me."

Cameron didn't wait to be invited. She followed him over, recognizing the portable fingerprinting device they used out in the field now.

"Got a hit," the technician said. "Monica Riddle. Has priors. Solicitation. Prostitution."

"Address?" Cameron asked.

"Last known was LA."

"Morales, where would these girls work? Truck stops? Hotels?" Andrea asked.

"Both, yes. We don't have the manpower to monitor the truck stops. Fender lizards, they call them," he said. "There are a few popular stops here along I-10 but the biggest two are on

I-40. One west of Barstow, the other west of Needles. There might be five or six hundred trucks parked a night. A lot of girls work those two."

"That's San Bernardino County?" She seemed to recall the big truck stop as they'd driven down I-40 on the way to Barstow.

"Right."

"So really, Needles isn't that far from here," Cameron said.

"Not far, no. Head up Highway 95 from Blythe. It'll take you right into Needles. You thinking trucker?"

Cameron hesitated, wondering if she should voice their suspicion this early in the case. Yet it was obvious that a trucker would be a prime suspect. "If this girl worked the stops, then yes, a trucker," she conceded.

CHAPTER EIGHT

"I feel like we've left Lola alone too much," Andrea said. The kitten had been all over them when they'd stopped at the rig to shower and change before heading to Palm Springs to meet Reynolds and his team.

"I know. It's tough working a case that's all over the map."

"Maybe when this is over, Murdock will give us some time to go back to Sedona. I can clean out my things and we could park for a week or so," she said, envisioning hiking the red rocks.

"Maybe so," Cameron said. "Do you miss it?"

"Sedona? Some, yes. Jim and Randy. I miss the routine," she said.

"Second thoughts then?"

"About this? Oh, no. I wouldn't go back, if that's what you're asking. You were right. I was stagnant there. But it was what

I needed at the time," she said. "Of course, I didn't count on falling in love with you," she added, watching a slight blush cross Cameron's face.

"You know, if you ever do have second thoughts, I want you to tell me. The constant travel, no place to put down roots—I'm used to that. If you need a home, solid ground, then you—"

"I have a home," she said, stopping Cameron. "It's not something I'm used to, no, but it's home. You and Lola make it home."

"And the job?"

Andrea smiled. "The job is perfect. I have a great senior agent showing me the ropes."

Cameron laughed, then reached over and squeezed her thigh. "Thank you."

Andrea captured her hand, holding it lightly as Cameron drove. They slipped into an easy silence, their fingers caressing. A simple touch, but one which served to reinforce the bond they had. Partners and lovers—a pairing that seldom worked out. But right now, she had no fear for either. They worked well together despite using nearly opposite means to achieve their goal. They were good partners. But they were better lovers. The fact that they separated the two as easily as they did gave her hope that they could make this work long term. She brought Cameron's hand up, kissing her knuckles gently before lowering it again.

"I love you," she whispered.

Cameron squeezed her hand but said nothing. And that was okay.

She watched the desert flash by them on her right as they drove the Redlands Freeway, the interstate bouncing from Indio to Thousand Palms and on to Palm Springs, the cities all flowing together. Cameron followed the GPS to the hotel where Reynolds was staying. It seemed he had taken her advice and secured one on the east side of the city.

"This is nice," she said. "Fancy."

"Taxpayer dollars at work," Cameron said. "Apparently Murdock's budget hasn't been cut."

Cameron held the door open for her and they bypassed the lobby, heading to the elevators instead. Reynolds said they had five rooms on the third floor.

"Do you know anyone on his team?" she asked.

"Murdock said he kept Jack Temperton from Collie's team. Jack's been around longer than anyone. Don't know about the rest," Cameron said, pausing to allow Andrea to exit the elevator first.

"This way," Andrea said when she saw the room chart on the wall. Their shoes sank into the plush carpet and she felt terribly underdressed. They were both still in jeans and boots, although she'd chosen a button-down shirt instead of the T-shirt Cameron had sported. She glanced at Cameron now, the deep blue T-shirt tight against her skin, her sandy blond hair a nice contrast. "You need a haircut," she said absently.

As if on cue, Cameron ran her hand through her hair and nodded. "Too unruly for you?"

"No. You do unruly well. It's bordering on shaggy."

A few more steps and Cameron stopped. "Here we are," she said, rapping her hand loudly on the door.

It opened quickly and Reynolds flashed a brilliant smile at them, his teeth inordinately white against his ebony skin.

"You made it. Come in." He nodded as Andrea passed. "Deputy Sullivan, good to see you again."

"*Agent* Sullivan," she corrected. "Thanks."

"Of course." He directed his gaze to Cameron. "*Very* Special Agent Cameron Ross," he said with a smile. "Come meet my team."

Sprawled across the suite were three other men and a woman. The men all wore suits and ties and the woman—a strikingly attractive brunette—was in a skirt that showed off long, well-toned legs. Andrea felt uncomfortable in her jeans, but Cameron looked as confident as ever. The woman stood and walked over, glancing once at Andrea and dismissing her, her eyes focused on Cameron instead.

Andrea arched an eyebrow at being overlooked so easily by the beautiful woman. Dark skinned, sharp features—she didn't appear to be American.

"Cameron," the woman said, the name rolling off her tongue with a slight accent. Italian, Andrea guessed. "Our paths cross again. How lovely."

Andrea watched Cameron's reaction, wondering if this woman was friend or foe.

"Carina," Cameron said rather formally. "How are you?"

"Much better now," she said with a flirty smile. "Hopefully we will have time to reacquaint, yes? It was so much fun the last time we were together."

Andrea's eyes narrowed at the obvious innuendo. Not friend nor foe. Just an old lover. She felt the stirrings of jealousy, and she had to remind herself of the warning Cameron had issued earlier. Nonetheless, she had to bite her tongue as the woman leaned closer, kissing Cameron on both cheeks in greeting. She finally cleared her throat, her gaze now locked with Cameron's, who had the grace to blush.

"This is my partner, Andrea Sullivan," Cameron said. "Carina Moretti."

The woman studied her—Andrea assumed she was trying to decide if they were lovers or not. Andrea politely stuck her hand out which Carina reluctantly took.

"A pleasure," Carina said and quickly turned her attention back to Cameron.

"How do you two know each other?" Reynolds asked.

"We had a joint mission," Cameron said evasively. "Years ago."

"Five, to be precise," Carina added.

He nodded. "Well, let me introduce everyone. Cameron, you know Jack, of course," he said. "Sullivan, this is Jack Temperton. That's Eric Scales and then our computer expert, Rowan Casper."

Andrea nodded at them. Jack was an older man, his hair graying at the temples. Eric Scales was almost too pretty to be an agent. Dark hair and eyes, smooth skin, he wasn't shy about letting his gaze travel across Andrea's body with a bold smile. Rowan Casper was painfully thin with dark glasses and wispy blond hair. His features appeared almost delicate compared to that of the handsome Scales.

"Quite a team, Reynolds. Five of you?"

"I started with four, but Murdock urged me to add my own computer guy. Jack, as you know, is a weapons expert. Eric is my undercover guy. He's quite talented. And Carina speaks five languages besides being somewhat of an explosives whiz."

"Yes, I remember you had a fondness for blowing things up," Cameron said dryly.

Carina laughed, making her appear even more beautiful. Andrea hated her.

"So dinner first? Or do you want to get down to business?" Reynolds asked.

"Business. We'll skip dinner," Cameron said, surprising Andrea. "We've had a really long day and we've still got to drive back to Indio tonight."

"Murdock strongly suggested dinner," Reynolds reminded her. "A chance for us to get to know each other since we'll be working together on this one. A bonding if you will."

"You'll only be assisting on this one, Reynolds," Cameron countered. "Our rig is in Indio. That's why I suggested you put your hotel base there. It's more centrally located than Palm Springs."

"Rig?" Scales asked.

"Motor home," Andrea supplied.

"Really?"

"It's FBI custom built," Cameron said. "A traveling office."

"So you won't be staying here at the hotel with us?" Carina asked. "Pity."

Andrea tried not to scowl. *Pity, my ass.*

"Did Jason Tremble really design your computer setup?" Rowan asked, his eyes lighting up as if Jason was a rock star.

"He really did," Cameron said. "I didn't realize he was so famous," she said. "Next time I talk to him I'll—"

"You *talk* to him?"

Cameron glanced at Andrea with an amused smile and a quick roll of her eyes.

"I've emailed you both coroners' reports from the first two victims," Andrea said, speaking to Reynolds. "The body that was found today, we should have the post by midday tomorrow."

"But you think it's the same killer?"

"Yes. Everything was the same. We'll just have wait on tox."

"We're going with prostitutes," Cameron said. "The first two victims are unidentified, but this last one's prints got a hit."

"Monica Riddle," Andrea supplied.

"Last known address was in LA. We don't know where she worked. Our thinking is truck stops."

"Why?" Carina asked. "That's hardly glamorous."

"And prostitution is?" Andrea asked.

"Agent Sullivan found a pattern from about eight years ago that matches this one," Cameron continued. "Victims were wrapped in a sheet, not a tarp. Phenobarbital wasn't used though. There were four bodies in all. Two were identified by fingerprints, both worked as prostitutes."

"That's a stretch, isn't it?"

Cameron stared, one eyebrow raising. "Jesus, Reynolds, you learn that line from Collie?"

"He taught me not to assume," he said.

"Yeah. He also told you Patrick Doe was only a figment of our imagination and didn't believe our theory then either. But, oh, guess what? He's dead now," she said.

"Come on, Ross, there's no need to bring Collie into this," Jack said. "He was a good man."

"Right. *Was.* So quit acting like he's still here. If you want to work with his mindset, then get the hell out of my case," she said loudly. "We can do this ourselves. But I won't have you questioning every goddamn thing we bring up just because that's what Collie used to do."

There was silence in the room, and Andrea watched their faces as they stared at Cameron. It seemed even from the grave, Collie could push her buttons.

"That was uncalled for, Ross. Collie was our colleague and team leader," Reynolds said.

"Yeah? He was also a jerk."

Carina's eyebrows shot to the ceiling then a slow, sexy smile formed. "Oh, Cameron," she said, "you still have that fire within you. It's *so* attractive."

Eric spoke for the first time, his glance going between Carina and Cameron, a smile growing with each pass. "Just how well did you two know each other?" He laughed. "Because I'm getting a visual and it's looking pretty good."

Cameron's blush confirmed Andrea's suspicion that they were lovers, but she couldn't help smiling at Eric's playfulness. Thankfully, that seemed to ease some of the tension in the room.

"Okay guys, can we get back to the case, please," Reynolds said. "I'm sorry, Cameron. Continue with your...*theory*."

Cameron glanced at her and Andrea thought there was a bit of an apology in her eyes. She wondered if it was because of her outburst...or because of Carina.

"If we can pinpoint where she worked—Monica Riddle— then that might give us an idea of her killer. Our thought is it's a trucker, but that's pure speculation. If Monica worked a truck stop, then speculation becomes probability."

"We have an unusual tattoo on vic number two. A lion's head," Andrea said. "If I could get all of your email addresses, then I'll supply each of you with a copy of it, as well as the coroners' reports. I'll also include the file I put together of the murders eight years ago.

"Since phenobarbital was found in the victim, I've asked Murdock to run down any vet clinics that may have reported a burglary recently. They would have been required to list any drugs that were missing. Not sure how much that'll help us, other than to get a better location."

"It could always be someone who works at a vet clinic," Jack said. "An assistant or someone who is stealing."

"Maybe someone pays him for the drugs," Eric added.

"Of course those are possibilities," Cameron said. "And if that's the case, then it's a dead end. Patrick Doe not withstanding, serial killers normally work alone. If you're buying phenobarbital and the media is reporting that these girls were injected and killed with phenobarbital, then don't you think your supplier is gonna throw up a red flag?"

Reynolds sighed. "So, I see that you really don't have anything then," he said. "Speculation only."

Before Cameron could speak, Andrea came forward. "We have what little evidence there is," she said. "Actually, there is *no* evidence. We have matching tarps with no prints. That's it. We have ID'd one victim, so that's all we have to go on. Trace her whereabouts and try to determine where she was last seen. That's our course of action."

"If your computer whiz here could locate truck stops within, say, a hundred-mile radius, then that gives us someplace to start. Since her body was found in this area, we'll concentrate our search here," Cameron said. "There are seven of us. We can break out into two or three teams, show her picture around as well as the tattoo."

"I'll be happy to join your team, Cameron," Carina offered.

"I already have a partner," she said, glancing at Andrea. "If Rowan can email us the list of truck stops, then we'll head out in the morning. There's a large one near Needles that I'm really interested in."

"I guess we'll concentrate in this area," Reynolds said. "And I suppose you were right. Palm Springs is a bit out of range. Perhaps we should relocate to Indio."

Cameron nodded. "Yes, you should. Enjoy your last night of luxury then. We need to head back," she said. "We'll be in touch tomorrow."

"I've set up a group email," Rowan said. "I'll add you and Agent Sullivan to it, then send it to you. We can communicate that way. I'll also list everyone's cell numbers. If you'd reply with yours, that would help."

"Sure." Cameron made a show of glancing at her watch, then she flicked her eyes at Andrea. "Ready?"

"Yes."

"We'll let you get on to dinner then," Cameron said.

"Good to meet you, Ross," Eric said. "And you, Agent Sullivan," he said, walking over and taking her hand. "It's going to be a pleasure getting to know you."

He was simply too pretty and charming to be offended by him so she smiled good-naturedly. "Likewise," she said.

"Me, too," Rowan said without looking up from his laptop.

Reynolds held the door open for them and she noted Carina's eyes never once left Cameron. *Oh, this is going to be so much fun.*

They were silent as they waited for the elevator and Andrea

wondered if Cameron was going to explain Carina or if she was only going to offer an explanation if Andrea asked.

Once inside the elevator, their eyes met and Andrea raised hers questioningly. Cameron let out a heavy breath.

"What do you want to know?"

"Lovers?"

"Yes."

Andrea nodded but said nothing.

"You're thinking I make a habit of sleeping with everyone I work with, right?"

"I was thinking no such thing. But now that you mention it, do you?"

"No. Carina and I worked together for nearly a year in Rome. She's...well, flirtatious."

"And beautiful."

"Yes, she is. We slept together. That's it. There was no emotional involvement for either of us," Cameron said. "I haven't seen her since."

"And she assumes you two will pick up where you left off?"

Cameron smiled. "Is that what you inferred from it all?"

"Yes. Didn't you? She dismissed me very easily. I doubt she thinks we're lovers," she said.

"Oh, I'm sure she suspects it."

Cameron motioned for Andrea to exit the elevator ahead of her, then guided her out to the parking garage.

"Is that why you changed your mind about dinner?"

"Partly. But I could see she was making you uncomfortable. And of course she was doing it intentionally." She held the door open to the truck and Andrea got in. "Besides, I'd rather pick up a pizza and have it back at the rig."

Andrea laughed. "Of course you would."

CHAPTER NINE

The truck stop was as busy as Deputy Morales had said. Literally hundreds of big rigs filled the fuel bays and parking lots, the smell of diesel thick in the air as engines rumbled.

"He wasn't kidding," Andrea said, her gaze going from one end of the parking lot to the next.

"It's like a small city. Restaurants, laundry, showers. Grocery store." Cameron had no idea where to start. She looked at Andrea. "What do you think?"

"Obviously the main hub is the convenience store and fuel. They're also open twenty-four-seven. Let's start there."

"If they support these women, they might not be willing to talk," she said.

"She's dead. They'll help us," Andrea said as she headed inside.

Cameron let Andrea take the lead. They waited until one of the clerks finished up with the customer in front of them. The smell of freshly baked pizza wafted through the air and Cameron's stomach did a roll.

"Don't even think about it," Andrea whispered.

Cameron gave a quiet laugh, turning her attention to the clerk instead.

"Excuse me," Andrea said. "I'm Agent Sullivan, this is Special Agent Ross." She discreetly flashed her FBI credentials, Cameron doing the same.

"Yes?"

"We're investigating a murder. We'd like to ask you a few questions."

"Me?"

Cameron noticed the trembling of the clerk's hands and the nervous twitch of her eyes. Unfortunately, FBI badges tended to have that effect on people.

"You're not in any kind of trouble, ma'am," she said quickly. "Do you have...working girls here?"

"Huh?"

Cameron glanced at Andrea for help.

"Prostitutes," Andrea supplied.

"Oh, no. Of course not," she said, her face turning red. "That's not allowed."

"I know it's not," Cameron said. "Look, is your manager here?"

"Yes," she said with relief. "I'll get him."

Andrea turned to her and grinned. "Why do you scare people?"

"Me? No, this one's on you." She stepped aside, gently guiding Andrea around the counter where they waited for the manager. "They may have two managers, one at night. If so, they would probably have a better knowledge of the *working girls*," she said. Her phone vibrated against her leg, and she pulled it out of her pocket, sighing when she saw Rowan's name. "I should have never given him my number," she mumbled. "Ross," she said, moving farther away from the counter.

"Rowan here again. I wanted to let you know that I found our vet clinic," he said.

Cameron drew her brows together, wondering when she asked him to search. "Murdock was going to run that down. What did you find?"

"Well, I've got a program that will dump data from several different databases and compile and sort at will. I downloaded the—"

"Cut to the chase, Rowan," she said impatiently.

"Sorry. A vet clinic in Morongo Valley reported a break-in ten months ago. Phenobarbital was on the list of drugs stolen."

"Good job. I'm hoping Reynolds is on his way there now?"

"Yes ma'am. He and Carina. Jack and Eric are going to talk to the police and see if there were any suspects."

"Great. Keep me posted," she said and disconnected quickly as the manager walked over.

"I'm Donald Auger, what can I do for the FBI?"

"Can we speak in private?" Andrea asked.

"Sure. My office is back here," he said, motioning between the rows of chips and peanuts to a back door marked 'private.'

They followed him inside what appeared to be no more than a cluttered storeroom with a desk shoved in one corner. A large monitor broken into four sections streamed surveillance camera footage and another one showed snapshots of the registers out front. There was only one visitor's chair and Cameron nodded at Andrea who claimed it.

"Sorry. I don't normally have visitors back here," he explained as he sat at his messy desk. "What can I do for you?"

"How well do you know the ladies who work the lots at night?" Andrea asked.

He didn't pretend to not know what she was talking about. "Look, we don't condone it, but we can't really keep them away. The security guys we hire are just for show really," he said.

"We're not here to bust you," Cameron said. "We have three dead women, two are unidentified. One had a tattoo on her shoulder." She glanced at Andrea who pulled up the photo on her phone and handed it to Mr. Auger. His eyes widened.

"Linda. Linda Blake." He took his glasses off and rubbed his eyes. "She's been around a while. Everyone knew her."

"When's the last time you saw her?"

"Maybe a week, maybe more. It's hard to know. They come and go."

"Does the name Monica Riddle ring a bell?"

He shook his head. "But they don't all use their real names," he said. "Linda actually goes by Lori Lou on the streets. What happened to Linda?"

"Her body was found along I-10," Cameron said, omitting any details.

"Damn," he muttered.

"Did Linda have any problems with any of the truckers?" Andrea asked. "Anybody ever threaten her?"

"No. She was well liked." Then he blushed. "I mean, you know. She's been around here on and off for ten years or so."

"Do you know her age?"

"She looked older than she was. It's a hard life for these girls. She may have been thirty," he said.

"On and off?" Andrea prompted. "What do you mean?"

"The girls will hang around for a few months, then next thing you know, they're gone. Six months later, they show up again."

"So no one would really consider them missing. Like Linda," Andrea said.

"Right."

"They get rides out with truckers?" Cameron asked.

"Yeah. Mostly. They take them to another stop along the way and the girls work that one for a while. It's like a circuit," he said. "Unfortunately, it's one most of them can't get out of."

"Do you think some of the girls would talk to us?"

He shrugged. "Hard to say. They don't trust cops. But if you want to talk to them, they come out at dark."

"What do you think?" Cameron asked as they sat in the truck, the AC blasting cool air around them.

"I think we're damn lucky to get a hit on our first stop," Andrea said. "But still, he picks her up here and then what? Where did he kill her? Did he promise to take her somewhere? LA maybe?"

"Does he have a bag with him, syringe all ready?"

"From where her body was found and here is over a two-hour drive. Is that all the time he has with her? You would assume he'd take her somewhere to kill her and not use his truck. Then there's the matter of the heads."

"So you're not liking the trucker theory now?" she asked. "Local?"

Andrea shrugged. "No, I don't think a local. Too dangerous. Too many people would know you."

"I agree. You can remain anonymous at truck stops. Pay by credit card at the pumps, you never have to go inside."

"Have we thought about that?" Andrea asked. "Credit card receipts?"

"What?"

But Andrea shook her head. "Never mind. I'm overthinking," she said. "We only have the one truck stop so far."

"Okay, yeah. If we can find where Monica Riddle worked, then we can have Rowan run receipts and see if we have a match at both places."

"Of course, seeing as how big this place is, we could have hundreds of matches." She paused. "What was Rowan's call about earlier?"

"He found a vet clinic," Cameron said. "Reynolds and Carina were going to check it out. Morongo Valley. Do you know where that is?"

"It's north of I-10. Not that far from Indio."

Cameron watched Andrea's reaction to the mention of her former lover. It was very subtle, but she could see a slight tightening of Andrea's jaw. It had been as much of a surprise to her as Andrea that they'd meet up with an old lover, much less team with her. She hadn't seen Carina since she left Rome, and she hadn't really given her much thought over the years. They were lovers, yes, but nothing more. And no matter how flirtatious or how many sexual innuendos she dropped, Cameron wasn't the least bit interested. She was no longer that person. What she had with Andrea was far more than she thought she'd ever have with someone...far more than she thought she even deserved.

"Burglary or rogue vet?"

Cameron smiled. "Burglary. But you have to admit a rogue vet would be much more interesting."

"Did he have details?"

"I didn't ask. Eric and Jack were checking with the police. He said it was reported about ten months ago."

"Will this help us?"

Cameron started the truck and pulled out to the highway. "Only if they have suspects." She glanced at Andrea. "What's next on the list?"

"Barstow."

"I don't remember seeing a truck stop," she said as she sped up to beat a truck.

"It's on the west side, before the city limits. We didn't take that route," Andrea reminded her. "By Rowan's notes, it appears to be as large as this one."

They were silent as she drove, Andrea reading through the notes on her phone. Cameron's gaze traveled across the desert, wondering at the attraction. While remote and wild, it held none of the charm that Sedona did, at least not for her. It appeared to be devoid of life—only sand and rocks, cactus and scrub brush with no vibrant green to be found.

"Tell me about you and Carina," Andrea said unexpectedly.

As was her habit, Cameron tried to find a deeper meaning to Andrea's request other than simple interest on her part. Was it just curiosity? Did Andrea feel threatened? So she shrugged nonchalantly.

"Nothing much to tell. We were in Rome. She was working for the CIA back then. We had a joint mission." She glanced at Andrea quickly, then back to the road. "It was a short-lived affair."

"Because you left?"

"Yes. Like I said, I haven't seen her since."

Andrea put her phone away. "She's very pretty. Glamorous. She could be a model."

"Yes," she agreed. "She's also very good at her job. Or she was back then. The sign of a good operative is to never let it get personal," she said.

Andrea stared at her. "Is that why you think you failed? You let it get personal?"

Cameron knew Andrea was no longer speaking about Carina but rather her days as a sniper, as the assassin she turned out to be.

"Yes."

Andrea reached over and rubbed her hand against her thigh, squeezing lightly. "I'm glad you failed then, Cameron. Killing should be personal. I'm glad you're not that person anymore."

Cameron covered Andrea's hand, holding it against her leg. It was one of the things she loved about Andrea. Such simple words, yet they had profound meaning to her. Andrea had no more questions and the silence settled around them again, their hands still linked as she drove toward Barstow.

CHAPTER TEN

After a fruitless visit to the truck stop in Barstow—no one had heard of Monica Riddle—they once again found themselves in Reynolds's hotel room. This time, a much less luxurious Holiday Inn in Indio, not far from the resort where the rig was parked.

"Clean entry," Eric said. "The alarm was disabled."

"With the code or a bypass?"

"Bypass. It wasn't anything sophisticated," he said.

"Police did the standard check on all employees, including the doctor himself. They didn't have video surveillance. It's just a small-town clinic, one doctor," Jack said.

"And no suspects?" Andrea asked.

Eric gave her a smile, a smile Cameron was growing to hate. He seemingly couldn't keep his eyes off Andrea. "Not a one."

"Besides the phenobarbital, propofol and ketamine were also stolen."

"And ketamine was on both coroner's reports," she said, nodding. "So we've found our source. Who's our guy?"

"I don't see your normal long-haul trucker pulling a vet clinic burglary," Andrea said.

"So back to thinking it's a local?" Cameron asked.

"I disagree with your partner," Carina chipped in. "Why not a trucker? The clinic is just off of the highway. He may pass it every time he travels this route. He would know it well."

Cameron again saw the slight tightening of Andrea's jaw, yet she hid it with a smile.

"I suppose you're right," Andrea said. "But it's a little conspicuous having a big rig parked in front of a vet clinic in the middle of the night."

"We can speculate one way or the other all day long," Reynolds said. "It doesn't really help us."

"Speculating is how you form possible scenarios," Cameron countered. "We have no evidence, no suspects."

"Speculating can send you down the wrong path," he said.

"At least it's a path, Reynolds. Unlike you, using Collie's habit of sitting on your ass until evidence is dropped in your lap," she said a bit louder than she intended.

"Are we going to start this again?" Jack asked. "Every time you two have a disagreement, Collie is going to be brought into it? Can't the man rest in peace?"

"I agree," Reynolds said.

"Great," Cameron said. "Quit acting like Collie and I'll quit bringing him up."

Andrea cleared her throat, her eyes purposefully avoiding Cameron's.

"How about dinner?" she asked. "I'm starving."

"Me too," Eric chimed in. "Perhaps we can discuss our evidence—or lack thereof—over a drink."

"Dinner is sounding better and better," Carina said as she moved beside Cameron, linking their arms together. "Maybe we could catch up, yes?"

Cameron's eyes flew to Andrea then realized everyone was watching so she nodded. "Sure."

"Okay, dinner," Reynolds said. "But I want normal food."

"Normal?" Eric asked.

"Yes. Not Mexican, not Italian, not Chinese. Normal. In other words, I want a steak." Then he looked at the group as he adjusted his tie. "Please tell me no one's a vegetarian on this team." He smiled when no one spoke up. "Great. Steak it is." He looked pointedly at Cameron and Andrea. "You two are going to change, right?"

"Change?"

"Clothes," he clarified.

"No," they said in unison.

Reynolds was a stickler for suits and ties, she knew, but Cameron didn't know he had a fetish about it.

"I hardly think what you're wearing is proper."

"Well, if they won't let us in, we'll have to settle for pizza or something," Cameron said with a smile as she glanced at Andrea.

Rowan was able to locate the most popular steakhouse with a few keystrokes and he announced that it appeared to be casual attire. Cameron was hoping for the opposite. Not that she wouldn't mind having a steak, but she was actually afraid of what Carina might be planning.

They settled on taking two vehicles and thankfully, Eric and Rowan got into Cameron's backseat before Carina could. Even then, for a second she wished her truck wasn't a super cab as she saw Eric's eyes following Andrea's every move as she brought the monitor to life.

"Sweet," Eric murmured. "You have an onboard computer?"

"Yes."

"Always connected?"

"When we have service."

Rowan stuck his head over the seat. "Did Jason design this?"

Cameron and Andrea exchanged amused looks. "Yes," she said. "When they asked me what I needed, they put this together along with the motor home's computers at Quantico."

"What kind of computer do you have in your motor home?" Rowan asked. "Do you have a server? Do you—"

"There's a lot of stuff," she said. "I don't know what all of it is, and Jason won't let me touch most of it so he logs in remotely. But yes, there is a server. I've got some algorithms that Jason wrote that I can run."

"How cool," he said. "I'd love to see your setup sometime. Do you know how big your server is?"

Cameron had to stop herself from rolling her eyes. Jesus, he wanted to do the geek-speak with her. "He said it's a beefy server, whatever that means," she said.

"Can I see it sometime?"

Cameron again glanced at Andrea. "Sure."

"Calm down, man," Eric teased. "You got a hard-on for her computer. We get it."

Rowan blushed profusely but thankfully sat back without asking any further questions.

Ten minutes later they were pulling into the crowded restaurant parking lot and Cameron wondered how much work they would be able to discuss if the place was packed. She scowled as Eric politely held Andrea's door open for her while she got out. Rowan tried to do the same to her but apparently the look on her face scared him away.

"Be nice," Andrea whispered as they waited for Reynolds's group to join them.

"I'm hoping for a 'no jeans' sign on the door," she murmured back with a smile.

As soon as they were led to a table, Andrea and Cameron became separated as Carina took the opportunity to sit next to Cameron. Andrea found herself between Eric and Rowan with Cameron at the opposite end. She smiled a thank you when Eric held her chair out for her. He was attentive, and she hoped it was only politeness on his part.

"So, what's a pretty gal like you doing in a job like this?"

She laughed. "Same thing as you are, I guess."

He grinned. "Can't be the money. Love of country?"

She shrugged. "Once a cop, always a cop?"

He leaned back as a waiter placed a glass with water next to him, then he put his arm behind her chair and moved closer.

"So you really live in a motor home?"

"Yes, we really do."

"Pretty crowded for two people, isn't it?"

"A little. But the loveseat makes into a bed, so we still have our own space."

He laughed quietly. "I'm going to guess you don't even know how that loveseat works, do you?"

She felt a blush but could not hide it. She doubted it would do any good to deny it. "Is it that obvious?"

"Oh, it's not talked about if that's what you mean," he said. "But obvious, yes." He leaned closer, his voice quiet. "Because Cameron is giving me the stare down."

"I don't know why. She's got Carina all up her ass," Andrea said without thinking.

Eric laughed loudly causing everyone else at the table to stare at them. Again, she felt a blush and only dared to meet Cameron's eyes briefly.

"Sorry," he said to the group.

"Something funny? Want to share?" Reynolds asked.

"No, no. Andrea just...made a funny," he said. "Sorry," he whispered to her.

Andrea sipped from her water, trying to contain a smile. This was the first time she'd even spoken to Eric one-on-one and already they were co-conspirators. She chanced a glance across the table, only to find Cameron's attention wrapped up in Carina.

"Do you know her?"

He followed her gaze. "Yes, I know her. She's a vixen," he said. "She knows you and Cameron are together, yet she's going to do everything she can to bed her."

"Really? Why?"

He shrugged. "That's what she does. Men or women, she doesn't care. It's her game. But she's damn good at her job. Top-notch, when she's on the clock. When she's off the clock, she likes to party. And now she's set her sights on your partner. Of course, they do have a history, I'm assuming."

Their conversation was interrupted by the waiter and Andrea joined everyone else in ordering a steak. Most ordered wine or something stronger, but she decided to join Eric and ordered a beer instead.

"Are you seeing anyone? Married?" she asked after their beer was served.

"No. Marriage isn't conducive to this line of work," he said. "You have a case, you may have a couple of days in between, maybe a week. It's hard to jet back home to a wife and kids."

"Don't you want that?"

"I don't know. I always thought someday I'd have that, but this is what I'm used to. Military. You move around all the time."

"You never learn to put down roots?"

"No, you keep moving. What about you?"

She shook her head. "Not military, no."

"Really? I thought that was a prerequisite."

"LAPD. Then I was a deputy in Sedona. That's where I met Cameron."

"On a case?"

"Yes. Patrick Doe."

"Oh. The one where Collie—"

"Yeah," she said quickly. The image of Collie sprawled out on the rocks, his throat sliced open, was something she could still vividly picture. Thankfully, he did not ask any questions.

"I was in Sedona once," he said. "Years ago. Lovely place."

"Vacation?"

"No. Furlough. I was in between tours." He smiled and she again thought how handsome he was. "I was on my way to visit my parents and I met this girl. She was all into the spiritual stuff and Sedona had all these places where, what do they call them?"

"Vortex," she supplied.

"Yeah, that's it. There were different spots where the vortex energy was supposed to be very high." He grinned and finished off his beer. "Don't know about that, but she was plenty full of energy."

"Ditched your parents, huh?"

"Yep. Spent a week in Sedona with her." He paused as the waiter came around. "I'll have another beer. Andrea?"

"Yes, I'll have another," she said, taking the opportunity to glance at Cameron. Even though Cameron was pretending to listen to Carina, Andrea knew she was keeping an eye on her and Eric.

"If I was at a place in my life to settle down, I would have chased her," he continued. "She was unique. She brought out a side of me that no one has before. Or since."

"How long ago was this?"

"Oh, six or seven years ago, I guess. Never saw her again after that." He leaned closer. "Even though Carina is all over her, Cameron is keeping a close watch on us."

"Yes. Carina is practically in her lap," she said quietly. "I think I hate her."

He smiled. "Are you jealous?"

Andrea glanced again at the pair. "I'm not sure. I should be, shouldn't I? She's a beautiful woman who's an ex-lover of hers. I should be."

"I think Cameron only has eyes for you. But it has to drive you crazy. It would me," he said.

"Don't think I haven't considered shooting her already."

He laughed again, and again conversation ceased around the table as all eyes were on them. They were spared having to explain as dinner was thankfully served.

Surprisingly, discussion of the case was put on hold as everyone seemed content to make small talk over dinner. The steak was very good and Andrea enjoyed Eric's company, managing to ignore the chattering couple across from her. Actually, Carina was chattering. Cameron was quietly eating her dinner, glancing up occasionally.

As their eyes held across the table, Andrea wondered which of them was more jealous. Cameron's eyes seemed to be full of questions.

CHAPTER ELEVEN

The drive back to the rig was made in silence and Cameron didn't know if it was her doing or Andrea's. She, for one, was afraid of what Andrea's reaction was to the evening. Carina had monopolized her time and attention throughout the meal, so much so that she and Andrea hadn't even exchanged words. Of course, Andrea wasn't lacking for conversation. Pretty boy Eric had apparently kept her amused, judging by the laughter the two of them shared. She was nearly embarrassed to admit that she had been jealous of the good time they seemed to be having.

She sighed as she disabled the alarm, letting Andrea go first up the steps. Lola was waiting for them and Andrea scooped her up, cuddling her against her neck as she walked inside. Cameron locked the door, then went to the fridge and got a bottle of water, the silence finally getting to her.

"So, you and Eric seemed to get along well," she said as she followed Andrea down the hall.

"Yeah. He's a nice guy. I really like him." Andrea stopped at the bathroom door. "And you and Carina looked like you were getting along really well too. Catch up, did you?"

Cameron swallowed. "Some."

"Good. She's very beautiful. I'm sure you enjoyed having her sitting practically in your lap."

"Look, Carina is Carina. I promise you there's nothing there. Nothing at all."

Andrea smiled. "I know. I'm just teasing you."

Cameron was confused by how easily Andrea dismissed it. Maybe Andrea didn't care that Carina was throwing herself at her. While Andrea brushed her teeth, Cameron leaned against the door.

"So tell me about Eric," she said, hating the pang of jealousy—and insecurity—she felt.

Andrea looked up, meeting her eyes in the mirror. "What about him?"

"Well, he's an attractive guy, he obviously likes you."

"Likes me? Seriously, Cameron?" Andrea wiped her mouth. "He's a guy. I'm a lesbian. You do know what that means, right?"

"Yes, but he's a really attractive guy. What better way to say 'Hey, I'm good. I nailed a lesbian'." As soon as she said the words, she wanted to take them back. She was acting like a damn teenager and she knew it.

"Nailed? Did you just say *nailed*?"

"You know what I mean."

Andrea shook her head and smiled. "You're way off base here, sweetheart. He actually reminds me of Mark. He's so easy to talk to."

"Oh, I...oh," she said, now embarrassed. Mark had been her best friend, her buddy. How silly of her to think something romantic might occur with Eric.

Andrea came over and touched her arm, rubbing her fingers lightly across her skin. "Get ready for bed, okay?"

She nodded, her gaze lingering on Andrea as she left. She didn't know why she was feeling insecure all of a sudden. What she and Andrea had, it was good, it was true. Carina could dance naked in front of her, and Cameron knew she wouldn't even be tempted. Andrea held her heart. She finally pushed off the door, taking her turn in the bathroom. As she was drying her face, she heard Andrea in the kitchen, talking softly to Lola as she readied the coffeemaker for morning. Cameron met her own eyes in the mirror and smiled. Little domestic things like that made her so content, so happy...made her realize that it had been missing for so many years. Missing and she didn't even know it.

She looked past her shoulder, seeing Andrea lounging in the doorway, much as she'd done earlier. She turned around, wanting nothing more than to take Andrea to bed. There was a bit of a hungry look in Andrea's eyes that thrilled her. But that must wait.

"Listen," she said, "I think we should split up."

Andrea's eyes widened and she took a step back. "*What*?"

Cameron frowned, seeing the look of disbelief and panic on Andrea's face. "What? No, no. God, Andi, no," she said quickly. "The case. That's all."

"Jesus, Cameron," she said as she let out a deep breath. "You scared the crap out of me."

"I'm sorry. No, I mean when we're out. I don't trust them. Reynolds and Jack were trained by Collie. You can tell by their questions, their attitude, they don't like the way we're running this," she said. She raised her eyebrows. "You think I'm overreacting?"

Andrea shook her head. "No. You're probably right."

Cameron ran her fingers through her hair, brushing it back on the sides, trying to split up everyone in her mind. "Two teams," she said finally. "I can't believe I'm even thinking this but, we could let Rowan come in here and play with the computers. He could coordinate us through phone and email." She paused. "I'll take...I'll take Eric and Reynolds. You take Jack and Carina."

Andrea raised both eyebrows in surprise, then shook her head. "No way," she said.

"Why?"

"I'm not taking Carina."

Again, Cameron was confused. "I thought you'd like it better if she was with you instead of me. I mean, you think she's trying to get in my pants, right?"

Andrea laughed. "She *is* trying to get in your pants. But I don't want her with me. There's a chance I might shoot her. No, I'll take Eric and Jack."

Now it was Cameron's turn to pause. Eric was a guy—albeit a very attractive guy—and that should give her no reason to be jealous that they might spend time together. Really, did she think Eric was a threat to her relationship with Andrea? Really? A straight guy?

"What's going through that pretty head of yours now?" Andrea asked as she closed the distance between them.

"Nothing," Cameron lied.

"You know I don't believe you." Her hands rested at Cameron's waist. "But that's enough talk. I think we're off duty now."

Cameron nodded, recognizing the look in Andrea's eyes, knowing that soon she would be naked and giving herself to Andrea. It was a hungry, possessive look, one that she loved.

"With all that flirting Carina did with you," she said, her hands pulling Cameron's shirt out of her jeans, "I think I need to remind you that...you belong to me."

Andrea pulled her shirt off in one motion then made quick work of her bra, the cool hum of the AC chilling her skin. Cameron felt her pulse pounding in her ears as Andrea lowered her head, her lips capturing a nipple. Cameron's head fell back as Andrea's tongue and teeth tugged at it and she couldn't contain a moan.

"You're mine," Andrea murmured, her mouth moving against the scar on her chest, finding her lips just as her hand slid between their bodies, cupping her, pressing the seam of her jeans against her center.

"Yes," Cameron hissed, her breathing labored now as she pushed against Andrea's hand. But Andrea's hand stilled, moving again to cup her breasts.

"Come to bed," Andrea said against her lips. "I have a long night planned."

Cameron's shirt and bra lay where they'd fallen as she followed her blindly into the bedroom, their hands clasped tightly together.

CHAPTER TWELVE

"Don't screw up anything."

"Can I call Jason if I do?"

Handing the number, along with Jason's email address to Rowan was something Cameron might live to regret as he clutched it tightly in his hand like a prized diamond.

"And don't let Lola out."

"Who names a cat Lola?" Reynolds asked as he stared at the ball of fur curled up on her usual spot on the loveseat.

Cameron ignored him, more concerned with Rowan as his fingers flew across the keyboard.

"You have access to everything with this," he said in awe. "Are you sure I can get clearance?"

"Murdock said he'd clear it. I told him to call you directly." She looked around, seeing Carina inspecting the rig. She'd made her way into the bedroom and Cameron was thankful she and Andrea had tidied up that morning. Their clothes had been strewn about, the bed a rumpled mess as Andrea had indeed made Cameron hers last night. Cameron felt the now familiar flutter in her stomach as she remembered Andrea taking her, leaving her mark upon her breast as she did.

"Nice," Carina said as she caught Cameron watching her.

Cameron turned back to Rowan. "Look for Monica Riddle. She must have used a street name. Find out what it was and where she worked."

He nodded. "I'll access her police records. They would have known aliases."

"If we find out where she worked then our next step is to start pulling credit card receipts and see how many matches we get for both the stop in Needles and the one where she worked." She raised an eyebrow. "Can you hack?"

He grinned. "Well, yeah."

"No way, Ross," Reynolds said. "We do this by the book."

"When you have your own case to work, you can do it by the book. We don't have the time it would take to get a subpoena to access credit card accounts."

"And there's a reason for that. Privacy," he said. "And Rowan works for me, not you."

She was about to point out the obvious, that Rowan was right now sitting—drooling—at *her* computers, taking instruction from her, but she could still hear Andrea's whispered words from earlier that morning. *Be nice.* So, she simply gave him a smirk of a smile and turned and winked at Rowan instead. "Let's hit the road then."

Carina took the backseat, letting Reynolds ride shotgun. The plan was to hit the big truck stop in Barstow again and show Monica's picture around and hopefully get some of the girls to talk. Now that the sheriff's department had officially released the case to them, they were free to work it without stepping on anyone's toes. The picture was a mug shot from five years ago when Monica was eighteen, but it was all they had. Andrea and her group were heading to Needles to do the same.

"How long have you and Agent Sullivan been partners?" Carina asked from the back.

Cameron refrained from glancing in the mirror to look at her. Carina was baiting her, nothing more. "A few months," she said evasively.

"Not counting the time in Sedona?" Reynolds asked.

"Oh, yes, Patrick Doe," Carina said. "Reynolds has told us all about it." She leaned forward and put an arm along the backrest. "Did you really jump off a cliff?"

Cameron flicked her eyes at Reynolds who gave her a coy smile. "It was more like a high ledge than a cliff," she said.

"Still taking risks, I see."

Carina had monopolized the conversation at dinner the other night, filling Cameron in on her exploits since the last time they'd seen each other. Cameron, on the other hand, had shared very little. That wasn't going to change, so she ignored Carina's comment.

"So if we find traces of Monica, what then is our plan?" Reynolds asked.

"Credit card receipts."

"I told you—"

"And I told you this was my case," she said. "If you want to play by all the rules, then get off of Murdock's team. You should know by now we have more leeway than most."

"Collie—"

"Jesus Christ, Reynolds, not Collie again."

"I'm just saying, we're not above the law. And arbitrarily gathering credit card receipts is a breach of privacy."

"And I don't care. I'm trying to stop a serial killer who is raping his victims then cutting off their goddamn heads. I don't care about privacy," she said.

"That evidence won't stand up in court."

She laughed. "You really think this will make it to court? He's a dead man the minute I see him."

Reynolds stared at her, slowly shaking his head. "Now I know why Collie wanted to distance himself from you. You're dangerous, Ross. Out of control."

She laughed again. "No, Collie wanted to distance himself

from me because he disliked me. It had nothing to do with the job and everything to do with a raven-haired beauty in Greece who chose me over him."

Carina laughed from the back. "Do tell, Cameron. This sounds like fun. Maybe she was someone I know."

She glanced in the mirror and smiled. Yeah, there were some fun times during her military days. She was young and reckless, everything was a thrill. She hadn't really lied to Andrea, but she never told her the extent of her adventures...or how many lovers she'd had. Nameless, faceless lovers, most. Carina being one of them.

"And for the record, I'm not out of control."

"What exactly is it we're hoping to accomplish?" Jack asked as they sped through the desert, just on the outskirts of Joshua Tree. Instead of taking I-10 all the way to Blythe and up Highway 95 to Needles, the GPS was taking them through the desert where they would intersect with Highway 95 just south of Needles. It was still over a two-hour drive.

Andrea turned in her seat and glanced at Eric with a frown. It was the third time Jack had asked the question. Eric leaned forward and tapped Jack on the shoulder.

"You didn't like her answers the first couple times you asked that question?" Eric laughed. "Or are you getting forgetful in your old age."

"So we show her picture around. Then what? So what if someone recognizes her? I deal in facts and concrete evidence. Neither of which seem very abundant."

"If someone knows her, or can remember a date, we pull security video. Or someone may remember the guy she was with." Andrea tried not to lose her patience with Jack, reminding herself that they all had military training, not police. Sometimes snooping for clues and asking questions was all you had. Like now.

"Or maybe someone remembers what his truck looked like," Eric added.

"At least it gives us a timeframe," Andrea continued. "We don't know if he holds them somewhere for days before killing them or if he kills them the same night. All we know about Linda Blake is that she hadn't been seen around there for a few weeks. That's way too vague to do us any good."

"The whole thing is vague," Jack said. "All this driving around to the middle of nowhere. Hell, if something goes down in Barstow, we're hours from there."

"Logistics is a problem, yes," Andrea said. "But it is what it is."

Thankfully, Jack had no more questions or comments and the drive continued in silence. That is, until Eric reached to the front and tapped her shoulder. She turned around, seeing the playful look on his face.

"So, whose idea was it to split up?"

Andrea glanced at Jack before answering. "Cameron's."

"And who picked sides?"

She smiled. "I did."

"I see. Still afraid you might shoot?"

"Shoot who?" Jack asked. "Carina?"

Andrea and Eric exchanged glances and Eric shrugged. "She's a bit obnoxious, don't you think."

Jack snorted. "A bit? Hell, everything is always about her. She's been there, done that and did it a lot better. I told Reynolds she wasn't going to be a good fit but he wanted a female and she was available."

"Equal opportunity employer," Andrea murmured, causing Eric to laugh.

"She's got credentials, I'll say that for her," Jack said. "CIA operative. Seems like she's taking a step down."

"Maybe her cover was blown," Eric offered.

"Maybe she wanted something new," Andrea said, thinking of Cameron and how she'd grown weary of that life.

"Well, I'm just glad I don't have to ride with her," Jack continued. "I'd rather listen to Rowan talk computers than listen to her."

Andrea glanced back at Eric, matching his smile. She had no idea the normally quiet, stoic older man would be so vocal in his dislike of Carina. She sighed as she looked out the window again, watching the endless desert flash by, her eyes drawn to some distant mountains on the horizon. Splitting up their teams was a good idea but she found she missed Cameron's presence. She allowed her mind to wander back to last night, picturing Cameron's face as she climaxed, hearing the whispered *Andi* as Andrea had continued to suckle her breast long after the tremors had left her body.

"What did you break?" Cameron asked when she saw Rowan's name come up on the console.

"Do you have any idea how fast your server is? I ran one of your algorithms—"

"You're *playing* with my algorithms?"

"I was just testing them. Jason is a genius. I mean—"

"Please tell me you didn't call just to talk about computers."

"Oh, no. Sorry. I got a name for Monica Riddle."

"Great," she said, quickly losing patience with him. "You want to give it to us or what?"

"Sorry, Cameron." He paused. "Can I call you Cameron or do you prefer Special Agent Ross?"

"Jesus Christ, Rowan, what's the goddamn name?"

"She...she either went by Angel or sometimes Rose."

"Okay. Good job, Rowan," she said.

"There's more. There's a sister. She lives in Redlands. I've emailed you the address and her phone number, in case you wanted to contact her. She's a bank teller. Gets off work at four thirty. Picks her kid up at daycare, then home by five thirty."

She laughed. "Excellent work. You can call me Cameron."

"Thank you. I hope you don't mind about the algorithm. I just wanted to see some of Jason's work."

"Play all you want," she said as she touched the screen to disconnect. "Where did you find him?" she asked Reynolds.

"Murdock recommended him."

"He's good."

Carina sighed. "He's a nerd. He's only twenty-five. Hasn't even lived yet."

"He got his PhD at twenty-one," Reynolds said.

"Like I said, a nerd."

Cameron wondered what she ever saw in Carina. Well, other than a sexy body. Back then, she hadn't realized how negative Carina was. Or maybe she just didn't care. Sex was an outlet for their stress and as she recalled, they used that outlet frequently.

"If someone can remember Angel or Rose, remember the last time they saw her, then I want Rowan to pull their security tapes and try to get footage. If we can't find anyone, then we'll need to hang around until the girls come out to work."

"What about the sister?" Reynolds asked.

"I'd like to talk to her too."

"How about you leave me at the truck stop? I can interview the girls. You and Carina can head to Redlands," Reynolds suggested. "Ask Agent Sullivan and her team to swing by and pick me up."

"They're at least two hours east of here."

"I can hang out. Observe."

She nodded. "Okay. Let me call Andrea."

CHAPTER THIRTEEN

"Alone at last," Carina said with an exaggerated sigh as Cameron pulled away from the noisy truck stop in Barstow.

"Alone?"

"Yes. You have to admit Reynolds was getting on your nerves too." She smiled and pursed her lips. "And we can finally catch up."

"What is there to catch up on?"

"Oh, come now, Cameron. You must have fond memories of our time together? I know I do," Carina said as her hand reached out to lightly stroke Cameron's arm.

"Fond memories? I don't know if I would call it that, Carina," she said. "We were nothing more than fuck buddies."

Carina laughed. "Yes. That's what made it so delightful." She let her hand drop to Cameron's thigh. "Would it be forward of me to say I'd like to pick up where we left off?"

Cameron bristled at her touch, amazed that Carina would be so bold. She stopped her hand before it slipped between her legs.

"Not interested," she said.

Carina's eyes widened in surprise. "Seriously?"

"Seriously."

"My, you have changed. Your exploits are legendary."

Cameron shook her head. "Not really. I believe you hold that honor."

Carina again let her hand fall to Cameron's thigh. "If I didn't know better, I'd say you're involved with someone. But the Cameron I remember wasn't into that sort of thing."

"People change. I'm not the same person I was back then." She glanced at her. "The missions we were on, we never knew if each day was going to be our last."

"Maybe that's why the sex was so good."

Cameron removed her hand again. "I'm still not interested."

"Surely you and Agent Sullivan aren't involved," Carina said.

Cameron said nothing.

"Oh, Cameron darling, she is *so* not your type."

"You think not?"

"No. You always went for the more worldly, glamorous types."

"Oh? Like you?"

Carina smiled and for a third time placed her hand on Cameron's leg. "Yes, exactly like me. Your Andrea is far from that. Not that she's not attractive. She is. She just seems so young, so naive."

"Naive? She hasn't lived the life we have, no, but she's not been spared from life's cruelties."

"So how long have you been lovers?"

"I never said we were." She glanced at her again. "And take your hand off of me."

Carina did but her smile was coy. "Are you in love with her, this partner of yours?"

How wonderful would it have been to be able to say, yes, she was in love. Madly, crazy in love. But she couldn't. "You know that's against the rules."

"Yes, love is definitely against the rules. Sex, not so much." Carina shifted away from her finally. "I should warn you though, I believe Eric has his sights set on her. When I talked to him earlier, he was planning a nice, romantic dinner out."

Cameron felt that seed of doubt creep in again, that tiny nibble of jealousy. She hadn't had a minute alone today to talk to Andrea and here she was, speeding down the highway toward Redlands, hoping to catch the sister at home. Andrea would be dining out, no doubt at a nice, fine restaurant with Eric. Not grabbing a pizza and taking it back to the rig, not staying in and making dinner herself, but going out, something they rarely did. She wondered if Andrea missed that. Maybe they should make it a point to go out more often. But really, any time she mentioned it, Andrea was content to stay in. As was Cameron. It was the quiet, alone time that they both seemed to savor. Now Carina was placing doubt in her mind. No, *trying* to place doubt. All Cameron had to do was think back to last night, the way Andrea had made love to her, her murmured words and soft kisses telling her how true their love was. No, she wouldn't fall into Carina's trap. Not this time.

"I hope he takes her someplace really expensive then," she said. "I usually only splurge on pizza."

That seemed to put Carina off enough that she quietly stared out the window, leaving them to continue the drive in silence. They hit heavy traffic in San Bernardino and she glanced at the monitor, noting that she would be turning left onto I-10 in a few miles. She contemplated calling Andrea, just to let her know where she was but that would be just an excuse. Reynolds would fill her in. Besides, she didn't want her to think she was checking up on her. She needn't have worried, however, as a soft beeping indicated a call. Instead of tapping the monitor to answer, she grabbed her phone instead. She knew they would not be able to say anything personal, but she didn't want Carina to listen to every word.

"Hey," she answered. "What's up?"

"Hi. Just wanted to check in," Andrea said. "We have Reynolds and we're now heading back to Needles."

"Why back?" she asked.

"We were able to talk to three of the girls who work the lot. They weren't giving us much, but Eric used his charm and finally got them to talk," she said with a laugh and Cameron heard Eric's voice in the background teasing Andrea. She bit down the jealousy she felt at their easy camaraderie. "There's a girl missing. Street name is Susie Bell. That's all I got. They haven't seen her in over three weeks. Young girl about twenty, they say. Could be Jane Doe 23," Andrea said.

"Okay. What's the plan?"

"She was staying at a cheap motel in Needles. We want to check it out, talk to the manager."

"Did Reynolds get anything in Barstow?"

"Not really. They knew her as Angel, but no one could pinpoint when the last time they saw her."

"Let's get Rowan to go over the security tapes. Maybe we can—"

"Already on it," Andrea said. "It'll be late when we get back. It's about two and a half hours from Needles to Indio."

"Yeah. We're almost in Redlands. It's only an hour to Indio. I'll take care of things at the rig." Meaning Lola, mainly. It was going to feel empty without Andrea around, she knew.

"Okay. Well," she paused. "Me too, Cameron."

Cameron frowned. *Me too?* Then she remembered their conversation from last week when Andrea accused Cameron of being afraid to say *I love you*. She laughed now, sporting a grin.

"Yeah, me too," she said, hearing the soft chuckle from Andrea as she disconnected.

"Anything new?" Carina asked.

"They have a possible lead on the Jane Doe. They're on their way back to Needles with Reynolds."

"Oh. Well it looks like it'll just be the two of us for dinner then. How convenient."

"I think I'll let you and Rowan share dinner. I need to spend some time with my cat."

"Oh Cameron, a cat? I thought surely that furry thing was your partner's. I can't see you with a pet."

"Like I said, people change." She merged into traffic on I-10, heading to Redlands.

She followed the GPS directions and only a few blocks past the freeway they were in a residential area. The homes were modest but well kept. She turned into the driveway of the sister's home.

"They all look alike," Carina said, glancing down the street.

"Yeah. I would hate living here." She got out, wondering if perhaps they should have called first. She didn't know if they would walk in on a grieving sister or not. She heard footsteps on the other side of the door but it was not opened.

"Who is it?"

"FBI," she said, holding up her FBI credentials to the peephole. "May we come in?"

The door opened revealing a slightly overweight woman, older than Cameron was expecting. She held on tightly to the door.

"Yes?" she asked nervously.

"Melinda Appleton?"

"Yes."

Cameron sighed, wishing Andrea were here. She was better at this part of the job. "I'm Special Agent Cameron Ross. This is Carina Moretti. I'm sorry, but we're here about your sister."

"Why would the FBI be interested in Monica?"

"May we come in?"

"Of course." She opened the door wider. "Please excuse the mess. I wasn't expecting company."

"No worries," she said, following Melinda inside. They walked through the living room which was cluttered with children's toys. The TV was on and a small girl was lying on the floor watching cartoons, oblivious to their presence. The kitchen counter was covered with bags, indicating Melinda had just come from the grocery store. She immediately began unpacking them as she motioned for them to sit at the table.

"I just got home a little while ago. My husband won't be home for another hour," she explained.

"We won't take up much of your time," Cameron said as she sat down. "When was the last time you saw Monica?"

"A couple of years, I guess."

"You weren't close?" Carina asked.

The woman shook her head. "Monica was...messed up. I can't blame her really. Our mother was a drug addict. Monica was around it all the time. I tried to get her out of the house when she was in high school but our mother wouldn't allow it." She opened the fridge and put in a carton of eggs. "I don't think Monica really wanted out. She was hanging around with the wrong crowd, you know what I mean? She was in and out of trouble."

"Did you know that she was arrested?"

"For prostitution? Yes." She smiled. "That's actually how I met my husband. He's a probation officer. We both tried to reach her, but she wasn't interested."

"Where's your mother now?"

"I have no idea. I haven't seen her in four or five years."

Cameron paused. "Do you know the circumstances of Monica's death?"

The woman looked away quickly. "Yes. It's horrible." She shook her head. "But it's hard to think of her as my sister. I'm eight years older. I moved out of the house as soon as I could. I worked and put myself through college, but I couldn't get her out. I finally stopped trying."

"But you kept in touch?" Carina asked.

"No, not really. She came around when she needed money. The last time, Joey—that's my husband—he told her not to come around anymore. We have the baby now." She smiled. "Well, not a baby. She's nearly three. But we didn't want Monica around. Not like she was. Like I said, she was messed up."

"Any other family?"

She shook her head. "We never knew our father. I have an aunt who lives in Pomona, but we don't really keep in touch. She's the complete opposite of our mother so you can imagine they weren't close when we were growing up."

"Do you know where Monica worked?"

"Worked? She didn't work."

"I mean—"

"Oh. Prostitution." She took a deep breath and closed her

eyes, as if to chase away the thought of her sister being a hooker. "I know she was up in Barstow a lot. She seemed to prefer to hang out at truck stops." She shook her head. "I really didn't ask a lot of questions. I didn't want to know."

Cameron wasn't sure what she was hoping to find, but they learned nothing new really. She stood up, handing Melinda Appleton her card.

"Thank you for your time. If you think of anything else," she shrugged, "please call."

"Why is the FBI on this case?"

"Monica wasn't the only girl killed," she said.

"I heard about the lady they found out near Indio. Is it the same killer?"

"We believe so."

"Was she a prostitute also?"

Cameron smiled politely. "I can't really discuss the details of the case with you. Again, thank you for your time. We can see our way out."

"That was a complete waste of time," Carina said when they'd settled back in the truck.

"Yeah. I think I was expecting to find a grieving sister," Cameron said as she drove them back to the freeway. "At least Barstow is confirmed. Reynolds told Andrea that Monica went by Angel. No one could pinpoint when they last saw her so Rowan is going to go over security."

"We have estimated times of death on all three victims?"

"Yes. So without knowing when they went missing, we have no idea how long he holds them, if at all."

"A trucker or a local?"

"Could be both," she said, something she and Andrea had discussed. "Number one, a trucker."

Once they got out of the heavy city traffic, the trip back down to Indio was made quickly and silently. Driving through the pass into Coachella Valley, they passed a huge wind farm, the blades of the turbines spinning round and round in the constant breeze. The barren mountains were a backdrop for the giant windmills, the white a perfect contrast of the brown drab surroundings. As they approached Palm Springs, Cameron declined Carina's offer of dinner. Instead, she drove straight on to Indio and the rig, happy to see that Rowan was already running programs to pull credit card receipts.

"A lot are going to be useless though. Company credit cards."

"Surely they have a truck associated with them."

"Yeah but that's just one more thing to sort through." He pointed at one of her computers. "Let this one run. Don't touch it," he said.

She cocked an eyebrow. "You do realize that this is *my* office, right?"

"Sorry. Yes. But please don't touch it. Hopefully by morning I'll be able to put some data together for you." He looked at her expectantly. "That is, if I can come back here and play with your stuff again."

She laughed. "Sure, Rowan. It's all yours. Now let's go. I'm tired and hungry."

After dropping them both off at the hotel, she picked up a pizza for dinner then settled back at the rig. After a long shower, she sat in her recliner in shorts and bare feet, fighting off a purring kitten who was trying to steal the pepperoni from her pizza.

She sighed, wishing Andrea were there with her. She glanced at her phone but refrained from calling. If Andrea needed anything, she would call.

CHAPTER FOURTEEN

"My God, this is a dump," Eric murmured as they followed the manager to room number eleven.

Andrea had to agree with him. Most of the outside lights were dark, bulbs broken or missing. Beer bottles and cans littered the area, and she saw what looked like a diaper against the chain-link fence.

"She paid for a month," the manager said. "Haven't seen her in weeks though."

"She pay cash?" Andrea asked.

He laughed. "You think I'm going to take a check from someone?"

"I don't suppose you see an ID when you book a room?" Reynolds asked.

"No," he said. He unlocked the door and pushed it open. "She signed it Susie Bell. That was fine by me."

"Step aside, please," Andrea said as she reached in and turned on the light. The bed was unmade and there was a towel tossed on top. Black pants were draped over a chair and two pairs of heels were lying on the floor. "Check the bathroom," she said.

"We got a brush," Jack said, pointing to the table.

"Toothbrush in here," Eric said from the bathroom.

"Great. Bag it." She turned to the manager. "I'm going to seal off this room. No one enters. Understand?"

"I could lose money. Someone may need—"

"She paid for the month. We still have a few days left." Then she smiled. "Besides, it looks like you have quite a few empty rooms should you have a sudden demand. This room stays."

He nodded. "Okay. No one enters."

"Jack, call Needles PD. Let them know what we have. I'll call the sheriff's department. We'll need their lab to run this for DNA."

"Even if DNA matches, that doesn't really help us," Jack said. "Susie Bell?"

"At least she's not Jane Doe 23," Eric said.

"Let's wrap this up," Reynolds said as he adjusted his tie. "This place is filthy."

Reynolds was still dressed impeccably in his suit and tie, even after spending most of the day at a truck stop in Barstow. At least Eric and Jack had ditched their ties. She was probably the only one comfortable after such a long day.

"I'm starving," Eric said. "Burgers on the way back?"

"Sounds like a plan," she said, wanting nothing more than to get back to Cameron. It was really the first day they'd spent any significant time apart and she found she missed her terribly.

After making calls to the Needles PD and San Bernardino Sheriff's Department, they were finally on their way back to Indio. She was beyond exhausted, having been on the road the majority of the day. The others must have felt the same way as they all ate their greasy burgers and fries in silence.

It was nearly midnight when they dropped her off at the rig. She quickly said her goodbyes and hurried to the door. She paused, wondering if Cameron would have armed the security or not. As a precaution, she went to the keypad and punched out the code, thankful she did as the familiar "all clear" sounded.

She entered quietly, thinking Cameron was in bed. She found her large frame curled on the loveseat, Lola tucked in against her stomach, both of them sound asleep. She couldn't help but smile, her heart filling with love at the sight. This was home. Her lover asleep, no doubt after waiting up for her, she succumbed, curling up as best she could. She spotted the pizza box and shook her head. Was she surprised?

Andrea knelt down beside her, gently stroking her arm. "Hey," she whispered.

Cameron jumped, her eyes opening immediately. They softened when they saw her and she sat up, flexing her shoulders.

"God, Andi, what time is it?"

"Late. After midnight."

Cameron reached for her, pulling her closer. "I missed you. Today, all day, I missed you."

Andrea nodded. "Me too." She leaned forward, kissing her softly. "I have thought about doing that for the last two hours," she whispered, letting her lips linger.

Cameron tangled her fingers in her hair, holding her close. "Did Eric take you out for a romantic dinner?" she asked before kissing her.

"When would we have been able to slip away from Reynolds and Jack?" Andrea leaned back, watching her. "We grabbed burgers on the way back. Way too late to eat but we were starving." She tilted her head, her eyes questioning. "Why would you think that?"

"Something Carina said. It doesn't matter."

Andrea stood, pulling Cameron to her feet too. She slipped deeper into her arms, letting them wrap around her as she buried her face in Cameron's neck.

"You do know what she's doing, right?"

"Yes."

"Good." She pulled out of her arms and took her hand. "Bed. I'm exhausted."

They went about their nighttime routines, Andrea feeling like she could fall asleep on her feet, but she forced herself through a quick shower. She'd been working eighteen hours straight, something she'd done many times before. There was just something about being in a car all day that zapped the energy from her.

She turned off the bathroom lights, then made her way down the short hallway to the bedroom, the soft light of the lamp illuminating the room. She found Cameron sitting up against the pillows, her breasts shadowed but bare. Lola was already in a tiny ball down by her feet, her preferred sleeping spot.

Andrea stood at the side of the bed, watching Cameron watching her. As tired as she was, she couldn't resist the look in Cameron's eyes. She slowly took off her shirt, revealing her breasts to Cameron. She could see Cameron's chest rising as her breathing increased. She slowly lowered her panties, seeing Cameron's tongue wet her lips. God, after last night, she thought she'd be sated, but the sight of Cameron watching her, knowing she was aroused, made Andrea forget all about the fatigue she'd been battling. She lifted the covers, finding Cameron as naked as she was. She slid closer, bending her head to Cameron's breast, her tongue bathing the nipple, feeling it harden against her lips.

"I love you," she murmured before taking it inside.

Cameron moaned, her hands finally reaching out to touch her, moving across her skin, lower to cup her hips and bring Andrea between her legs.

"I love you, Andi," she whispered, finding her mouth. "I missed you so much today."

Andrea wondered if it was her insecurity showing, or just the fact that Carina had filled her head with Eric, but Cameron nearly clung to her, her mouth possessive as she kissed her.

She decided it didn't matter which. She rolled over, letting Cameron's weight settle over her. She sensed Cameron's need to be in control tonight, much as she'd been last night. She parted her thighs, opening for Cameron, feeling her wetness coat her skin. Her hands moved slowly across Cameron's strong back, down her sides then back up again, sighing softly as Cameron's tongue teased her nipple.

"I don't like being apart," she murmured, arching into Cameron as she suckled her breast. "God, I love when you do that," she breathed.

Cameron moaned again, moving to her other breast. Andrea held her head tightly against her, her hips beginning to move against Cameron, her arousal reaching a fevered pitch. She wanted to beg Cameron to take her already but she knew Cameron wouldn't be rushed tonight. Her mouth moved ever so slowly downward, making Andrea squirm with desire. She raised her hips, pressing hard against Cameron, moaning when they made contact, but Cameron pulled away, her mouth continuing its downward path.

"Cameron, do something," she breathed. She felt Cameron smile against her skin.

"I thought I was." She lifted her head, her gaze smoldering. "Much like you were last night."

Andrea tried to smile as she remembered how she'd teased Cameron mercilessly, but her aroused state made it difficult to do anything other than urge Cameron to continue. She closed her eyes, pushing Cameron down, pleading for her to hurry.

"I promise I'll never do it again," she managed between breaths.

"Promise?"

"God, Cameron...yes, I promise."

Cameron laughed quietly, allowing Andrea to guide her. When Cameron spread her thighs, Andrea groaned, her fists clutching the sheets, her chest heaving. She lifted her hips, offering herself to Cameron. Cameron didn't prolong it any longer as her tongue snaked through her wetness, swirling around her clit, making Andrea moan louder. She tried to keep her eyes open, wanting to see Cameron as she made love to her, but her head spilled back as her hips rose, Cameron's mouth claiming all of her, sucking and nibbling until Andrea exploded, her body jerking violently as she climaxed against Cameron's face.

She was spent, too exhausted to even move and she felt Cameron gather her close, heard her whispered words, but her eyes remained closed as sleep claimed her immediately.

CHAPTER FIFTEEN

The motor home was crowded as everyone tried to find a place to sit. Lola was hiding in the bedroom under a pillow, and Cameron closed the door on the frightened cat. Reynolds was in the middle of a tirade. He'd just found out Rowan had been running the program to retrieve credit card receipts. Cameron thought she'd let him have his say before she interjected.

"I am the leader of this team. Me," he said, tapping at his chest. "You work for me. You do not work for Special Agent Ross." Cameron could see the vein bulging in his neck as he continued yelling at Rowan. "I thought I made myself clear. I told you—"

"Give it a rest, Reynolds," Cameron said as she'd had enough of his ranting. Rowan looked like he was about to cry. "We needed the receipts. Why do you think Jason wrote all of these programs for me? So that we can wait and get a nice and tidy subpoena?" She shook her head. "No. So that we can get what we need when we need it. So lay off Rowan. He was just doing as he was told. Murdock gave the okay on this."

"Murdock? Then why the hell didn't he run it by me."

"Because he doesn't have to. Now sit down already. Jesus, it's not even nine o'clock and you've already stressed me out." As if on cue, Andrea handed her a cup of coffee, their eyes meeting briefly.

"When will they have DNA back on the stuff from the motel room?" Jack asked.

"They said they'd put a rush on it," Andrea said. "I hope today."

"Okay, let's go over everything we have so far." Cameron nodded at Rowan, who had been busy putting together a timeline and best guesstimates. "Rowan's been having a little affair with my computers in there so let's see what he's got for us."

Rowan blushed profusely as he stood in the kitchen, a laptop held in his hands. His eyes darted around the room nervously and Cameron wondered if this was the first time he'd had to address anyone like this. She didn't know much about him but she guessed being on Reynolds's team was his first assignment. He cleared his throat before speaking.

"Remember a lot of this is speculation based on...well, we don't really know when they were abducted. Now—"

"Speculation seems to be the only thing we have here," Reynolds said with a hint of irritation in his voice.

"Speculation is my middle name," Cameron said with a smile. "Go on, Rowan. Speculate away."

"Let's start with the first victim, Jane Doe 23. If she turns out to be Susie Bell, the missing girl from Needles, she was last seen approximately three and a half weeks ago, give or take a day on either end of the equation. The profile on Susie Bell that Andrea supplied me with is a blond female, age twenty-one. She had a history of drug use, according to her associates, so that fits the coroner's report for Jane Doe 23." He looked up nervously, avoiding Reynolds but smiling slightly at Andrea. "I should say approximate age twenty-one, which also fits in the range the coroner reported."

"Age is probably not a factor in how he chooses his victims though," Eric said. "The second victim, Linda Blake, was thirty-one."

"Neither is hair color a factor," Jack added. "Both Monica and Linda were brunette. If Susie Bell is Jane Doe 23, she was blonde."

"If we go by the last time they were seen—which as I said is an estimate—versus when their bodies were found, he is holding them for shorter periods each time. Again, that's if Jane Doe 23 is Susie Bell." He clicked quickly on his laptop. "By the way, I'm running a face recognition program against the security tapes from Barstow, trying to get a last visual on Monica Riddle."

"Let's take this in order," Cameron said, seeing Reynolds start to fidget as Rowan was bouncing all over the place.

"Sorry. Okay, victim one was found twenty-one days ago. Susie Bell's been missing twenty-six days, give or take. Victim two, Linda Blake, was found eight days ago now. We have no known last seen date other than she may have been missing a couple of weeks. I'll run that security file next for face recognition to see if I can get a better date."

"So once a week or so he grabs a girl," Eric commented.

"Approximately. Monica Riddle, our most recent victim, found two days ago, again was thought to have been missing a week. If that holds true, he grabs them, holds them for nearly a week, then dumps the body. But there was a longer gap between the first and second victims. Two weeks. Only one week before the third killing. In all three cases, time of death was twenty-four to thirty-six hours from when the victim was found."

"Not surprising as they were most likely dumped at night, found the next day," Carina said.

"But tox report showed Jane Doe 23 had cocaine in her system. She had to have been using while being held, if our timeline is correct," Rowan said.

"If it's correct? This is crazy, Ross," Reynolds said with a shake of his head. "We have nothing. This is just grasping at straws."

"What would you rather do, Reynolds? Sit around on our asses, hoping some evidence will fall in our laps?"

"Actually," Andrea said. "It's not all that crazy. If Jane Doe 23 was a user, then most likely she had a supply with her. In her purse, for instance. So when he nabs her, he finds it. Maybe they do a line together. Maybe she's an addict, maybe she's freaking out so he gives it to her."

"Again, more speculation," Reynolds said.

"Right," Cameron agreed. "Plausible? Possible? Probable?" She smiled. "Yes. Now, Rowan, tell me what my lovely computer spit out on your receipts."

"Oh, yeah, that was cool," he said as his fingers again tapped quickly on his laptop. "I pulled data on credit and debit card transactions," he said, glancing quickly at the disapproving Reynolds. "Then I dumped all of that into one of Jason's programs to sort out company cards by individual drivers. I was expecting a huge return since our dates and times are a little imprecise, but there are only twelve hits."

"Explain, please," Carina requested.

"Well, I first used an estimated date of abduction. Well, the computer did," he said. "Do you want me to tell you the program I used? Because—"

"Just the facts," Cameron said.

"Okay. So what I did was put in all of our data, with a range for disappearances and the coroner's times of death. Using only the two truck stops in Barstow and Needles, twelve hits came back where the same credit card was used during all three timeframes."

"Have you run their names?" Reynolds asked.

"I've got eight company credit cards and four individuals. I've separated the eight out into distinctive trucks." He glanced at Cameron. "I've not yet been given the okay to hack into their servers to get truckers' names."

Cameron nodded. "Do it." She expected Reynolds to protest but he kept quiet.

"So we're going to stake out the stops?" Eric asked.

"That's what I would do," Reynolds said. "We could get help from the local PD or sheriff's department."

"Absolutely not," Cameron said.

"Why not? If we want to prevent—"

"We're not trying to prevent another murder," Cameron said. "We're trying to catch the bastard."

"We don't want to alarm him," Andrea said. "If you plan to rob a bank and you get there and you see cops patrolling—extra security guards—then most likely you're going to abort. We don't want him to abort."

"There's more," Rowan said. "I used an algorithm to determine the next most likely hit. I've got an eighty-two percent chance he hits tomorrow night, a sixty-three percent chance for Thursday night. The likely hit will be at the Barstow truck stop, not Needles."

"How can you know this?" Carina asked.

"Because the data complies, using—"

"Because the computer said so," Cameron interjected. "With the range you've given, are all of the hits during the week?" she asked him.

"Yes. In fact, Wednesdays got the highest probability."

"So, the *computer* says he's going to abduct someone tomorrow night? In Barstow?" Reynolds asked. He looked at Cameron. "You actually believe all this stuff?"

"How do you think we caught Patrick Doe? You think we just accidentally happened to be on that trail the night he brought up his next victim?" She stood, pacing in the tiny space that was available. "But what do we do with this information? Like Andrea said, we don't want to alert him."

"We pose as a potential victim."

Cameron's eyes flew to hers. "What?"

"I'll go undercover as a hooker. We can—"

"No," she said forcefully. "Absolutely not."

"I agree with Cameron," Carina said. "It would hardly be believable. There is nothing," she said, pointing at Andrea, "that says *hooker* here. You couldn't pull it off."

"I have experience," Andrea said, glancing at Cameron. "I could pull it off. I just don't have the outfit."

Cameron felt panic tighten her chest. She knew that determined look in Andrea's eyes. And here, in front of everyone, was not the time for Cameron to plead her case.

"Okay. So you go under. We wire you. We follow you." She shrugged. "Is that the plan?"

"Yes."

"And so what happens when you have the wrong guy? How do you get out of it?"

"Not tonight honey," Eric said as he rubbed his temples. "I have a terrible headache."

They all laughed, even Reynolds. But Cameron still didn't like it.

"I think our guy travels," Andrea said. "I don't think he's one who parks for the night. I think he picks up our girls, maybe with a promise to take them to the next stop."

"Maybe he offers them more money if they'll go with him," Eric suggested.

"He could use that as a ruse for company," Jack said.

"Grasping at straws again, people," Reynolds said.

"I think our guy does the soliciting," Andrea said. "I think he approaches the ladies first."

"Why do you think that?" Carina asked.

"Because if your intent is to kill, do you chance waiting to be approached? What if it's a busy night? One of the ladies that works the stop might not ever come to your truck. So you're all geared up to kill but you have no victim."

"Makes sense," Eric said. "But how do we target him when we don't even know who he is?"

Andrea glanced at Rowan. "He'll give us a name with the highest probability."

"And how will he do that?" Reynolds asked.

"Look, Reynolds, do you really need to know how algorithms work?" Cameron asked. "Once he finds the names of the twelve, he'll dump that in along with their traveling history." She raised an eyebrow at Rowan. "Right?"

"Right. I'll be able to trace their movements using the receipts. The algorithm will tell us who is most likely our guy."

"And that's how you want to work this?" Reynolds asked.

"I'm not crazy about having Andrea be the target, no," she said, glancing at her. "But we don't have a lot of options."

"I can be the target," Carina said, giving her a flirtatious smile. "I can pull off the hooker act."

Cameron shook her head. "No offense, Carina, but I haven't

worked with you in a lot of years. I trust Andrea with this. Not you."

"Well, she is your...*partner*," Carina said. "No offense taken."

"Okay, let's let Rowan get to work," she said. "Reynolds, divide your team. We need the post and tox reports on Monica Riddle. We also need to get with San Bernardino's crime lab and see if DNA is back on Susie Bell. We need this today so push them if you have to."

"What will you do?"

"Andrea needs an outfit for tomorrow. We'll be shopping. We need to test out her wire and bug too. I'll need Rowan for that. Then we'll have to put together a plan for how we're going to make sure Andrea has eyes on her at all times." She looked at her watch. "Let's meet up at your hotel at seven. We'll order in. Chinese or something. Then we'll go over everything again."

Eric put his arm about Andrea and pulled her close. "I think your name should be Cherry Ann," he said. "How about it?"

"Cherry? Really?" Andrea shook her head. "I don't think so."

"No? It's perfect."

"No."

"Then how about Candy?"

Andrea laughed. "I like Candy better than Cherry. But I think I'll just stick with Andrea."

"Not nearly as much fun," Eric said and kissed her cheek quickly before following the others out.

With a slight blush on her face Andrea looked at Cameron, who raised her eyebrows but said nothing.

"Well, I guess I'll get to it," Rowan said.

Cameron took Andrea's hand and led her back into the bedroom, closing the door again behind them. Lola was curled on the pillows and didn't even bother to lift her head.

"Can we talk about it now?"

"There's nothing to talk about," Andrea said.

"I don't like it."

"You don't get to make that decision."

"The hell I don't. This man is a monster. I don't want you anywhere near him."

Andrea put her hands on her hips and stared at her. "Do you think I can't handle it?"

"That's not it and you know it."

Andrea sighed, then moved closer, letting her hands roam up Cameron's arms. "Why are we bothering with this conversation? We both know it's a done deal, Cameron."

Cameron pulled her into an embrace. "I know, Andi. I just don't like it."

Andrea kissed her, letting her lips linger. "I think I fell asleep on you last night," she said.

"Yes, you did."

"Well, we'll have to take care of that tonight, won't we?"

Cameron closed her eyes and just held her tightly for a long minute, wishing they could spend a lazy day together. She finally released her.

"Shopping?"

"Yes. I'll even let you buy me lunch."

"It's a date."

CHAPTER SIXTEEN

"This egg roll is fantastic," Eric said as he licked the corners of his mouth. "Good choice, Ross."

Andrea had to agree, and she wished she'd ordered more than two. She looked at Cameron who had yet to touch hers. She was busy reading the coroner's report on Monica Riddle.

"No drugs in her system other than ketamine and phenobarbital. Yet according to everyone, she was a user. Even her sister said as much."

"So unlike Jane Doe 23, she didn't have anything on her. Any drugs in her system were out by the time she was killed."

"Rowan, you get a video match?" Cameron asked as she picked up her carton of kung pao chicken.

"The last footage of Monica was six days before her body was found. It was at six twenty-three p.m. as she left the convenience store."

"And Linda Blake?"

"So far nothing."

"What about Susie Bell?"

He shook his head. "No. They only keep surveillance footage for two weeks."

"Okay." She rubbed her eyes, and Andrea could tell how tired she was. "So no new data to enter other than we have confirmation on Susie Bell?"

"No. And I put in the date and time for Monica but it didn't change the results."

"What time are we going out?" Jack asked.

"As soon as it's dark, I want Andrea in place," Cameron said. She put her Chinese food aside and reached for her bottle of water. "Rowan, let's go over the logistics."

Rowan wiped his hands on a napkin then pulled his laptop closer. Andrea, too, put her food aside. As good as it was, she'd suddenly lost her appetite. Talking and planning was one thing. But laying it all out, going over the procedures, brought it closer to home. Tomorrow night, she'd be putting herself out there, hoping their guy took the bait. And hoping in all of their planning they didn't leave the smallest thing out.

"We've got a tracking device that Andrea will attach to the truck." He glanced at her. "Stick it on the door, under the cab, inside or out. Doesn't matter. It's magnetic, so anything you can find. I've implanted a microphone in these earrings," he said, holding up a small gold loop. He then held up a gaudy yellow plastic watch. "I've also put a tracking device in the watch, just in case Andrea is separated from the truck."

"Will she have an earpiece too?" Carina asked.

"No. We didn't want to take the chance he might spot it," Rowan said.

"A weapon?"

"Not on her," Cameron said. "She'll conceal one in her purse. Reynolds, did you let Barstow PD know what we're doing?"

"Yeah. I spoke to the chief. He wasn't thrilled with the idea but said they'll be ready to assist if need be."

"Good." Cameron turned to Eric. "You, Jack and Carina will be in one vehicle. Reynolds will ride with me. Rowan will rig up our communication where we can all be on—listen and talk—at the same time. You'll also have a feed of Andrea's mic. Once she's in the truck, we follow."

"And you think he's going to just take her to where he does his killing?" Jack asked.

"Yeah, that's the plan."

Andrea saw them all looking at her, perhaps because she'd been quiet through it all. She and Cameron and Rowan had been over it several times already, so she didn't feel the need to say anything. She'd been undercover several times in LA, usually for a drug sting, but she knew how to play it. The worst part would be maneuvering in heels. She calmly looked back at them as she picked up her last egg roll and took a bite.

"So did you get a sexy outfit?" Eric asked, his eyebrows wiggling teasingly.

"Strapless," she said after she swallowed. "You'll love it."

"Oh, I'm sure I will," he said with a grin.

"Did Cameron pick it out?" Carina asked with a sly smile.

"Actually, she did," Andrea said. She'd spent very little time around Carina, thankfully, but she had a strong dislike for the woman. Andrea had a hard time believing that she and Cameron were once lovers.

"Well, she does have excellent taste. Or rather she did." Carina rolled her eyes to Cameron. "Remember that black, sleek dress you got for me in Rome?"

Cameron frowned. "No. I don't recall," she said with a shake of her head. "But I think that's all we have for today. Unless some new developments occur, let's take it easy tomorrow. We might be up all night. I want to be in Barstow by six so let's meet back here at three tomorrow." She glanced at Rowan. "You'll have a name?"

"Yes. It's running now. Jason is awesome, by the way. I've never seen such a complicated program. It's using data from like ten different sources and is sorting—"

"Yeah. Right." Cameron smiled. "He's a genius."

"I'll come over in the morning and compile it all."

"Wonderful. Can't wait."

Andrea hid her smile as Cameron's gaze landed on her. She knew Cameron didn't like the plan they had set up, but someone had to be the bait. She wasn't really crazy about the idea herself. Getting inside a truck and driving away with a man who could possibly be a serial killer didn't exactly thrill her. Cameron raised her eyebrows in a silent question and Andrea nodded.

"See you guys tomorrow," she said.

Their short drive to the rig was made silently and they both went about their nighttime routines, sidestepping each other in the small bathroom. Andrea didn't need an explanation from Cameron. She knew Cameron was worried and this was her way of dealing. She found Cameron in bed, cuddling the purring Lola who was stretched out in her arms.

"She misses us," Cameron said.

"When this is over, let's ask Murdock for some down time," Andrea suggested as she pulled the covers back on the bed. "I miss us too."

Cameron put Lola down at the end of the bed and rolled over, pulling Andrea closer to her. "Me too. I don't like this whole *team* stuff." Her hand slid under Andrea's T-shirt, boldly cupping her breast. "You're not going to do anything stupid, right?"

Andrea smiled. "Shouldn't I be asking you that?"

"There aren't any cliffs around. I think I'm safe."

Andrea rolled toward her, entwining their legs together. "Please don't worry about this so much. Nothing's going to happen. Besides, you'll be following right behind me."

"I know. I just have a bad feeling about this."

"I'll be fine." She nuzzled Cameron's neck, inhaling her unique scent. While she would have been content just to snuggle, her hands slid across Cameron's soft skin, making their way to her breasts. Cameron's breath hitched and Andrea's lips found their way to Cameron's mouth. "I love you," she murmured.

Cameron rolled them over, settling her weight on top of her. Their eyes met and held, then Cameron lowered her head, kissing Andrea softly.

"I love you too."

CHAPTER SEVENTEEN

The smell of diesel fuel and the constant rumbling of engines permeated the air. Cameron tapped her foot nervously, her eyes jumping from one truck to another, wondering how they were going to find their guy in this crowded lot.

"You really think Rowan's on target with this guy?"

Cameron flicked her gaze at Reynolds, then back to the trucks. "It's not just Rowan, it's the algorithm. You put in the data, it gives you a probability."

"Sixty-eight percent? Is that high?"

"The more data you have, the higher the accuracy," she said. "It's all we have. If he's not our guy, we go on to the next one." She eyed his clothes with a raised eyebrow. "Really Reynolds? We're on a stakeout and you're in a suit? Couldn't you have dressed down a little to fit in with our surroundings?"

"This is what I wear."

"At least take your tie off. Jesus, even an idiot could make you for a cop."

He sighed but finally loosened his tie before removing it. Her gaze went back to the trucks. It was full dark now, only a sliver of a moon visible in the sky. She could see people moving in the shadows, walking between the parked trucks. Some stopped to talk, others kept moving, heading to the convenience store or the showers. The name Hank Waters popped up with a sixty-eight percent rating. The troubling part was that he didn't register in the system. Not anywhere. Rowan had pulled his name from the credit card receipts for the small trucking company he works for, based out of Riverside. No hits in the system meant he was using a false identity, probably driver's license as well. Her gut told her he was their guy, but it seemed too easy.

"Cameron, his card's been used. Bay Four," Rowan said, his voice loud and clear over the console speaker.

"Copy that." Andrea was in Eric's car, parked in the back and out of sight. "Show time." She heard a car door open and close, assuming Andrea was on the move.

"We're going to swing around, see if we have a visual," Eric said.

"Slow and easy, Eric," she murmured. She took a deep breath, trying to quell the tightness in her chest. She had a bad feeling that she couldn't shake. She'd learned over the years to trust that feeling, but there was nothing she could do about it now. The plan was in motion.

Andrea thought the chewing gum was a bit much but Eric had insisted. She chewed deliberately, concentrating on walking in heels, something she was not used to at all. She swung her hips, smiling as a trucker gave an exaggerated whistle.

"Like what you see, sugar?" she asked as she kept moving. The tight strapless dress hugged her body, so short it barely covered her ass. She'd added black fishnet hose and a garter belt that peeked out enticingly. When she'd modeled it for Cameron her jaw had dropped open, and she'd pushed Andrea back into the dressing room, taking several minutes to let her know just how enticing it was. She smiled at the memory of their quick make-out session, still picturing Cameron's flushed face as the saleswoman had knocked on the door, asking if they were okay.

She clutched her purse tighter as she approached Bay Four. Her only means of defense was a small caliber handgun hiding inside along with a phone. The phone was an afterthought, but Cameron wanted her to take it. *Just in case.*

She slowed her walk, wishing she knew who their target was, other than the truck in Bay Four. She turned her head, trying to see if anyone was about when she walked right into the solid chest of a man. She instinctively held her hand out to steady herself, trying to remain in character.

"Hey, big fella. You startled me."

"You lookin' to play?"

"That depends." She took a step back, sizing up the man. He was tall, easily over six feet, his frame muscular. A stubby beard indicated he hadn't shaved in several days. He was close enough to smell tobacco on his breath and she had to stop herself from turning away. When she finally met his eyes, she saw a soulless man in front of her and the tiny hairs at the back of her neck stood out. She knew instantly he was their guy.

"I'm lookin' to take a drive," he said.

"And you want company?" She tilted her head. "It'll cost you more."

He smiled, a smile that never reached his eyes. "I can pay."

"Two hundred," she said.

"That's it?"

She took the gum out of her mouth and tossed it aside. "Two hundred to get in your truck. And then another two hundred when I get out."

He pushed aside a well-worn NASCAR cap and scratched his head, seeming to contemplate her offer. She was worried that perhaps she'd shot too high but he nodded. "Deal."

She glanced at the dusty red rig in the bay, the trucking company's logo just a faded puzzle of letters on the door. "That yours?"

He nodded. "Give me just a second to finish up."

"Sure, honey. You take your time," she said, giving him a flirty smile. When he walked around the truck, her smile faded. "I hope you guys can hear me. I'm in. I'm putting the tracker on the truck now," she said quietly as she walked into the bay. Diesel engines rumbled loudly under the cover of the bays, and she doubted they would be able to hear her any longer. She looked about, making sure he was still tending to the fuel. His back was to her and she slipped the small magnetic box from under her garter belt and nonchalantly attached it to the fender of the truck.

She was about to make her way out of the bay when he turned around, looking past her. She turned, surprised to find another man walking toward her.

"About damn time, Hank," the man said. "You couldn't have called?"

Andrea stood still as the two men approached each other between the two rumbling trucks. She put her hands on her hips and smiled broadly.

"We doing double duty? It'll cost you more," she said to her target.

"Jesus, Hank, you still picking up fender lizards?" The man looked at her and shook his head. "No thanks, honey."

"Where you parked?" Hank asked.

"Bay Twelve." He tipped his dirty hat at them. "See you next round."

Andrea's arm was squeezed hard as Hank Waters led her away. She turned back, confused, as the other man got in the truck in Bay Four—with her tracking device—and drove away.

Oh fuck.

"I can't hear a goddamn thing, Rowan. Clean it up," Cameron said.

"I'm sorry. That's the best I can do. The engines are too loud."

"This is not helping us," she said.

"Okay, they're on the move, pulling out. I'm putting it up on your screen now."

Cameron took a deep breath, then started the truck. "Eric, you copy?"

"Yeah. We don't have a fancy console like you have but it's up on our phones."

"Stay behind me," she said as she drove slowly through the parking lot, her eyes darting between the red dot flashing on the animated map and the trucks surrounding them.

"Don't follow too close," Reynolds said.

"I won't," she murmured as she pulled onto the highway, letting the big rig in front of her gain some speed. "Signal is strong, Rowan. Good job."

"Okay. I'm overriding our feed with Andrea's. It'll run continuously, but you can talk over it now."

A few seconds later, Andrea's voice could be heard.

"What's your name, sugar?"

"Does it matter?"

"Well, I just like to know what name to scream out," she said.

Cameron smirked. "She's a natural."

"Henry. But they call me Hank. What's yours?"

"You can call me...Candy."

This time Eric laughed. "I win," he said, referring to the names they'd tossed out for Andrea to choose from.

"Candy? I like that."

"So, where are we heading? I'm used to doing my business right away, you know what I mean?"

"I got a place. I don't like the truck."

"Yeah? So where's my two hundred bucks?"

"I'm good for it. Don't worry."

"Baby, I'm not worried. My legs don't spread for free."

Reynolds chuckled beside her. "She's good. You think this is our guy?"

"It sounds like it. But something's not right. It's too easy." She tapped the wheel, keeping an even distance between her and the truck they were following.

"You know, I used to be married," Andrea said. *"I wasn't always in this line of work."*

"But you like it, right?"

"Baby, I'll make it good for you, don't worry."

"I ain't worried."

"I would like to know where we're headed though."

"Why so curious?"

"I don't want to get too close."

"Too close?"

"My husband was a gambler. When we lived in Vegas, he lost everything. Our savings. Our house. I left his ass and moved to LA but I couldn't find work."

"You got a job now."

"Yeah, and I'm good at my job, baby, don't you worry."

"I bet you are. I can't wait to find out."

"I just get nervous now whenever I'm heading to Las Vegas. Bad memories."

Cameron frowned, her gaze going to the red dot on the monitor heading steadily toward Los Angeles.

"What the hell?"

"What?" Reynolds asked. "What's wrong?"

"Didn't you just hear what she said? Rowan, activate the tracking device on her watch."

"What for? We have a strong signal already."

"Just do it." She took a deep breath, her chest tight. She waited only seconds for the monitor to change. "Son of a bitch," she murmured.

They were following the wrong truck.

CHAPTER EIGHTEEN

"Eric, stop that goddamn truck and find out where the hell our guy is," she said as she slammed on her brakes, causing horns to honk around her. She bounced across the median, barely conscious of Reynolds beside her. Her hands were tight on the wheel, squeezing painfully as they bounded across the highway, now heading east instead of west.

"What the hell is wrong with you? Are you trying to get us killed?"

"Rowan, how far out?" she asked, ignoring Reynolds.

"Based on their speed and—"

"Just give me a guess."

"Twenty-three point four miles."

"Twenty-three point four miles," she repeated. "Great," she murmured as she sped up, passing cars at an alarming speed. She almost felt like they were flying down the highway. Judging by the grip Reynolds had on the dash, they were. "You're turning white, man."

"Not funny," he said.

"You don't talk much, do you?"

"You talk too much."

"Just trying to get to know you, baby."

"We'll have plenty of time for that."

"Yeah? I hope it's soon. I don't normally do this, you know."

"What?"

"Travel. Most just want it in their rig."

"Yeah? Well, I'm different. I think you're going to like it."

"Hey guys," Eric said, drowning out Andrea's conversation. "Got the truck. Tag team drivers. They switched trucks in Barstow. The truck Andrea is in is heading to Vegas on I-15."

"Eric, find out everything he knows about our guy. Then find out who manages the trucking company. We need to know who the hell Henry Waters is. Copy?"

"We're on it."

"You know, those guys work for me, not you."

"Shut up, Reynolds."

She glanced at her speed as she neared a hundred, thankful the traffic wasn't too heavy. She passed another truck, then glanced at Reynolds.

"Sorry. I know they're your team. But Andrea is mine."

"I know you're worried. We'll get there. If you don't kill us first."

"Hey, what are you doing?"

"What does it look like? I'm taking your purse."

Andrea swallowed down the panic she was feeling, trying to stay in character...praying Cameron was not still following the other truck.

"Baby, why do you want my purse?"

"Shut up."

"What did I do?" Her eyes widened as he opened her purse.

"Well, well. A gun." He flicked on the overhead light in the cab, taking the gun out. "Take off your jewelry."

"What's wrong with you? You're scaring me. I think I want you to stop."

"Too late for that, pretty lady. Now take it off."

"Why?"

"Because you're a cop, that's why. You probably have a bug on you. Now take it off."

She tried to laugh. "A cop? Why do you think I'm a cop?"

"I can smell it. Now do it. Put it in the purse."

He waited—watching—while she removed the watch and earrings. She couldn't hide the watch from him, but she needed to hide the earring with the mic. Their plan was unraveling quickly, and she needed to hold on to something linking her with Cameron. She felt real fear for the first time as his soulless eyes watched her.

"You don't want to do this," she said as she dropped the watch in the purse, then made a show of taking off her earrings.

"Oh, I do want to do it," he said. When his eyes turned back to the road she stuck the earring under her garter belt, then dropped the other one in the purse. "And I'm going to love to fuck you. I've always wanted to fuck a cop. And I'm going to fuck you until you bleed."

"Goddamn bastard," Cameron said between gritted teeth. "Rowan, how far are we?"

"His speed is slowing. They're eight miles ahead."

"Jesus, that's too far."

"What are you doing? You can't just throw my purse away."

"I just did. Now shut up."

Cameron and Reynolds both looked at the monitor, seeing the red dot stop moving, while the green, indicating her truck, crept closer.

"Rowan, talk to me," she said.

"She's obviously still got the earring on her."

"Can you locate her with that?"

"No. Not...not with what I have. I mean, I could try but it would take...could take an hour. The best I can—"

"We don't have an hour. Give me something," she said quickly, interrupting him.

"Okay, based on his average speed of sixty-eight, I can calculate their distance from where our tracker stopped. We should still be able to locate the truck."

"He's got a place, he said. That means he's getting off the highway." She pounded her fist on the steering wheel. "How the hell did he make her for a cop?"

"Serial killers are not dumb," Reynolds reminded her. "They're calculating. Meticulous about details."

"She played it right," Cameron said. "Right down to the damn garter belt."

"I think that might have been it," Reynolds said. "New clothes. Hookers don't have new clothes."

"Oh come on. The man's not going to know whether the clothes are new or not."

"Attention to detail, remember. Something must have clued him in."

"What are you doing? Why are you turning?" Andrea asked.

"Shut up."

"Where are you taking me?"

"I think you know where I'm taking you. You owe me a fuck, remember?"

"Look, you don't want to do this."

"I said shut up."

The slap they heard and Andrea's soft cry afterward was deafening in the silence that followed. Cameron tried to keep it professional, she tried to think of it as any other mission, but her heart wouldn't let her. Her body was tense, aching.

"Goddamn it, Rowan. Talk to me," Cameron said. They had just passed the marker where Andrea's purse had been thrown.

"Based on his speed, still seven miles ahead of you."

"Pull up a map. Show me a satellite."

"Will you watch the road," Reynolds said as she zipped around a slow-moving car. "I can check the map."

"He was turning. Do you see the road to the right that heads to the Nevada border?"

"Yeah. See it."

"I think he turned off the highway," Rowan said.

"You think?" she asked tersely.

"Okay, there's a private road to the left, about a mile down. It looks small though," Rowan said. "Can an eighteen-wheeler make it down something like that?"

"I see it," Reynolds said, pointing the monitor. "Any dwellings?"

"Yes. There's a building of some kind," he said. "It's at least a half mile off the highway."

"Anything else?" Cameron asked. "We need to be sure."

"There's another road, about a mile farther," Rowan said. "But based on my calculations, I don't think they were that far."

"You better be right," she murmured, her rigid gaze fixed on the highway. "Get us some backup," she ordered. "And an ambulance."

CHAPTER NINETEEN

Andrea winced as he grabbed her arm, pulling her roughly across the seat and out of the cab. She nearly twisted her ankle as the high heels folded under her. Catching her balance, trying to formulate a plan, she found herself staring into the barrel of the gun he'd taken from her purse.

"That way," he said, motioning to what appeared to be a long-abandoned shack. "I want you alive, but don't think I won't shoot you."

She nodded, not trusting herself to speak. She dealt with victims her whole career, never once truly understanding their fear. Right then, at that moment, she felt it deep in her soul. She listened absently at the whir of traffic, thinking they were a good half-mile away from the highway, maybe more. She wondered if Cameron was rushing to find her.

Surely she was. Andrea knew she had time. He liked to play with his victims. She shivered, thinking of all the things he would most likely do to her. She was beginning to understand it all. He grabbed his victims and drugged them, holding them here most likely while he finished his route. Then he would come back and have his fun. He could hold them here for days. If his truck route stayed the same, he could stop in anytime he liked without causing suspicion.

She nodded slowly, turning toward the building. Her police training told her to try to disarm him but she hesitated. Surely Cameron was coming for her. What if she couldn't disarm him? She wasn't Cameron. She wasn't trained in martial arts, she wasn't as strong. If she failed, he might indeed shoot her. Or worse. No. She had to play this out. This was the plan. So she walked on, feeling him close behind her, imagining she could feel his foul breath on her neck. Imagining she could hear Cameron coming for her.

"Stop."

She did as she was told, waiting. She heard keys jingling, then the barrel of the gun touched her back as he reached around her to unlock the door. He pushed her inside, not bothering to turn on any lights. She squinted into the darkness, seeing little.

"This way."

Again, he unlocked another door and shoved her inside. She blinked several times as a bright light was turned on. What she saw made her gasp. A bloody table complete with shackles for arms and legs, a countertop lined with needles and vials. She turned quickly, flight instinct taking over, but he was prepared. She registered the electric shock in her neck, was conscious enough to recognize the Taser before her limbs gave way.

"Jesus Christ, where's the fucking road?" Cameron yelled.

"Almost there," Reynolds said.

"One more mile," Rowan said.

Cameron's hands were sweating, her heart pounding loudly in her ears. The only sound from Andrea's mic was of him dragging her, and then the sound of chains. There was a rustling sound and her gut told her he was removing her clothing. There was static, then deadly silence. He'd apparently found the mic.

It seemed like an eternity—the last few miles. She was driving as fast as she dared. Reynolds was right. They would be of no help to Andrea if they had an accident, but her fear was real. She was terrified of what he was doing to Andrea...what he was going to do.

Andrea shook her head, still feeling numbness in her right shoulder. She tried to move, then felt the chains digging into her flesh. She was cold and only then did she realize she was naked. She lifted her head, her eyes wide. An IV was in her arm, a clear liquid slowly dripping. *Oh, dear God.*

"Welcome back," he said as he inserted a needle into a vial.

She blinked several times, fear blocking any sound from her throat. She shook her head again, trying to clear her mind, trying to focus.

"I learned something in prison," he said as he smiled at her. "I was a good boy. I got to work in the infirmary. You learn a lot in sickbay," he continued. "How to give shots. How to properly set an IV." He laughed. "What drugs do what. That kind of stuff."

She yanked hard on the chains, crying out in pain as her skin tore from the force.

"I got you now, don't I?" He laughed again. "But what am I going to do with you?" He ran his hand up her leg between her thighs and she flinched. "I must say, compared to the others, you look mighty good. Fresh."

"Take your hand off me," she managed.

"I'll do what I please," he snarled, grabbing her breast roughly and squeezing hard until she cried out.

She strained against the chains, trying to pull away, only to have him squeeze harder. She relented, biting her lip until he finally released her.

"Oh, yes. You're going to be fun to fuck. I might keep you a little longer than the others." He gave a sickly laugh. "Of course,

I like to fuck them dead too." He threw his head back and laughed harder. "Oh, yes indeed I do."

She groaned as he raised the syringe, showing it to her, the needle glistening in the sharp light.

"Do you know what this is?"

She shook her head.

"I think you do. You want it fast and quick? Or do you want it slow? Slow...drip by drip." He waved the syringe in front of her face, her eyes following its jerky movements. "Slow. I think slow," he said.

"No," she whispered, finally turning her head away. She tried to fight it but she couldn't. The last thing she saw was a bloody rag on the floor before her world went black.

"Hold on," Cameron said as she turned sharply, her tires squealing as she left the highway and bounced onto the dirt road that shot out into the desert. A horn honked behind her but she hardly noticed, her only focus was Andrea as she sped down the bumpy road.

"There." Reynolds pointed. "There's the truck."

Her headlights flashed across the truck and she skidded to a stop, not even taking the time to kill the engine. She had her weapon drawn as she raced to the door.

"Protocol, Ross," Reynolds called after her. "This is a crime scene."

"Fuck protocol," she snapped. "That's my partner in there."

She kicked the door with all of her force, the old wood splintering as the lock broke. She leaned against the wall in the darkness, motioning for Reynolds to take the opposite. She held up one finger, then another, then moved along the wall, seeing light pouring out from beneath a doorway. She pointed and he nodded. She hesitated at the door, so afraid of what she'd find inside. Then, with a deep breath, she brought her foot up, kicking in the door easily. Her eyes swept the room, finding an empty kitchen, save for a lone table and two chairs.

"Goddamn," she muttered, then turned, hurrying back out into the dark hallway. "Reynolds? Anything?"

He snapped on his small flashlight, shining it along the wall until they found another door. There was no light seen under the door and she stood by it silently, listening, but there was no sound from within. She stepped back, one powerful kick opening the door. The air left her lungs when Reynolds's light flashed across Andrea's body.

"My God," she whispered.

"Focus, Ross," Reynolds said, his light flashing in the corners of the room, illuminating medical equipment that looked like it had been scattered in haste.

"Clear," she said. She turned, finding the light switch, nearly gasping as it all came into view. Dried blood covered the floor, the countertop, the table...and Andrea lay naked on top of it, chained by the arms and feet.

"We should," he said, clearing his throat as he stared, "we should secure the house."

But Cameron didn't move, her eyes were glued to Andrea, her heart filled with fear. She felt sick to her stomach. Andrea couldn't be dead. She just couldn't be. It was then she saw the needle sticking out of Andrea's arm, the IV drip, the vials. It jolted her into action, rushing forward, reaching out, then pausing, hoping to feel warm flesh, not cold. Her hand trembled as she touched Andrea's arm, relief flooding her as she saw her shallow breathing. She jerked the needle out of her arm and flung it to the countertop. She did the same with the IV, tugging it out of her arm, feeling remorse as blood seeped out from her actions.

"Oh, God," she murmured, bending low, feeling her faint breath on her face. "Hang in there, baby," she whispered. She looked up, seeing Reynolds staring. "Find the goddamn keys," she said as her hands tugged at the chains.

"She's alive?"

"Yes."

They both looked up, hearing sirens in the distance. Their backup, she hoped.

"Here," he said, tossing keys at her.

She fumbled with them, finally finding one to open the locks and release the chains holding her arms. When she did so, they fell helplessly off of the table, dangling lifelessly beside it. She went to her feet, glancing at Reynolds who was trying to avert his eyes.

"Find me something to cover her, please."

But there was nothing in the blood-filled room. Reynolds took off his suit coat, handing it to her.

"Use this."

"Thanks. Remind me not to give you shit anymore about wearing a suit all the time," she said as she covered Andrea the best she could. She tucked her arms along her sides, bending down again, making sure she was still breathing. She patted her face several times. "Wake up, Andi. Wake up." The sirens were loud now, the emergency lights flashing against the window. "You go. I'll stay with her."

After he left she very nearly broke down, her chest still so tight with fear. She choked back tears that were threatening. She didn't have the luxury of tears. Not now. She squeezed Andrea's hand tightly, making herself move away. It was a contaminated crime scene already so she didn't bother with proper protocol as Reynolds had suggested.

An empty vial lay on the countertop, tipped on its side. Two others were beside it...waiting. There was a pile of unused syringes, all still neatly wrapped in their plastic containers. She glanced around the room, her eyes landing on a bloody saw, pieces of mangled flesh caught in the blade. She turned away, trying not to picture Andrea meeting the same fate as the others.

"In here," she heard Reynolds say and she stepped aside as two paramedics rushed in.

They unceremoniously ripped off Reynolds's jacket, leaving Andrea naked again.

"What do we have here?" one asked as he held a stethoscope to Andrea's bare chest.

Cameron was about to protest when Reynolds grabbed her arm. "Come on. Let them do their job."

"Yeah. Okay." She pointed to the countertop. "There's an empty vile. Ketamine."

The paramedic only nodded and Cameron supposed it wasn't his place to ask questions. That was her job.

"Come on," Reynolds said. "We have a job to do too."

She nodded, knowing it was true, but she felt like she was abandoning Andrea. She glanced back once again, seeing her ashen complexion, so unlike the normal healthy, vibrant glow that she associated with Andrea.

Out in the hallway, there were four San Bernardino sheriff's deputies waiting for instruction. She almost wished Reynolds would take over as her emotions were all over the place but she took a deep breath, summoning up the best professional face she could muster.

"Is this it?" she asked, looking at them.

"Crime scene team is en route. They're about fifteen minutes out," one of them said.

She nodded. "Our guy slipped away. He took to the desert, I guess. Check the perimeter. We didn't hear an engine so assume he's on foot."

They nodded, all dispersing quickly.

She walked into the makeshift kitchen, the only room where a light had been on. Reynolds stood watching her.

"Why was this light on?" she asked, not really expecting an answer.

She looked around, seeing an old dorm room sized refrigerator in a corner, a tiny microwave sitting on top of it. There was a set of cabinets—shelves, no doors—on one wall. There was nothing there but a couple of plates and a can of beans. There was a sink, but no faucet. A bucket of water, half empty, sat beside it.

"Electricity, but no running water."

"Explains the mess in the other room," Reynolds said.

"No running water, yet not a shred of evidence was ever found on the bodies," she mused. She stepped back, looking at the room as a whole, frowning. The table and chairs were off center.

"What is it?"

She squatted down, seeing that the old dusty rug had been moved. "Son of a bitch," she murmured. She pulled the rug back, revealing a door.

"Trap door," Reynolds said. He bent down, reaching for the handle but she stopped him.

"Don't be stupid," she said as she lay down on the filthy floor. "Give me your flashlight."

She shone it along the seam of the door, slowly lifting it. She felt the tightness and stopped, seeing what appeared to be trip wires on the latch. She let out a breath, gently closing the door again.

"What?" he asked.

"It's wired."

"Wired?" He shook his head. "He wouldn't have had time to wire it. Chances of there being a bomb down there are slim."

"Yeah, well you're goddamn crazy if you think that."

She jerked her head up, hearing the rolling of the gurney in the hallway. She got up and went to the door, thankful they had covered Andrea finally.

"How is she?"

"Vitals are good."

She felt some of the tension leave her body and she nodded. "Where will you take her? Vegas?"

"Needles. CRMC."

She raised an eyebrow. "I'm not from around here."

"Colorado River Medical Center," he said as they quickly wheeled Andrea away.

They had no sooner left than three crime scene investigators arrived. Cameron held up her FBI credentials to them, pointing to the room Andrea had been held in.

"Did you guys work the scene where the headless woman was found east of Barstow?" she asked.

"Yeah," one said. "Jesus Christ," he murmured when he looked in the room. "Is this it?"

"We think so."

"Where the hell do you start?"

"It's been contaminated," she admitted. "Us two," she said, pointing to Reynolds. "And paramedics. We had a live victim." She almost choked on the word, hating to call Andrea a victim.

"We'll sort it out," he said, the other two already getting to work.

"Do any of you know anything about bombs?" she asked.

The lone female of the group looked up and shrugged. "Just enough to be dangerous. What do you have?"

"Trap door. Trip wires," she said.

"I'll take a look."

She got down on the floor much as Cameron had done, lifting the door slowly. She stopped and nodded, lowering the door again.

"Yep. Trip wires."

"So the simple matter of cutting them should be safe?" Cameron asked.

"They're looped over the bars on the latch. That's your pressure point. Cut the wire as close to the center as you can. Make sure there's not a secondary wire." She studied the floor. "Even so, the blast radius is probably right here at the opening. I doubt it's rigged to blow up the whole place."

She left them with that word of advice and Cameron and Reynolds stared at each other.

"She *doubts*?" Reynolds said, apparently now convinced there could be a bomb.

"Swiss army knife?"

"No."

The woman stuck her head back in the door and tossed a pair of heavy-duty scissors at Cameron, which she caught in one hand.

"Thought you might need those," she said, winking at Cameron before joining her team again.

Reynolds shook his head. "Flirting at a crime scene. We've lost all sense of professionalism."

"Yeah. Especially you, without a coat and tie," she said dryly, resuming her position on the floor. She glanced up at Reynolds. "Would you rather do this?"

"No, you're doing fine."

Cameron pulled the trap door up again, stopping when she could see the wire. "Get down here. I need you to hold the flashlight."

He hesitated, looking first at the filthy floor then at his properly pressed pants, then back to the floor.

"Don't piss me off, Reynolds," she said. "It's been a really bad night so far."

"God knows what's been on this floor," he muttered as he joined her, holding the light under the trap door like she'd asked.

"Over here," she said as she scooted down. "There. See it?"

"Yeah."

She took a deep breath. "On three," she said quietly. She closed her eyes briefly. *Please don't let us blow up.* "One, two... three," she said, snipping the wire.

They were both quiet, waiting, then grinned at each other.

"No big bang," she said. "That's a good thing."

"You think he's down there?"

Cameron pulled her weapon. "If he is, he's a dead man," she said fiercely. "Open it up."

He lifted the door slowly, flashing his light along the door as if looking for more wire. Then he flung it open and it landed against the rickety table with a crash. His flashlight illuminated the room, looking like nothing more than an underground root cellar. Cameron went down the steps first, nearly afraid the old ladder wouldn't hold her weight as each step made a creaking sound.

"Whoa," she murmured.

Reynolds landed softly beside her, his light held fast on the explosives.

"Where the hell did he get C4?" she asked quietly.

He moved his light around the room, finding what appeared to be a tunnel. "There," he said, making a move for it.

She grabbed his arm. "What do you think you're doing?"

"Let's go after him."

She shook her head. "You're insane. First of all, there's a wad of C4 staring at us that I'm not real crazy about. Secondly, if the door was wired, then there are probably booby traps, maybe more C4. No way."

"What's with you? I always heard you'd go in head first and ask questions later. You getting scared in your old age, Ross?"

Cameron very nearly accepted his challenge, but she realized the answer to his question was pretty simple. She no longer had only herself to think about. In the past, yeah, she wouldn't even consider *not* going into the tunnel. But now there was Andrea, now she had someone who loved her. Her responsibilities, her priorities had changed. Because she had changed. But not so much that she couldn't glare at Reynolds with a near snarl on her face.

"Why do you keep putting up the challenge flag? I'm sick of it. You learn that shit from Collie?"

"I'm just saying, we have the bastard. Let's go after him."

"And I'm saying you're goddamn crazy, Reynolds. You're dressed in your fancy, pressed suit, shiny shoes and you want to go running blind into a tunnel?" She felt the pressure of the day settle on her shoulders as her voice got louder. "That's fucking insane. You want to blow yourself up, go ahead. That's fine. But you let the rest of us get the hell out of here before you do anything so goddamn stupid," she yelled, feeling the vein in her head about to explode.

"Ah...excuse me."

They both looked up, seeing two of the sheriff's deputies looking down at them.

"If you guys are through yelling at each other, we have something you might want to see."

Reynolds looked back to the tunnel, as if still considering it, then climbed back up the ladder, Cameron close on his heels.

"We need a bomb squad," she said to one of the deputies. "Close this trap door. Gently. There's C4." She shook her head as she followed the others outside into the darkness. It's a wonder they didn't blow the whole damn building up earlier when they'd just tossed open the door without a thought. She'd seen unstable C4 detonate from only a cough.

"There's a shed over here. It was locked up tight," he said, showing them the broken lock. "I ain't never seen nothing like this my whole life. I hope to never again."

"Trophy room?" she asked.

"What?"

"You found the heads?"

He nodded, then stepped aside so she could enter.

An old dusty lightbulb hung on a wire, swaying now with the

desert breeze that blew in. It swung gently back and forth, the shadows dancing with its movement, skeletal and decomposed heads going from light to dark to light again, like a bad horror movie.

"Jesus Christ," she murmured, absently taking the large flashlight one of the deputies handed her. She covered her nose with her shirt, breathing through her mouth. The heads appeared to be attached to a sturdy peg or dowel stick, displayed along shelves, just like a hunter might display his kill. Which was exactly what he was doing.

"There's so many," Reynolds said quietly.

"Seventeen."

Cameron shone her flashlight at each one, some so old they were just bones, others decayed, still others with flesh on the bones. She flashed to the most recent, expecting to find their three women. Instead, she found four heads.

"What the hell?"

"There's a body we haven't found," he said.

"There are apparently a lot of bodies that haven't been found."

"We got more," the deputy said. "In here."

There was an open doorway going into a small room. There, hanging on hooks and piled on the floor were clothes and shoes, some purses and jewelry, even a couple of pretty hats. The light landed on the dress and shoes Andrea had been wearing—the latest addition to his collection.

"Goddamn bastard," she said. She glanced at the deputy who was standing in the doorway. "Get one of the CSIs. They're going to need to call in help on this. There'll be an FBI forensics team sent in too."

Back out in the fresh air, she took deep breaths, chasing away the decomp that still lingered on the latest victims. She tried not to picture Andrea like this but, damn, it had been close. If he'd thrown the watch out earlier, if Andrea hadn't alerted them to the fact that they were following the wrong truck, she'd still be in there, chained to that table, waiting for him to play whatever sick little games he liked. Waiting for him to eventually get tired of her and...and kill her like the others.

"Hey, you okay?"

She glanced at Reynolds and shook her head. "No." But she didn't elaborate, not feeling the need to share her thoughts with him. By the look on his face, she didn't have to. He knew exactly what she was thinking. "Call Murdock, would you? Get a team sent down to help with all this," she said, motioning to the shed.

She walked over to her truck, realizing she had never turned it off. As she leaned in to kill the engine, she heard Rowan's frantic voice.

"Can anybody hear me? Anybody?"

"Rowan?"

"Cameron? Thank God!"

"Oh, man. Sorry."

"Please say you found her."

"Yeah. They took her by ambulance to Needles. I'm headed that way."

"Is she okay?"

"She was drugged. Sedated. Something." She watched Reynolds as he approached. "I think she'll be okay." She cleared her throat. "Have you been in contact with Eric?"

"Yes. They've got the manager of the trucking company. They're holding him in San Bernardino."

"Hold him overnight. We'll be there in the morning." She motioned for Reynolds to get in. "I'll be in touch, let you know how Andrea is."

"Does this mean you didn't get the guy?"

"No. He had an escape...tunnel or something." She turned to Reynolds. "You give them our contacts?"

"Yes. But they said it would be days, if not weeks, before they had it all sorted out."

She nodded, then turned the truck back down the dirt road to the highway. "Rowan, we found where he kept the heads. There were seventeen. Some appeared to be decades old. But of the recent ones, there were four, not three. San Bernardino County is processing the evidence. Can you monitor that for me? Keep us up to date with what they find until we get a team in here?"

"Sure. No problem."

She sighed. "Thanks. Good work tonight, Rowan. Talk to you tomorrow."

"Thanks Cameron. Good night." A pause. "Oh, and you too, Special Agent Reynolds."

Cameron smiled. "He's a good kid. Sharp."

"Yes, he is." He stared at her. "You want me to drive?"

"No, I'm okay. It's been a long-ass day, but I just want to check on Andrea." She hated feeling uncertain, especially in front of Reynolds, but she needed some reassurance. "You think she's going to be okay, don't you?"

"Yes," he said without hesitation. "I think she'll be just fine."

CHAPTER TWENTY

Cameron's chest felt tight as she stared into the brightly lit room, a crisp white sheet covering Andrea. Other than an IV drip, she appeared to be just sleeping. Her color was good, not the pale, ashy color she'd had earlier.

"May I help you?"

Cameron glanced at the nurse, noticing the constant low beeping of the monitor on the wall, Andrea's vital signs updating by the second as the numbers continued to change. She cleared her throat, then held up her FBI credentials.

"I'm Special Agent Ross," she said. "I'm just here to check on my agent." She finally moved into the room, her eyes again going to Andrea's face.

"We had to sedate her. She—"

"Sedate her? She was sedated when she came in. I don't understand."

"When she came to, she ripped the IV out of her arm and attacked the doctor," the nurse said with a slight smile. "Pompous ass that he is, I'm glad she took a swing at him," she said quietly, looking over her shoulder to make sure she wasn't overheard. "We had to restrain her. He gave her a sedative so that he could examine her."

"She was abducted and drugged. Using an IV. So I guess she—"

"Oh, my. Well, we didn't know. She was nearly hysterical. She kept calling for someone named Cameron. I assume that's her boyfriend. Or husband. Maybe you could find him? She would probably be more settled if he was here."

Cameron felt a sting of tears but blinked them away, somehow feeling as if she'd failed Andrea by not being here for her. She nodded at the nurse, her hand reaching out to touch Andrea's.

"It'll be awhile before she wakes up. You look like you could use some coffee," she suggested.

Cameron sighed. "Coffee? No. I need something much stronger than coffee."

The nurse leaned closer. "There's a bar a couple of blocks down. Is that what you mean?"

Cameron smiled her thanks. "I'll be back shortly."

She found Reynolds waiting, his phone to his ear. He motioned her over when he saw her.

"Jack says the trucking manager is throwing a fit. Demands an attorney," he said.

She shook her head. "No. If we suspect terrorist activity, we don't have to follow all of the Miranda rights," she said.

"Terrorists? That's reaching a bit. Even for you."

She smiled. "We found explosives. Could be a hideout of a terrorist cell."

He studied her for a moment then nodded. "Okay. I'll buy it." He went back to his call with Jack and Cameron waited while he gave the other man instructions. When he put his phone away he looked at her questioningly. "Well?"

"They had to sedate her again. Seems she attacked the doctor," she said with a smile.

"She's your partner. I'd expect nothing less," he said with a smile, showing a sense of humor Cameron hadn't seen before.

"Come on. I'll let you buy me a drink. We have about an hour."

They walked down the dark sidewalk silently. Cameron in her dirty jeans and T-shirt, Reynolds in his suit pants and tie, minus the jacket that he'd covered Andrea with. It was now part of the crime scene. Her boots were silent, his dress shoes making a nearly metallic clicking on the concrete.

It was late, or early, depending on how you looked at it. The bar was sparsely populated, only a handful of tables occupied. Some of the patrons were dressed in street clothes, others still in scrubs, no doubt having just come from their shift at the hospital.

They chose the bar instead of a table and Reynolds motioned for the bartender. "What would you like?" Reynolds asked her.

"Bourbon. Straight up."

The bartender waited, patiently wiping down the bar. Reynolds held up two fingers and the bartender nodded.

They both sighed, then smiled at each other as their drinks were served. They silently touched glasses.

"You married, Reynolds?"

"No," he said with a shake of his head. "Like everyone else on this team, I'm single. I'm not sure this job and marriage is a good mix. This line of work is not really conducive to marriage. Neither was the military."

"You got someone?"

He smiled. "I have a *friend*," he said. "In Chicago. I see her whenever I get back there. But she knows our relationship will never be permanent. I don't think she'd want it to be. She's a surgeon. Dedicated." He watched her for a moment. "You?"

She smiled. "Who would put up with me, Reynolds? Besides, I'm a loner. Always have been."

"Yeah, but now you've got a partner," he said.

She shrugged. "I needed someone to watch my back. We bonded quickly in Sedona. For not having trained together, we just seemed to be in tune with each other. That's what you want in a partner."

He smiled and tossed back the rest of his drink. "You two look really close. That's good."

"Yeah. We're close."

He looked at her drink and she nodded. He held up two fingers again to the bartender.

"So? You and Carina?"

"That was a long time ago."

"She doesn't really fit in with the team, does she?"

"No. But she's good at what she does. This must seem very tame to her," Cameron said. "Why did she leave the military?"

"She is actually on loan from the CIA. Had a botched mission. Civilians died, including her lovers."

Cameron raised her eyebrows.

"A man and his wife."

Cameron shook her head. "What was she thinking?"

"From what I understand, that was common for her."

"I suppose," she said, remembering the sexual appetite Carina had. "So? Her request to get out?"

"No. The brass suggested she take a break. She's on leave. For at least a year. They handed her over to Murdock."

She nodded, taking a sip from her fresh drink. "Eric seems good. Jack is Jack."

Reynolds laughed quietly. "I'm surprised you haven't shot Eric yet. Or at least punched him out."

Cameron looked at him questioningly.

"You know, for how he flirts with Andrea."

Cameron felt the slightest of blushes threaten. "I wanted to shoot him. Andrea wouldn't let me."

Reynolds laughed outright. "Don't worry. He knows what the score is. We all do."

"Really?"

"Really. It's a dangerous position, Cameron. I'm sure you know that. You let your emotions override your training." He looked at her pointedly. "Like tonight."

"If breaking protocol saved her life, I'd do it every time."

He studied her intently for a long moment. "Is it the real thing? Or just an affair?"

Cameron didn't know why she was trusting him, but she was. "I'm in love with her. It's not just a passing affair. She's—" She paused, not knowing how, or even if, she could explain Andrea's importance in her life. So she just shrugged. "Not an affair."

He nodded again. "I like you, Cameron. I don't always agree with your tactics, but I like you. Collie made you out to be this rogue agent who was out of control and who wouldn't play nice." He smiled. "I see that too, of course. Not that I think you're out of control, mind you." He finished off his drink and slid the glass away from him. "You and Andrea seem to be a good fit. If it works for you, then great. But just be careful. We still have a serial killer to catch. That's our top priority."

She tipped her glass at him before swallowing the last bit of it. "Thanks Reynolds. I like you too. Even if Collie trained you." She stood and shoved the barstool back. "Thanks for the drinks."

CHAPTER TWENTY-ONE

Andrea sat on the edge of the bed, still feeling a bit out of it, but she was determined to prove she was fine. She just wanted to get out of there. She glanced at her arm, a dark bruise showing where she'd ripped the IV out earlier. She rubbed it, avoiding the bandage they'd placed there. The doctor—who she had slugged earlier—had released her. Whether or not it was because he truly thought she was ready to be discharged, she wasn't certain. He'd kept a safe distance, even after she'd apologized for the fourth time.

"Andi?"

She jerked her head up, then nearly collapsed as she tried to stand. Cameron rushed to her, strong arms holding her tight against her solid frame.

"God, Cameron," she murmured, clinging to her, burying

her face against Cameron's neck. She knew this wasn't the time or place for this but she couldn't possibly let her go. Only when she saw Reynolds watching from the doorway did she pull away.

Cameron, too, took a step back, but she kept a hand on her to steady her. "Should you be up?"

"I've been released. I just want to get out of here."

"Are you sure? I mean—"

"I'm very sure." She glanced at Reynolds, then back to Cameron. "Did you...did you find him?"

Cameron shook her head. "No."

"We found an underground tunnel," Reynolds said. He came fully into the room. "Agent Sullivan, you did a fine job tonight."

She wanted to laugh. No, she wanted to cry. She found she was too tired to do either. She knew they'd want a briefing but she was still too raw, too emotional. She shivered as she remembered his hands on her. When she'd woken up—the second time—the first thing she asked the nurse was whether she'd been raped or not. Her relief was visible as the nurse assured her she had not been.

"If it's okay with you, can we go over this in the morning? I just want to go home."

The drive back to Indio was made in near silence. Andrea had taken the backseat, letting Reynolds ride up front with Cameron. She'd positioned herself so that she could see Cameron in the mirror, but the rocking motion of the truck lulled her to sleep. She'd not even stirred when Cameron dropped Reynolds off at the hotel.

Now, nearly three in the morning, she stood holding Lola, watching as Cameron moved about the rig, getting ready for bed. Cameron had been attentive, but quiet. Too quiet. Andrea knew exactly what was going through her mind.

"You want to talk about it?" she finally asked.

Cameron looked at her but shook her head. Before she turned

away, Andrea saw her tears. She put Lola down, then grabbed Cameron's arm as she tried to move away.

"Come here," she said.

She thought Cameron was going to resist but she relented, letting Andrea pull her into her arms. Cameron's tears were silent at first and Andrea rubbed her back, letting her cry. Then a sob escaped and Cameron clung to her as she wept.

Andrea squeezed her own eyes tight, not willing to give in to her emotions. Not yet. Cameron needed this right now. Andrea could wait.

"I'm sorry," Cameron mumbled against her neck. "I feel so weak."

"You're not weak, sweetheart," Andrea whispered.

"I am weak," Cameron said as she pulled out of her arms. She wiped at the tears on her face, rubbed a finger under her wet nose. "I'm very weak." She took a step away from her as if trying to get herself under control. "I could hardly do my job. I was so worried about you," she admitted.

"But you did do your job. You found me. You saved me."

"What if I hadn't?" Cameron ran her hands through her hair, pacing now. "Maybe this was a mistake. I'm not sure I can do this."

Andrea tilted her head. "What are you talking about? What's a mistake?" She raised an eyebrow. "Us?" Andrea was taken aback, not knowing exactly where Cameron was going with this. "Us?" she asked again, motioning between them. "This is a mistake?"

Cameron nodded. "I can't keep worrying about you. I can't keep being afraid I'm going to lose you. I could have lost you tonight, Andi. Then what?"

Andrea felt a touch of anger, but she knew Cameron hadn't intended to sound so selfish. It was just her vast insecurity rearing its ugly head again.

"So we're back to that?" She walked closer to Cameron, standing just in front of her. "Your sole existence is not dependent on me. Just like mine is not dependent on you. I love you. You love me. What we have is something...what we have—us—is something I've only dared to dream of. That's why we're afraid.

That's why it hurts when we think about losing the other." She took Cameron's hand, holding it tightly. "I feel it too. If we didn't have what we have, then you wouldn't be so afraid. So this is not a mistake. This is beautiful what we have between us."

Cameron's eyes searched hers but she didn't say anything.

"Would it be better if we didn't work together? If you had a different partner?"

"God, no. No. I wouldn't trust anyone else." She dropped Andrea's hand, moving away again. "I almost went crazy tonight."

"But you didn't. You did your job."

Cameron met her eyes, holding them. "It was so close, Andi. Too close."

Andrea took a deep breath, hoping to assuage her fears. "Cameron, our goal was to get him to lead us to his safe house. That was the goal. When I realized he'd made me for a cop, I could have done something. I had a gun. When he took it, I could have disarmed him. I could have grabbed the wheel and rolled his truck, something. But I knew you were behind me, I knew what our goal was. I knew you were coming for me. I didn't want to abort the mission." She reached out, cupping Cameron's face with one hand. "I knew what my job was and I did it. Just as you did."

Cameron finally nodded, turning her head to kiss Andrea's palm. Andrea watched as her eyes slid closed and a soft sigh escaped.

"I'm sorry," Cameron finally said. She tried to smile. "It just occurred to me how selfish I've been."

Andrea did smile. "Yes."

Cameron gave up the fight, pulling Andrea into her arms. "Now, do *you* want to talk?"

Andrea shook her head. "I'm tired. I just want to go to bed. I just want you to hold me. Keep me safe."

Cameron nodded. "I'll do my best."

Andrea kissed her neck, then moved to her lips. "That's all I ask."

CHAPTER TWENTY-TWO

Andrea stood behind the glass mirror, along with Eric, Jack and Carina. Rowan was at the rig again, which he'd dubbed "control central." Reynolds and Cameron were in the interrogation room, questioning the manager of the small trucking company.

"*Where was he headed?*" *Reynolds asked.*

"*I told you. Vegas.*"

"*Then where?*"

"*Then he swings down Ninety-five to Needles.*"

Eric leaned closer. "You okay?"

It was the second time he'd asked. She smiled and squeezed his arm. "I'm fine. Just tired."

Carina watched them but said nothing. Jack's eyes never left the glass.

"And his name?"

"I already told you. Henry Waters. That's all I got."

"Henry Waters died in 1957. We pulled your records. You pay him in cash. Now who is he?"

"I told you. I don't know."

"Why did you pay him in cash?"

"We pay a couple of guys in cash."

Andrea watched Cameron as she stood in one corner, letting Reynolds do the questioning. She could tell by the look on her face that she'd had enough.

"Jesus Christ, Reynolds."

Cameron nearly shoved Reynolds out of the way as she grabbed the man by the collar of his shirt, slamming him against the wall.

"Listen, little man, I've had enough of your bullshit. I want to know his goddamn name. Now!"

Eric gave a quiet laugh as the man's mouth actually quivered.

Carina, too, laughed. "She's so sexy when she's like that."

"She sure is," Andrea murmured.

"He's an ex-con. I'm not supposed to hire ex-cons, but I can't keep drivers so I do what I can. A cop put in a good word for him. I thought it was cool."

Cameron released him. *"What's his name?"*

"Leonard Baskin."

"And the cop?"

"Buddy Burke. From Barstow. It's his half-brother."

Andrea saw Cameron's shoulders stiffen. She, too, recognized the name. He was the officer from Barstow who had showed them where the first body was found. Cameron was already walking out of the interrogation room, phone to her ear.

"We move the rig to Barstow. Reynolds, pack up your team," she said, pausing as her call was obviously answered. "Murdock? We got something."

Chief Hudley of the Barstow police department looked from Cameron to Reynolds in disbelief, still shaking his head.

"No way my officer is involved. No way."

Cameron leaned forward. "We just want to talk to him."

Cameron watched the muscles in his jaw clench and unclench. He finally reached for the phone.

"Contact Officer Burke. Have him return to the station." He glanced at Cameron. "You may speak with him, but this is in no way an interrogation. I know Buddy. He's a good cop."

"I'm not saying he isn't. It's his half-brother we're interested in."

"And this will be kept confidential. I don't want—" His phone buzzed, interrupting what Cameron feared was going to turn into a lecture. He nodded without speaking, then hung up. "Burke is not responding."

Cameron stood, pacing. "Do you have a locater on his car?"

"Yes, we can track it. It's going to take a little time. I'll need to get the tech guys to—"

"I want to be involved in this. I can have my—"

"No. This is my officer. This is my jurisdiction. The FBI gets to back off," he said, pointing at her.

Reynolds was about to protest but she stopped him. "Come on." She pulled out one of her cards and tossed it on the chief's desk. "Keep us in the loop."

Once out of his office, Reynolds spoke. "What's going on? You never back down like that."

Cameron took out her phone, already dialing. "We have our own tech guy. We don't need his." Rowan answered immediately. "I need Buddy Burke's home address. Then I need you to locate his patrol car."

"Is this my okay to hack their system?"

"Yes. Just be quick about it. Call Andrea with his home address. Reynolds and I will go after the car."

The Burke home was in a newer subdivision, all of the houses looking somewhat the same. Children's toys lay scattered in the driveway, as if a game had been interrupted. While Jack and Carina went to the back of the house, Andrea and Eric walked slowly to the front door. The drapes were pulled making it impossible to see inside. Eric nodded at her and she knocked rapidly on the door.

"Mrs. Burke?" she called. "FBI." There was no sound from within and she knocked again.

Eric reached down to try the door, finding it unlocked. "Our lucky day," he murmured as he pushed it open.

They went in with weapons drawn. The house was quiet and dark, indicating no one was home. Andrea stepped into the kitchen and froze. Blood was splattered on the walls and countertops. She went to the back door, using the bottom of her T-shirt to open it for Jack and Carina.

"Careful where you step," she said quietly.

Eric rounded the corner into the living room and stopped up short.

"Holy fuck."

Andrea came up behind him, staring in disbelief as she slowly lowered her weapon.

"Dear God," Carina murmured beside her. "They've been butchered."

Working the streets of LA, Andrea had seen horrendous crimes before but nothing could have prepared her for this. The woman, who she assumed was Mrs. Burke, was laying on the sofa, her belly ripped open, her intestines spilling out to the floor. Two children—toddlers—lay on the carpet. Their fate was that of their mother, one also had her throat slashed. A third child, a boy, was tied to a chair, intact except for a bullet to the head. A gun was lying on the coffee table, the same gun taken from Andrea's purse the night before.

She turned away, unable to look. Eric and Carina went into the room, stepping over the bodies on the floor, seemingly unaffected by it. No doubt they'd seen horrors like this in their military days. Were they immune to it all?

"Why don't you call Cameron?" Jack suggested, giving her an out. She nodded numbly, going back into the kitchen and out the back door.

She held her phone tightly, staring at the neat privacy fence, the flower bed that was planted with assorted cactus, the swing set with two red seats, one of them moving slightly from the breeze. A tricycle lay tipped over at the edge of the patio. She went to it, righting it again. She couldn't help but feel responsible. If they'd captured the guy last night, if she'd stopped him, then this family would still be alive.

Her body was trembling, and she fought to get herself under control. She would be no good to the team—to Cameron—if she broke down. She squeezed her eyes shut, trying to push the bloody scene from her mind, trying to push last night from her mind.

Several deep breaths later, she finally felt composed enough to call Cameron, who answered immediately.

"We've got a crime scene," she said evenly. "Four bodies."

"Burke?" Cameron asked.

"No. Wife, three...three kids."

Cameron paused. "Are you okay?"

Andrea shook her head. "No. No, I'm not," she admitted, not wanting to pretend otherwise. "They're butchered," she said, echoing Carina's words.

"Okay. I'll let Barstow PD know," Cameron said, keeping her professional mask in place. "Rowan got us a fix on the car. We're heading there now. When you're finished there, meet us back at the rig."

"Yeah. Okay," she said.

"Andi?"

"I'll be fine, Cameron. Be careful."

"Always."

Andrea crossed her arms, trying to remain emotionless and failing. The last two days had taken their toll. She'd only managed a couple of hours of sleep—she wished she'd taken the doctor up on his offer of sleeping pills. Her dreams were real—the bloody table, the smell of death, the syringe and vials, his soulless eyes, rough hands as he grabbed her breasts. Cameron had found her sitting in the dark that morning, Lola on her lap, untouched coffee beside her. They hadn't really had time to talk, not that Andrea had even wanted to.

Now, all she wanted to do was curl up beside Cameron and close her eyes and let sleep take her away from all this. Unfortunately, that wasn't an option.

"There's the car," Reynolds said.

The sunlight reflected off of one mirror, twinkling at them as they drove down the bumpy desert road a short distance from the highway. Cameron could see the driver's door was flung open. She slowed, wanting to be cautious, even though her gut told her the car was empty.

Reynolds got out first, his weapon drawn. She followed, going to the passenger side of the car.

"Empty," Reynolds said.

"Got blood," she said. "On the dash."

"Steering wheel too."

"Could be transfer from the house." She looked around, trying to find footprints, anything to indicate in which direction he'd gone. "Look at this," she said, squatting down. "Motorcycle? Dirt bike?"

"Maybe that's how he escaped us last night," Reynolds said.

"A smaller motorcycle, maybe. But a dirt bike? They're noisy as hell. We would have heard it."

"So where's Burke? And why ditch the car like this? It's not really hidden. What's the purpose?"

Cameron turned in all directions, seeing the endless brown desert, the occasional smattering of creosote bushes, cactus, the hulking shapes of rocks. She shielded her eyes to the sun, looking nearly longingly at the distant mountains. She impatiently wiped the sweat from her brow.

"He's got Burke somewhere. I don't think he killed him. He needs him."

"So why the car?"

They heard sirens and knew that Barstow PD was closing in on their location. She smirked. "About time." She looked around again, back to the motorcycle tracks. "A diversion," she said.

"A diversion?"

"Yeah. Make us think he ditched the car here and took off on foot. Let us concentrate our search here."

"First of all, nobody takes off on foot out in the desert. Secondly, he would have known we'd find the tire tracks."

"Not necessarily. The way the wind blows the sand around, they would have been covered up in no time. He didn't count on us finding the car this soon."

Reynolds shook his head. "Nothing but damn speculation."

"Are we going back to that again? Shit, Reynolds, I thought we, you know, bonded or something last night," she said as she headed back to her truck. "Let's go before the cavalry gets here."

CHAPTER TWENTY-THREE

"You're wasting time," Cameron said, her voice as loud as his. "He's not anywhere near the goddamn car."

"You don't get to make that call. And I have a mind to file a complaint against you," he said.

"Won't be the first time," she said as she glared back at him.

"I specifically told you to stay away."

"I'm telling you the car is a diversion."

"Don't presume to tell us how to do our job," he continued. "We're not some rogue FBI team. We're processing the scene at the house, not you. We're by the book. That'll take all day, at least. We're getting the car towed in. They found multiple prints. They—"

"They'll belong to the half-brother, Leonard Baskin, my

goddamn serial killer," she said, pointing at him. "The FBI has jurisdiction on this one."

"You don't have any jurisdiction over my crime scene. None. Right now, you have no evidence that your serial killer and this family's murder are related."

"It's the goddamn brother, of course they're related," she nearly yelled, frustration creeping into her voice. "Don't be an idiot."

His eyes flashed at her. "This is my town, my officers, my case." He stood in front of her, inches taller. "My case. Not yours. So you back off right now. If you want to go chase your serial killer, get the sheriff's department's help. It started out as theirs anyway. But in Barstow, I'm in charge. Not you. *My* case," he said again.

Cameron felt her anger boiling just under the surface, but she kept her voice as even as she could.

"No sir. It's not your case." She pulled out her phone, never breaking eye contact with the chief. She waited only a few seconds before it was answered. "Murdock? The chief of police here in Barstow is not cooperating. In the least. You better do something about it before I shoot him."

Andrea felt a presence behind her and she turned, surprised to find Carina watching her. She was still in the backyard, sitting on the steps, watching the empty red swing sway back and forth. Truth was, she was mesmerized by it, the wind moving it to and fro.

Before Barstow PD got there, Eric and Jack had already begun to question the neighbors. Eric was chumming it up with some of the officers now, asking questions about Burke. The place was crawling with cops, some official, some curious, most in shock as the reality of the situation hit home.

Andrea hadn't been able to go back inside. She kept seeing his face, the soulless eyes. She could picture him doing this, could picture him killing them. She wondered if he'd made Burke watch or if Burke was involved somehow. No, even the most deranged father could never do this to his family. At least she hoped not.

Carina sat down beside her, dressed in an expensive suit and heels. Andrea thought again what a beautiful woman she was. She was perfectly made up, not a hair out of place, her dress pants as pressed as Reynolds kept his. She took a moment to look at her own jeans, her T-shirt that clung to her in the heat, the scuffed boots that had seen many a mile of trail in Sedona. She and Carina were like night and day.

"That was quite gruesome in there," Carina offered.

"Yes."

Carina rested her arms on her knees, her gaze following Andrea's out to the swing set.

"Last night must have been frightening for you."

Andrea turned to look at her but Carina kept her gaze on the swing. She nodded. "Yes. I was terrified."

"I was held captive once," Carina said quietly. "For nine days. In Sudan. They did...they did unspeakable things to me."

Andrea literally saw her shiver at the memory. She turned, waiting for her story.

"It was a rescue mission. I was supposed to get captured. There was a woman and child there. British diplomats. We were on a joint mission to rescue them and the other women and children who were being held there. They were all nothing more than playthings to be used for the soldiers' pleasure. Me included." Carina took a deep breath before continuing. "I had to gain the trust of the women, as many didn't speak English and were wary of me. But the rescue mission didn't turn out as we'd planned. There were twenty-eight people being held there. Eighteen women, nine children and me. We got the British diplomat out, but her child was killed. We only saved ten of the women and four children. It was a bloodbath." She looked at Andrea quickly, then away. "You get numb to it after a while. Sometimes you see so much of this, you forget they're people. They just become subjects, just another casualty of war."

Andrea shook her head. "I hope I never reach that place where I'm immune to it."

Carina offered a small smile. "No, I suppose you don't.

Sometimes the military turns us into nothing more than machines." She turned to look at her. "Cameron loves you, you know."

Andrea was surprised at her comment. "Yes, I know she does."

Carina's gaze went back to the swing set. "I tried my best," she said, smiling. "The night we were alone, I offered myself to her on a silver platter. She wouldn't have anything to do with me." She turned back to Andrea. "The Cameron I knew would have never turned me down. You must have some hold on her."

Andrea nodded. "Yes. Love. It's because I love her too."

Cameron sat quietly in the chief's office, her legs crossed, her fingers tapping impatiently on her thigh. She hadn't said a word, hadn't responded to his continued discourse as to why the Barstow PD should be in charge and not the FBI. She simply stared at him, barely hearing his words.

"We do know what we're doing. I know you think we don't," he continued.

Again, she said nothing as she willed his phone to ring. Finally, it did. He looked up, their eyes meeting, but he made no move to answer it. She smiled, then glanced at the phone.

"You're probably going to want to get that," she said.

"Chief Hudley," he answered quickly. "Yes sir. But—" He glared at Cameron. "I don't agree. I feel—"

Here it comes, she thought.

"Senator Orin?" He flicked his eyes at her. "I still don't think—" His eyes narrowed as he glared at her. "I see. Of course." He hung up the phone, then cleared his throat. "That was the mayor. I'm...I'm to give you full cooperation."

"Wonderful. You've only wasted twenty minutes of my time." She stood, making a mental note to thank Murdock. Apparently he wasn't kidding when he said he could pull strings. "I want to interview Burke's commander. I also want to talk to his closest friends. I want—"

He stood too. "I'm not going to let you run roughshod over my department."

"I'll do anything I damn well please," she said. "I don't give a shit if I piss someone off or hurt their feelings. I have a serial killer to catch."

"You don't really believe Burke's a suspect in this, do you?"

"No. I've heard what the crime scene looked like. He didn't do that. But whether he's helping his brother willingly or not remains to be seen." She pulled out her phone, calling Rowan. He answered immediately.

"I need some background on Leonard Baskin and Buddy Burke. I need everything you can find. And I need it right now."

"I'm good, Cameron, but I'm not that good." She heard him already tapping away at her computer. "Give me a few minutes."

"You've got ten. Share it with the group when you're done."

"Yes, ma'am."

"And don't call me ma'am," she snapped, turning to Hudley. "How many officers do you employ?"

"We have forty-three."

"My team is going to interview them all. I'll need names."

CHAPTER TWENTY-FOUR

Andrea jotted down some notes, waiting for the next cop to come in for his interview. So far, all she'd learned was that Buddy Burke was just a good old boy, following in his father's footsteps on the force. Everyone expressed disbelief that he could be involved in any of this. All she remembered about the man was that he had a fondness for smokeless tobacco.

"What's your name?" she asked, offering a smile.

"Crowley. James." He leaned his arms on the table. "Everyone calls me Jimmy."

"Okay, Jimmy. How well do you know Officer Burke?"

"Know him well. Me and Buddy came up together." He shook his head. "We were friends. I got a couple of kids too. His wife and mine would share babysitting if the other had something to do." He paused. "We live in the same neighborhood," he said, his eyes looking past her. "I can't imagine what hell Rebecca went through. And those poor kids."

Andrea knew well the hell they'd endured but she forced those images away. "What about his brother? Leonard Baskin? Do you know him?"

"Half-brother," Jimmy corrected. "He was a year older than us. He spent summers here when they were kids. We would hang out, play. But when he got older, he didn't come around much."

"What is your opinion of him?"

"He was kind of shy back then. Didn't really know us. Took nearly half of the summer before he would warm up, you know. He and Buddy were close though. They kept in touch throughout the year." He shrugged. "I haven't seen him in years though. Well, obviously, since he was locked up."

"When did he move here?"

"The first time was, what? Ten years ago maybe?"

Andrea nodded. "When he was arrested, did Buddy support him?"

"Oh, yeah. Buddy was convinced he was innocent."

"What did you think?"

"Hell, I'm a cop. They had evidence. The woman had the marks to prove it."

Andrea folded her arms on the table, leaning closer. "You know about the shack we found, right?"

"Yeah. Seventeen heads."

"When Baskin lived in this area before, there were four bodies dumped in the desert, all beheaded. That woman was lucky. It's also what sent him to prison and the killings stopped." She opened up a folder, glancing at the three photos of their victims. She placed them on the table for him to see. "They started up again. One found here near Barstow," she said, pointing to Susie Bell. "The other two were found on I-10."

He nodded but said nothing.

"It'll take awhile to get all the DNA sorted out, but we're confident that Leonard Baskin is our serial killer. Then and now. We're also convinced he killed Buddy Burke's family." She gathered the photos again. "And we're assuming he has Buddy. Whether it's by force or not, we can only speculate."

"Buddy loved his brother. But his family was everything to him. No way would he go with him willingly, not if he knew what he'd done to his wife and kids. No way."

"You're born and raised here?"

"Yes. Most of us were. Barstow is not a destination city, if you know what I mean."

"Where could they be hiding?"

Jimmy leaned back. "Hiding? It's the desert. They could be anywhere."

"Is there some childhood place they had? Is there perhaps another place like the old house he was using?"

"There are abandoned houses all over in the desert. Nothing where you could live though. I mean, no power or water. Just shelter."

She nodded. "The place where we found him, he had solar panels and batteries for power. No running water. Can you think of another place like that?"

He shook his head. "No, nothing comes to mind. I mean, like I said, it could be anywhere."

She sighed, having heard the same answer time and again. No one knew anything.

Cameron rubbed the bridge of her nose, shaking her head.

"Nobody knows anything. Nobody saw anything." She sighed, stating the obvious. "Nobody can offer a guess. Highway patrol has nothing. Sheriff's department has nothing. No activity on credit cards. No phone calls." She snapped her fingers. "Just disappeared."

She looked at the faces around her, all showing the weariness that she felt. They'd interviewed every officer, they'd interviewed neighbors. Jack had gone back to San Bernardino to interview the other truckers Baskin worked with. Nothing. She heard Rowan tapping away and she moved in the direction of her office.

"Rowan? Anything?"

He shook his head, not looking up.

"Cameron?"

She turned, finding Andrea standing close. She raised an eyebrow.

"It's late. We need a break."

She was about to protest. What they needed were answers. But they'd been at it nonstop all day, and she knew everyone was tired. She could see that in Andrea's eyes.

"Okay. Yeah." She ran a hand through her hair with a sigh. "Let's call it a night. Meet back here in the morning."

"You don't have to tell me twice," Eric said, offering a hand to Carina as he pulled her to her feet.

"We'll be over by eight," Reynolds said. "Rowan? You coming?"

"Yes. One sec," he called.

Reynolds eyed Cameron. "Do you know what he's working on?"

"He may be...searching some databases," she said evasively.

"In other words, I don't want to know?"

"Exactly."

Rowan came out, glancing at Cameron. "Let it run. Maybe we'll get a hit."

"I won't touch it," she promised.

She plopped down in her recliner once they'd taken their leave. She closed her eyes, listening to the shower. The RV park was a dump, but they hadn't had time to be choosy. The owner of the park hadn't been thrilled when Cameron had flashed her credentials at him. That was probably one reason he'd let them park in a secluded part, far from the other residents.

She gave a weary smile as Lola hopped in her lap, a quiet meow the response as Cameron threaded her fingers through her fur. She leaned her head back and closed her eyes. She, like the others, didn't even have a guess as to where Baskin and Burke might be.

Rowan was running a search, looking at property tax records. Burke was fourth generation in Barstow and records show the only property he owned was his house. While there were no family homes on record—his childhood home having been destroyed years ago—they were hoping to find something that may have once belonged to the Burke family. Something familiar where Baskin could hide.

"Hey."

She opened her eyes, finding Andrea watching her, her hair damp and slicked back from her face. She looked clean and fresh, but her eyes reflected just how tired she was.

Cameron pushed herself up, wrapping her arms around Andrea. "Go on to bed," she said, kissing her lightly on the cheek. "I'll be there soon."

"I need to get the coffee—"

"I'll get it, Andi. You're exhausted."

"So are you."

Cameron nodded. "Yes." She pulled Andrea closer, kissing her lips this time, letting them linger. "Now go to bed."

Andrea nodded, picking Lola up before turning away. Cameron got the coffee ready for morning, then slipped into the bathroom, intending a quick shower. Instead, she stood under the spray until the hot water ran out. She ducked her head into the cool stream of water, then stepped out. She didn't bother putting any clothes on as she brushed her teeth. She towel dried her hair, then combed it with her fingers. She was too tired to worry with it.

Andrea was sound asleep when she crawled in beside her. She moved closer, then smiled as Andrea's hands, even in sleep, found their way to her body. She pulled Andrea into her arms, closing her eyes as Andrea snuggled against her, never once waking. She had no time for any other thoughts as sleep claimed her, chasing Leonard Baskin and Buddy Burke from her mind.

CHAPTER TWENTY-FIVE

Andrea had to pee but it was too warm, too comfortable where she was so she ignored the urge. She lay on her side, Cameron curled protectively around her from behind. She slipped her fingers through Cameron's, moving Cameron's hand to her breast. She sighed as Cameron's fingers tightened.

"You trying to tell me something," Cameron murmured in her ear.

"No. I just wanted your touch. Is that okay?"

She felt lips kiss behind her ear and she closed her eyes, pulling Cameron's arms tighter around her.

"Did you sleep well?" Cameron whispered.

"Yes. I don't remember waking up once." She rolled to her back, her lips finding Cameron's. "Did you?"

"Yes." Cameron leaned up on an elbow, her fingers moving

in lazy circles over Andrea's breasts. Her nipples hardened immediately.

"Don't start something you can't finish," Andrea warned.

Cameron dipped her head, her mouth closing over one erect nipple. Andrea moaned, holding Cameron closer. She spread her legs, urging Cameron between them. Her hips arched, meeting Cameron's thrust. Her hands moved over Cameron's back, sliding down and cupping her, bringing her hard against her.

She moaned again as Cameron's mouth went to her other breast, her tongue swirling over her nipple. She could feel Cameron's arousal on her thigh and she arched again, opening to her.

"Do we have time?" she murmured, her body craving more.

Cameron didn't answer, instead, she took her lips in a fierce kiss, her tongue moving wildly inside Andrea's mouth. She felt Cameron's hand move between their bodies, felt fingers slip into her wet folds, opening her, exposing her clit.

"Oh, God," Andrea moaned, holding Cameron tight as their clits rubbed together, each thrusting against the other, slowly, grinding together in a perfect rhythm. She wanted to stay like this for hours, their bodies wet against each other. But they didn't have hours, and she gave in to her body's demand for release, her breath held as she shuddered, her body pulsing against Cameron's as she, too, gave in to her climax.

Their bodies were damp with perspiration and Cameron rolled off her, both of their breaths slowly returning to normal. Cameron reached for her phone, then groaned when she saw the time.

"They'll be here in twenty minutes."

Andrea pushed the hair out of her face. "Great, company," she said dryly, her body still humming from Cameron's touch.

Cameron leaned over, kissing her quickly. "I think to save time, we should shower together."

Andrea laughed. "Sweetheart, if we shower together, we'll never be finished in twenty minutes."

But they were, even after enjoying a few playful wet moments. They were both seated and sipping coffee when the team arrived. Cameron's hair had dried but Andrea's was still damp and she brushed at it now, chancing a glance at Cameron who gave her a soft smile before opening the door.

"It's like a hundred degrees already," Eric complained as he walked into the air conditioned rig. "How do people live out here?"

"It's a dry heat," Andrea said automatically. "You get used to it. Although it was never this hot in Sedona."

Rowan mumbled a hello and headed straight for the office. Cameron gave him a smile, then turned her gaze to the others.

"I trust everyone got a good night's sleep."

"Well, you two look like you certainly did," Eric said, then laughed as Andrea blushed.

Andrea looked at Cameron, pleased that she too sported a blush. And why not? Only a half hour ago they had been naked, making love.

"We slept...very well," Cameron said. "Thank you."

Reynolds cleared his throat, an amused expression on his face. "Coffee?" he asked.

"Sure. Help yourself," she said, pointing to a cabinet where they kept the cups.

"I got a call this morning from the sheriff's department," he said. "The tunnel was indeed rigged to blow so thank you for that."

"My pleasure," Cameron said.

"It came out about a hundred feet from the highway. Had a little ramp going up."

"Motorbike?"

"That's the assumption," he said as he took a sip of coffee. "Seeing as how this crowd likes to speculate, I guess we'll go with it."

Andrea was surprised by the gentle teasing of Reynolds. Apparently he and Cameron had moved past their earlier debates on the wisdom of speculation.

"No wonder we didn't hear anything," Cameron said. "It was a half-mile to the road."

"So you really think the patrol car was left where it was as a ruse?" Carina asked.

"I think he wanted us to concentrate our search in that

area, yes. We've found his house, his haven, so he's no longer comfortable. He feels hunted, which he is. I think he went to the only person he could trust—Buddy Burke."

"And maybe Buddy didn't want to help," Eric suggested. "Or maybe Buddy put two and two together and threatened to turn him in."

Andrea shook her head. "We met Burke. He didn't seem that bright."

Cameron nodded. "Yeah. All I recall of him was his constant spitting of tobacco juice and his questioning us if we were really FBI."

Reynolds snorted. "Imagine that."

"No, I think Buddy refused to help him so he had to be persuaded."

"By killing his family," Carina concluded. "Of course, if Burke had to watch all that, I can't imagine him even being able to function. That would drive most men mad."

Rowan came out holding up his laptop. "Got a couple of hits," he said. "Three really, but one place is currently occupied, so we can cross that one off." He sat on the edge of the loveseat, next to Carina. "There's an abandoned house that used to belong to the grandparents. Of course, they sold it way back in 1992 and it's had three other owners since then."

"Burke would have been what? Ten? Eleven?"

"Yes. Eleven. This place is located in the high desert area between Yucca Valley and Twentynine Palms. Then I found another property, this one no longer has a residence on it, according to tax records anyway. But I pulled up a satellite image and," he said, showing them his laptop, "you can see there are a couple structures here. A small shed or something. This one is here in the Barstow area, on I-15 near Newberry Springs."

"So right in his hunting area."

"Exactly. It's only a couple of miles from an abandoned water park. Used to be called Lake Delores but now Rock-A-Hoola," Rowan said with a grin. "That was the last name it used. It's just off of I-15. It's been closed down for the last ten years."

"Okay. Who owns the place near Barstow?"

"Creosote Properties," he said. "It's currently for sale."

"And the grandparents' place in the high desert area?"

"The bank now. The grandparents used to own both of these properties twenty years ago."

"Are they still alive?"

Rowan shook his head. "Both deceased."

"What about parents?"

"Divorced. Burke's mother lives in Bakersfield. No location on Baskin's mother. The father—who is the biological father to both Burke and Baskin—lives in Las Cruces, New Mexico. He's remarried."

"Bakersfield is close," Reynolds said. "Let's put a call in to the PD there, just as a precaution."

Cameron nodded. "It wouldn't hurt to have someone question the father as well, but I don't think Baskin would contact him. I think this is his war and I think it plays out here."

Jack, who had been silent, nodded. "I agree. This is his territory. This is where he lives, this is where he hunts, this is where he kills. He's familiar with things here."

"He may very well have any number of places where he feels safe. As we learned from the interviews, there are a lot of abandoned houses, businesses. A lot of places to hide," Eric said.

"I'm still at a loss about the patrol car," Andrea said. "Obviously he needs to hide. But why take the time to ditch the car? If it's to try to throw us off of a search grid, that's crazy."

"Is it?" Cameron asked. "Chief Hudley was ready to put his whole force in the area of the car."

"And the car was left to the north, miles away from any of these possible safe houses," Rowan said.

"Right. *Miles* away," she said. "Why is he taking the time for that, taking that chance that he'll get caught? Why isn't he hiding?"

"What are you thinking?" Cameron asked.

"I don't know," she said. "But it just doesn't feel right. The whole car thing makes no sense to me. If he's got Burke, why not just take him and leave the car? Why take the car out of the way and dump it?" She shrugged. "Maybe I'm overthinking it."

Cameron shook her head. "No. That's what we do. Speculate,"

she said, glancing at Reynolds with a smirk. "I want everyone to feel free to express their thoughts."

"I think he dumped the car as far north as he did to make us at least *look* in that direction," Jack said. "If he's headed south, to Twentynine Palms, then he'd have a good head start."

"Head start to what?" Eric asked. "The shootout?"

"And do we assume Burke is being held captive or is helping? He may have a police radio. He may know everything."

"Will he assume we'll find these properties? His grandparents are buried several owners deep," Reynolds said.

"That's the chance you take with speculating," Cameron said. "We may be off base with the whole thing. Hell, he may have headed south and is in Mexico already."

"I don't think so," Andrea said. "A serial killer is just that. He doesn't run. He keeps playing the game until he gets caught. This is just a little setback for him," she said. "He still has this compulsion to kill, to torture. What he did to the Burke family— will that satisfy him for a while?"

"I agree," Carina said. "Like Jack said, this is where he hunts, where he kills. I don't think he's running."

Cameron spread her hands out. "Okay then. Which property? South to Twentynine Palms?" She turned to Rowan with a raised eyebrow as he typed quickly on his laptop.

"From all the data that we have, plus plugging in these new properties, the highest probability is Twentynine Palms. Seventy-three percent. The property here near Barstow is only thirty-four."

Cameron glanced at Reynolds, then at Andrea. Andrea wasn't surprised by Cameron's next words.

"Reynolds and I will take Twentynine Palms. I want you four here."

Eric raised his hand to protest but Cameron stopped him. "We'll get the sheriff's department for backup. So will you."

"But why send four of us on the lowest percentage? If we—"

"It's not up for discussion," she said.

Andrea wasn't sure what Cameron's motive was regarding the others. For her, she knew—after what happened the other night—that Cameron would do everything she could to keep

Andrea out of a similar situation. A part of Andrea was angry at that and she would have her say later, but she knew better than to argue. As Cameron had said, it wasn't up for discussion.

It was over an hour's drive from Barstow to the high desert area near Twentynine Palms. Rowan was still at the rig, keeping up with both teams and providing GPS assistance and updates.

"Heard back on the DNA from the items they took from the motel in Needles," he said. "Match on Susie Bell. Not that it matters at this point."

"And the forensic team made it?"

"Yes. They're working out of Apple Valley."

Cameron glanced in the rearview mirror, seeing the two units following her. The sheriff's department had been nothing but cooperative. For that, she was thankful. There was no drama like there'd been with Chief Hudley.

"Want to tell me why you split the team up unevenly?" Reynolds asked.

"I think you know why."

"Yeah. You want us to have all the fun, I guess."

Cameron sighed. "She's pissed at me."

"No doubt."

"I mean really pissed," she said.

"I don't blame her."

"You think I'm wrong?"

"The way you're trying to protect her, she can't do her job. You're going overboard," he said.

Cameron smiled. "Funny. Those were pretty much her exact words."

"But?"

"But I don't think she's recovered—emotionally, at least—from the other night. Then, with what they found at the Burke house. Outwardly, she's acting like she's fine. But I know Andrea." Cameron looked at him quickly. "He had her chained to that bloody table, for God's sake. He drugged her. She was about to meet the same fate as the others. That's got to screw with your mind."

Reynolds shook his head. "I don't think you're giving her enough credit. She was a victim because we made her a victim. It was a plan we threw together chaotically that actually worked, which still surprises me."

"Considering it was based on speculation?"

"Mostly, yes."

"No. Partly speculation, mostly Rowan and the algorithms."

"But really, what are the chances we found our guy on the first try?"

Cameron laughed. "I believe the chances were sixty-eight percent."

Jack drove them down I-15 with Carina riding shotgun. Andrea was still a little miffed at Cameron and hated that they'd parted in anger. Well, anger on her part. Cameron had still been trying to reason with her.

"You're treating me like a goddamn child."

"No, I'm not. I'm not even treating you as my lover. I'm treating you as an agent who had a traumatic experience and needs to back away. If this had happened while you were still a cop, they'd make you see a shrink before returning to duty."

"That's bullshit. If we weren't sleeping together, you wouldn't be doing this."

"That's not true. If this were Carina, I'd be doing the same damn thing."

"Oh, well sure, since we're talking lovers and all. Why don't we try it with someone you haven't slept with?"

It was a childish thing to say, she knew, but she hated that Cameron didn't trust her enough to handle this. She wondered why she didn't trust any of them enough, since Cameron had sent them off together to what amounted to nothing more than a formality check. She knew from working in Sedona that thirty-four percent was nothing. It might as well have been ten percent.

"You okay?" Eric whispered.

"No. I'm pissed."

"Get into a little fight, did you?"

"This is bullshit," she said.

"What? This little trip we're taking?"

"Yes. We should have gone as a group to Twentynine Palms. Why trust the sheriff's department as backup?"

Carina turned to look at them, obviously overhearing their conversation.

"Cameron is following procedure," she said. "In the military, if you have two possible targets, you don't send all of the elite team to one and grunts to the other. Besides, she is trying to protect you, you know that."

"Yeah. That's the part that pisses me off."

"What does that say for the rest of us?" Eric asked.

Carina smiled. "Andrea and Reynolds are the only two who Cameron really trusts. We are the grunts, unfortunately," she said with a shrug.

That much was true, Andrea knew. Although she might also lump Rowan in with Reynolds. Cameron had come to rely on him so much. She knew Cameron trusted him. She hadn't called Jason even once to help with the algorithms, simply letting Rowan do his thing. The rest of them—Jack, Eric, Carina—no, Cameron didn't trust them. Not that they'd given her any reason not to, she just hadn't worked with them enough, or recently, in Carina's case.

She let out a heavy sigh, glancing out the window again. They were passing the old water park, palms still growing and flourishing on the site.

"Crazy idea for a water park, isn't it?"

She turned to Eric. "What? In the middle of the desert?"

"Not just that. It's in the middle of nowhere in the middle of the desert. There aren't enough people living out here. Who were they targeting?"

"Traffic from LA to Vegas," Jack said.

Eric laughed. "Yeah, right. I'm dreaming of slot machines and show girls, but I stop off for a quick play day on the water slides? I don't think so."

"Obviously their plan didn't work."

"Here's the road," Carina said as she followed the GPS on her phone. "Rowan? You still with us?"

"Yes. The road should dead end at the larger of the two sheds. The second shed is about two hundred feet north."

"Okay. We can see the first shed," she said. "I'm taking you off speaker." She glanced at the others. "Earbuds."

Andrea turned her phone on, dialing the number Rowan had set up for them. When she was connected, she put one earbud in. "I'm on," she said.

"Copy that," Rowan said. "Eric? Jack?"

"I'm on," Eric said.

"Me too."

"Okay. As Cameron would say, slow and easy."

CHAPTER TWENTY-SIX

Cameron turned down the driveway, the skeletons of long dead palm trees lining the sides. The house was fairly close to the road and in desperate need of repair. The constant wind and blowing sand had taken its toll, leaving the paint nearly stripped. An old, faded *For Sale* sign leaned haphazardly against the front porch, nearly obscured by a cactus left to grow unchecked.

There was no sign of a vehicle, no evidence that one had been down the driveway, but she knew how quickly tracks would get covered up out here. She stopped and got out, waiting for the four sheriff's deputies to do the same. Reynolds had his phone on and she nodded at him.

"Let Rowan know we're here. Find out where the other team is," she said before walking toward the deputies. "Two with me, two with Reynolds," she said. "We're doing a sweep of the house and then the grounds."

"The other team just checked in," Reynolds said. "No sign of vehicles. They're just now checking the sheds."

"Okay. You take the back," she said.

The front porch creaked under their weight. She peered in through a broken window, surprised that there was still furniture inside. Maybe someone was living here after all. She motioned for the deputies to stay to the side. She slowly opened the screen door, the old hinges protesting, suggesting they hadn't been opened in years.

She turned the knob. Locked. She was about to step back and kick it in when one of the deputies stopped her.

"I'll do it, ma'am."

She stepped away, then paused. "Don't ever call me ma'am again."

"Yes, ma'am...I mean, no, ma'am...no, I won't, ma'am."

"Jesus," she murmured, rolling her eyes. "Just do your thing."

One powerful kick and the doorjamb shattered, splintering the wood. He pushed the door open, then let Cameron go in first. Her weapon out and ready, she entered the small room which was indeed still furnished. The thick layer of dust indicated it was unused.

"Back here," Reynolds called. "Kitchen."

They headed for the sound of his voice, stopping up short. Burke was tied to a chair, one side of his head missing from a large caliber gunshot wound.

"Damn," one of the deputies murmured behind her. "So much for brotherly love."

Cameron flicked her eyes to Reynolds, then turned to the deputies. "Sweep the house."

"His service weapon is missing," Reynolds said, pointing to his empty holster.

"Judging by the hole in his head, I'd say it was used to kill him."

"Yeah. And we can assume Baskin has it."

The larger shed, while obviously abandoned, was in decent shape. Andrea guessed it was twenty-by-thirty. There were no windows and only a double door that was securely padlocked.

"Can I shoot it off?" Eric asked.

"How about we use bolt cutters," Jack said. He raised his eyebrows at one of the two sheriff's deputies who had accompanied them. "You got some?"

"Yes sir."

"Doesn't look like anyone's been here recently," Carina said as she walked around the side, her gaze fixed on the rocks and sand that surrounded the building. "No tracks."

"You can't go by that out here," Andrea said. "The wind moves the sand around all the time."

"Here you go," the deputy said, handing the bolt cutters to Jack.

They all stood back as Jack pulled the double doors open. A swoosh of hot air hit them, then nothing. The place was entirely empty. Using their flashlights, they went inside, inspecting the floor and walls but there was nothing other than the stifling heat. Andrea felt sweat trickle between her breasts and a lone stream fell down her cheek. She wiped it away impatiently, then turned to go back outside into the somewhat cooler temperature.

"Were we really expecting anything?" Eric asked.

"No."

"Come on," Carina said. "Let's check the small one."

Andrea holstered her weapon, then wiped again at the sweat on her face, seeing Eric do the same. Jack and the two deputies followed Carina to the shed.

"You guys copy?" Rowan's voice sounded in her ear.

"What's up?" Andrea asked as she and Eric followed the others.

"Reynolds checked in. They found Burke. Dead."

Eric turned and their gazes locked.

"Copy that," Andrea said. "Nothing here in the large shed. Checking the smaller one now."

"Keep me posted. I'll pass this along to Cameron."

"Yeah. Sure." She shrugged. "I guess that answers whether Burke was helping him or not."

"Got blood," Carina called.

Andrea and Eric turned, watching as Carina and Jack stood opposite the door, this one without a padlock. They had their weapons drawn, the two deputies beside them.

"Wonder why that one doesn't have a lock," she murmured out loud.

"Really. This one was locked up like it held gold or something. Yet empty. That one—"

But his sentence was cut off as an explosion literally blew the small shed apart. Andrea saw it all in slow motion—after all, she'd seen it before—her team consumed by the blast. In a blink of an eye, her breath was knocked from her as the force of the explosion blew Eric off his feet and square into her body.

It was déjà vu—the blast, the fire, the pain. Only this time, it wasn't her lover, Erin. It wasn't her best friend, Mark. No, but still, it didn't lessen the sting, the agony of it all.

She felt the hard desert ground beneath her, rocks cutting into her back. Eric lay sprawled on top of her, shielding her, his dead weight heavy on her chest. She let her head fall back, unable to fight the inevitable, her eyes closing as blackness enveloped her.

"There's nothing else," Reynolds said as they finished a sweep of the outside perimeter of the house.

"Rowan called in CSI?"

"Yes. They're on their way."

She put her hands on her hips, surveying the land around them, wondering where in the hell Baskin had slithered off to. "You think he's still on a motorcycle?"

"Pros and cons with that," Reynolds said as he wiped his brow. "He's a sitting duck if he is. Exposed. Yet he would be able to escape tight situations, much better than in a car." He shrugged. "What does your gut tell you?"

Cameron stared at him, shaking her head. "Still with the tie, Reynolds? It's a hundred and ten."

He wiped the sweat from his face again. "Tie or not, it's still fucking hot."

She laughed out loud, seeing the sheen of perspiration on his dark skin. "I do believe that's the first time you've dropped the f-bomb, Reynolds. Am I wearing off on you?"

"Hardly."

She looked back at the house, the desolate landscape surrounding it, the four deputies talking quietly among themselves. "My gut says he's on a motorcycle."

Reynolds nodded. "Mine too. I think perhaps—" He tilted his head, holding the earpiece tightly to his ear. "Hang on. *What?*"

Cameron frowned, trying to read Reynolds's expression. Suddenly the deputies were a flurry of activity as they all reached for their radios at once. Reynolds turned to her. "Get your phone."

"What is it?"

"It's Rowan. Get your phone."

A sense of dread settled over her as she fished out her phone. Her hand was trembling and she wanted to throw the phone down to the desert floor, not wanting to hear what Rowan had to say.

"Yeah. It's me."

"There was an explosion, Cameron. I've lost communication with the team."

Cameron's eyes flew to Reynolds, their gazes locking. "What do you mean you've lost communication? No one is answering you?"

"Not just that. There's no signal. I'm assuming the blast... well, it would have disabled the phones, obviously, if..."

Cameron was having a hard time breathing, the tightness in her chest sucking the air out of her. She cleared her throat, trying to focus. "Sheriff's department?"

"I've notified them, yes. They are already en route."

"Good. We're on our way." She paused. "You find out what the hell is going on, Rowan."

She strode purposefully to the deputies, them just getting the news too of the explosion.

"Do you know anything?" one of them asked.

She shook her head, wondering if her face gave away her nervousness. "No. But I need you four to stay here." She pointed at the house. "Secure the scene until the CSI team gets here."

"We know the drill."

Any other day, Cameron would have come back with a biting retort, but not today. She simply spun on her heels and headed for her truck. Reynolds intercepted her.

"Let me drive."

"Like hell," she spat out, trying to open the door.

"You're in no condition. Let me drive."

She glared at him, wanting to tell him to get his ass in the passenger's seat, but the look in his eyes was genuine, not condescending. She nodded.

"Fine," she said, hurrying around to the other side of the truck. "But I expect you to break every traffic law there is."

"Will do."

True to his word, Reynolds spun out of the driveway, sending rocks flying in all directions as he skidded around the corner and sped out onto the highway. Cameron held on, barely getting her seatbelt fastened as she was flung against the door.

She said nothing, her eyes staring straight ahead. She didn't dare think of what she might find. She couldn't bear it. All she could see was Andrea's face, her beautiful face trying to hide her anger that morning. Despite her pleadings, Cameron had sent her to the property which barely registered on the algorithm. They both knew it was pointless. That's probably why Andi was so mad at her.

"You're treating me like a child."

Cameron squeezed her eyes shut. No, not like a child. She was treating her like her lover. She was. She was doing anything she could to protect her. She slammed her fist on the dash.

"Goddamn it," she yelled. "There was supposed to be nothing there. Thirty-four percent is *nothing*," she said. "Nothing."

"Quit blaming yourself."

"Who the hell else should I blame?"

"How about Baskin?"

"I sent them there, Reynolds. I sent *her* there." She grabbed her chest as she felt her heart breaking. "I can't lose her," she whispered, cursing the tears that had started to fall. "Goddamn it," she said again, wiping angrily at her face.

Reynolds glanced at her but said nothing. He was literally flying down the highway and through her tears the desert was but a blur as they raced back to Barstow.

Andrea blinked her eyes several times, conscious of the body on top of her. *Eric.* She could smell the smoke of the burning shed and she tried to guess how long she'd been out. Not long, judging by the flames.

She pulled an arm free, reaching up to touch Eric, his skin warm against her hand. She nearly gasped when she felt a pulse in his neck.

"Eric...God, you're alive." She was afraid to move him but knew she must. Off in a distance she thought she heard sirens, or maybe it was just wishful thinking. "Eric," she said again. "I'm going to roll you."

He moaned as she did, moving him enough to sit up. She got him on his back and slid her legs out from under him. She immediately knelt by his side, gently patting his face.

"Eric, can you hear me?" There was a nasty cut on his head and an obvious knot forming. She leaned closer, speaking directly into his ear. "Eric? Come on, buddy, open your eyes."

Another moan and she saw his eyelids flutter. She squeezed his hand, waiting, but they never opened.

She finally looked around, seeing what was left of the shed. She spotted the bodies, all four mangled and burned. For an instant, her mind flashed back to LA, back to the ambush, back to her team, back to Erin and Mark. She shook the vision away, turning again to Eric whose hand was squeezing hers painfully.

"Can you open your eyes?"

"My...my ears are ringing," he whispered.

She nearly laughed, bending down close to his face. "So are mine."

The sirens were louder now and she knew they were coming for them. She reached for her phone, finding the facing shattered. She turned it on but got nothing. She patted Eric's pockets, looking for his.

"Stop that. I don't want Cameron to shoot me."

She glanced up, her smile turning into a grin as his warm eyes met hers. "Phone?"

"I had it clipped on."

She looked around them, but found no phone. She needed to contact Cameron. Rowan would have heard the blast and reported it. No doubt Cameron was frantic by now.

"The others?" Eric asked, trying to sit up. "Jack? Carina?"

She shook her head. "No. Just us. Now lie still. You have a nasty cut on your head."

He closed his eyes again. "It happened so fast."

"Yeah. They...they didn't know what hit them."

"I hear sirens," he murmured.

"Yes. They're almost here," she said, still holding tightly to his hand, so thankful he appeared to be okay. So thankful she wasn't left all alone again, the only one left alive to carry the guilt. She shook her head, clearing her thoughts. No, she wouldn't go down that road again. But God, she wished Cameron was here. She needed her. She needed her strength. She needed to look into her eyes and know that everything was going to be okay.

She smiled ruefully. Even if she did get a phone, she had no way of contacting her. Cameron's cell number was locked away in her phone. She'd had no reason to memorize it. And Rowan's temporary community number, as he called it, was there as well.

She sighed with relief as flashing emergency lights finally came into view, signaling her that help was on its way. Help for Eric, certainly. But for Jack and Carina? For the two innocent deputies who just happened to get assigned to them today? No. There would be no help for them.

CHAPTER TWENTY-SEVEN

Cameron snatched her phone up, seeing Rowan's ID. Her hand trembled and she was nearly afraid to answer. She finally took a deep breath, then nodded at Reynolds before answering.

"Ross," she said, her voice thick with emotion. "What do you have?"

"I don't know much, Cameron. All I've learned is from their radio communications."

"Okay." She swallowed. "How bad?"

"Cameron...there were four casualties. Two survivors."

She felt her breath leave her and she squeezed her eyes tight. "Andrea?" She brushed at the tears that fell again. "I need to know if Andrea is okay," she said hoarsely. "Please Rowan. I need to know."

"I don't know, Cameron. I'm just repeating what came over

the radio. I don't know the extent of the injuries. I've been trying to get someone to patch me through but it's a little chaotic, I'm sure. They had two of their own there too," he reminded her.

"Keep trying, Rowan. We're about fifteen minutes out." She disconnected, then glanced at Reynolds, no longer caring if he saw her tears. "Four dead," she said quietly. "He doesn't know... who."

Reynolds surprised her by reaching over and taking her hand. "Keep the faith, Cameron."

She nodded. "I can't lose her. I just can't." She wiped at her tears, angry with herself for her loss of control. "I swear, if you tell anyone about this, I'll shoot you myself."

He put both hands on the wheel, not letting up his speed. "You know, that was my team too," he said. "I didn't know Eric or Carina before this, but Jack, hell, I've known him for years."

"I know. I'm sorry, man. This whole thing is fucked." She squeezed the bridge of her nose hard, trying to remain focused. Unfortunately, Andrea was the only thing she could focus on. "My chest is so tight," she said, rubbing between her breasts. "I can't...I can't even think about her being one of the four." She tapped her chest hard. "She's in my soul, Reynolds. I know you don't understand, but she is. I feel like I'm losing control here."

"Yeah, I know."

"Don't say it," she said, glancing quickly at him. "I know what you're thinking. That's why they have rules for this sort of thing. But you can't help who you fall in love with." She paused, looking at him again. "I know, I know. We fell in love first, and then were partners. But I couldn't leave her behind in Sedona. I just couldn't."

"Does Murdock know?"

"Of course. He pretends he doesn't, but yeah, he's not stupid." She clenched her fists tightly. "It shouldn't be a problem," she said. "We're damn good partners. We work well together. We bounce ideas off each other, we...we *speculate*," she said with a smile. "She knows what I'm thinking sometimes before I even do." She leaned her head back. "I can't lose her," she said quietly.

"Almost there," he said. "Are you going to be able to hold it together?"

"If she's gone?" She shook her head. "No. And when I find this son of a bitch, I'm putting a bullet in his brain."

"Ross, we follow—"

"Don't start that shit. We aren't following any goddamn rules. He's a dead man." Her phone buzzed before he could reply and she held it up, showing him it was Rowan. "Jesus, I don't want to get this."

"Answer it. Better we know now than when we get there."

Her thumb tapped her phone, then she held it to her ear. "Rowan?"

"Andrea is alive," he said simply.

She let out a sob, then caught her breath. She was nearly ashamed at the relief she felt. "Who else?"

"Eric. They're going to take him. He's got a gash on his head from what I understand. Andrea is okay."

Cameron looked at Reynolds. "Andrea and Eric," she said.

He nodded, then turned his attention back to the road.

"Thank you, Rowan. I've been...well, I've been a little crazy," she admitted.

"I know. I imagine she's been too, not being able to contact you."

"You're right. I hadn't thought of that," she said. "I'll be in touch. We're almost there."

The relief she felt was palpable. She wanted to laugh out loud with it, she wanted to yell at the top of her lungs. Yet they'd lost two team members. She wasn't close to Jack but she'd known him for several years. Carina...well, she was nothing more than an old lover. She wouldn't even call her a friend. But she was a damn good agent. She was nearly an expert in explosives. How had she not seen it? What kind of trigger had he used?

"God, amazing," she murmured.

"What?"

"My brain is working again," she said. "Carina was an expert in explosives. How could she have not anticipated it? I mean, especially since we found C4 at the safe house."

She held on as he turned sharply, the desert road as bumpy as the rest they'd been on in the last week. A dozen flashing lights beckoned them. Reynolds skidded to a halt and Cameron jumped out even before the truck had come to a standstill. She glanced around frantically, her eyes bouncing from one deputy to another. Finally, she spotted Andrea, leaning in the ambulance, talking to Eric. She would have bolted in her direction if not for Reynolds's grip on her arm.

"There are a lot of eyes out here, Agent Ross," he said. "Play it cool."

He was so right, but all she wanted to do was run to Andrea and wrap her arms around her and hold her close. She squared her shoulders instead, glaring at him.

"*Special* Agent Ross," she corrected.

Andrea turned then, finding her. Their eyes collided, both trying to convey their feelings without words. Andrea finally nodded at her, a slight smile on her face. Cameron felt everything right itself in her world again.

Andrea was okay.

"She made it?"

"Finally," Andrea said, turning back to Eric. "Now quit arguing with me."

"I'm not arguing. I'm simply stating that I don't want to go to the hospital. There's no need."

"Your head hurts. You have ringing in your ears." When he didn't respond, she put her hands on her hips and raised her eyebrows.

"Okay. Yeah. My head hurts like a son of a bitch. And I've got bells going off. That doesn't mean—"

"Oh, God, you're as stubborn as Cameron, I swear," she said, grabbing his hand. "Please? Just to be safe. I promise I'll come and spring you out in the morning."

He squeezed her hand tightly. "You promise?"

She leaned closer, kissing his cheek. "I promise."

"You know, if Cameron ever ditches you..."

She laughed. "You are *so* not my type." She released his hand as they loaded him into the ambulance.

"Don't forget me tomorrow," he said.

"Not a chance."

She stood back, watching the ambulance pull away, stirring the desert dust as they left the scene. She felt eyes on her and she turned, not surprised to find Cameron walking her way. She stood back, her eyes glued to Cameron's.

"How is he?" Cameron asked.

"Probably a concussion. He's got a nasty cut on his head. Debris in his back...superficial, but still," she said, shrugged. "He'll be okay."

Cameron nodded, her eyes searching, looking for what, Andrea didn't know. Then Cameron grasped her elbow, leading her further away from the others.

"Are you...are you okay?"

Andrea nodded, her eyes never leaving Cameron's. "I'm sorry," she whispered, grabbing Cameron's hand, needing some contact. "I'm so sorry. All I've been thinking about is how we were angry with each other."

"I know," Cameron said, her fingers tightening around Andrea's. "Me too."

"Let's don't ever do that again. I love you. I love you so much," she said. "I don't want to ever be angry with you."

She could see the hesitation in Cameron, could see her chest heaving, her eyes dark with emotion. Cameron looked around them, everyone going about their jobs, no one watching them.

"Fuck it," she murmured, pulling Andrea into her arms.

Andrea clung to her, her tears falling hard and fast. She felt her body sag as all the emotion of the day took its toll on her. She buried her face against Cameron, soaking up her strength.

"It was just like before," she whispered. "Just like before. I thought I was the only one spared again. Eric was thrown into me, on top of me. He shielded me. Just like before."

"I'm so sorry, Andi. God, I thought Reynolds and I would be going into the firestorm, not you. I just wanted you to be safe."

"I know. And I was pissed at you for it." She pulled away slightly. "Maybe I wanted *you* to be safe and I was angry that you were putting yourself in danger ahead of all of us. It works both ways, Cameron."

"So maybe we just need to stay together so we won't both have to worry."

She wiped at her face, running her hand under her wet nose. She took a deep breath, then pointed to the large shed still standing.

"That one was locked. A huge padlock. Jack got one of the deputies to get bolt cutters from their unit. It was locked up tight, yet there wasn't a single thing inside. Not one thing." She paused, turning to the remaining rubble of the smaller shed. "Carina and Jack went first. The deputies followed. Eric and I were behind them. Carina said she found blood. That shed wasn't locked. Eric and I made the comment that there was no lock on that one and then...and then it just exploded as soon as she opened the door."

"As far as you know, she didn't check to see if it was wired?"

"No. I don't think she did."

She heard footsteps behind her and she turned, finding Reynolds there. His eyes were filled with concern and she surprised both of them by giving him a quick, hard hug. He held her for a moment, then stepped back.

"No worse for wear?"

She shook her head. "I'm so sorry," she said. "It was...it was so quick. They didn't...well, they didn't know what hit them."

He nodded. "Their bodies are...well," he shook his head, not finishing his thought. "Eric?"

"He's going to be fine. He didn't want to go to the hospital. Can't say I blame him, but I promised I'd get him out in the morning."

"Very good. At least—"

"Got a body," someone yelled from the burned-out shed.

The three of them turned, then rushed over with the others. The charred remains were unrecognizable. Judging by the positioning of the body, it appeared to have been folded into a large box of some kind.

"Headless."

Cameron turned to Reynolds. "The fourth victim?"

"What are you talking about?" Andrea asked.

"In his trophy room, there were four recent victims. We only had three bodies."

"So something happened that prevented him from dumping this one," she said. "Yet he still went hunting again. He picked me up."

"The killings were escalating."

"And still are," Cameron said. "The Burke family. Burke himself. Obviously Leonard Baskin felt no attachment to Buddy Burke." She turned to Andrea. "We found him tied to a chair, his head practically blown off."

"Same as the oldest child," Andrea said, remembering the scene in the Burke home.

"Maybe Burke betrayed him," Reynolds suggested. "Or refused to help him."

Cameron arched an eyebrow. "Are you *speculating*, Special Agent Reynolds?"

Andrea noticed a slight blush on his ebony skin and she smiled at him.

"Okay, so maybe you are rubbing off on me," he said.

Cameron led them out of the way of the CSI team who was sifting through the rubble. She followed Cameron's gaze as the last of the four victims were carried away. It hit her again how easily that could have been her they were carting off. Not Carina, not Jack...but her. Cameron must have sensed her discomfort and she put a steadying arm around her shoulders.

"Let's get back to the rig," Cameron said. "We need to give all this data to Rowan and see what he can dig up. See if he can find any sort of pattern with the algorithms."

"I need to fill Murdock in," Reynolds said. "Let him notify next of kin. Jack has a daughter," he said. "I don't really know what other family he had. Carina," he said with a shrug. "I don't know anything about her."

"She had a large family, from what I remember," Cameron said. "I think a couple of her brothers are in the military as well."

Reynolds eyed the rental car that Jack had driven to the shed. "I've already checked with the deputies. I'm clear to take the car. Where do you want to meet?"

"Pizza at the rig. We'll be doing a lot of speculating, I imagine."

"Okay. I'll bring some beer."

Cameron studied her for a moment and Andrea wondered what question Cameron was hesitant to ask. Finally, she motioned to the truck.

"Come on. Let's get you out of here."

CHAPTER TWENTY-EIGHT

Andrea stood under the hot water, glad they were at an RV park and not in a parking lot somewhere, even if the park was just this side of sleazy. She didn't want to have to worry about running out of water. She turned the handle, changing to cool water as she leaned against the wall, eyes closed. She was having a hard time reconciling her feelings. When she'd lost her team in LA, she'd been so consumed with guilt, it ate at her and ate at her until she'd nearly lost the ability to function.

Of course she recognized the difference. This time, she hadn't just broken up with her lover. They hadn't walked blindly into an ambush today, her lover taking the lead. The closeness she felt with her team was something that developed over time. She and Mark had been best friends since their time in the academy. It was only natural she would be more affected by their deaths than Jack's and Carina's. She barely knew them. It would have been different if it were Eric instead of Jack. She and Eric had bonded in a very short time. She would feel his loss. But the others?

Was she in danger of being like Carina? Immune to death after a while?

She finally turned the water off, wringing out her wet hair before stepping out of the shower. As she toweled off, she caught sight of her reflection. The last week had been a rough one. She hadn't been eating properly, she hadn't been sleeping right. She'd lost weight, she knew. And she was exhausted. She wished she could just crawl in bed and stay there, letting Cameron wrap around her, keeping her safe. She saw the irony of it. That's what Cameron had been trying to do. Keep her safe. Andrea had fought her, saying she didn't need Cameron to look after her. But she did.

Well, all of that would have to wait. Reynolds was on his way. Cameron had showered earlier, and she and Rowan were holed up in the tiny office, playing with the computers. Lola, who had become quite fond of Rowan, was last seen curled in his lap. She sighed as she leaned on the counter, still perusing her reflection. She brushed at her hair, wondering when they could find the time for a trim. Cameron, too, was downright shaggy. Another tired sigh and she pulled on shorts and a loose-fitting T-shirt, slipped her feet into a pair of Cameron's flip-flops and went in search of something cool to drink.

She stood at the fridge, staring in. Bottled water didn't appeal to her. Neither did the carton of orange juice that had barely been touched. A cold bottle of beer, did, however. She wondered when Cameron had bought them.

"Find something you like?"

She smiled, holding up the bottle. "You want one?"

"I think I do." Cameron called to Rowan. "You want something to drink?"

"Just water."

Cameron winked at her. "Good. More for us." She cocked an eyebrow, the playfulness leaving her face. "You feeling better?"

Andrea nodded. "Some. Tired." She took a swallow of the cold beer, smiling. "Good stuff."

"Yep. I ordered the pizza, by the way."

Andrea laughed. "No doubt you did."

"And Reynolds called. He's on his way."

"Murdock?"

"Yeah. I talked to him briefly. Reynolds had already called him. Murdock and Jack served together in the first Gulf War," she said. "He had already notified Carina's family."

"Did you know any of them?"

"No. Just from what she told me." Cameron reached up, gently stroking her cheek. Andrea leaned in to the touch. "Carina and I weren't what you would call close, Andi. Never. I regret her death, of course. Jack's too. But I was nearly paralyzed with fear," she said, her eyes never leaving Andrea's. "At first, Rowan only knew that there were two survivors. He didn't know who. I... I was praying you were one of the two. I didn't care about the others," she admitted. "I wasn't thinking like an agent. I was thinking like your lover."

Andrea finally shoved off the counter, moving close to Cameron, their bodies barely touching. "Thank you. Because right then I needed you as my lover, not as my senior agent."

Cameron leaned closer, their lips touching in the briefest of kisses. They both sighed, then stepped away, putting some space between them. Only a thin wall separated them from Rowan, and Reynolds would be there any minute, as would their dinner.

"I wish we were alone," Andrea whispered. "I need some *us* time."

"Me too. When this is over, Murdock said we could head back to Sedona. He'll give us a week."

"That's great." Andrea couldn't resist one more touch, one more kiss. "Tonight, however, I need you to make love to me," she said against Cameron's mouth. "Can you handle that?"

Cameron nearly growled as she pulled Andrea tight against her, her tongue dancing against her lips. "I can handle that right now," she murmured.

Andrea moaned, her body reacting to the contact like it always did, her hips sliding intimately against Cameron's. For a few seconds, they let themselves go, their kisses hungry as hands roamed freely. Andrea wanted to rip her own clothes off and Cameron's too, and just let Cameron take her to a place that was pure bliss, away from the chaos of the day. But a gasp and an embarrassed cough brought them back to the present.

A red-faced Rowan stood staring at them, his eyes darting around the room, landing on anything but them.

"My...my water," he said. "I just—"

Cameron cleared her throat, moving away from Andrea again, her hands brushing quickly through her hair. "Sorry, kid. I kinda forgot," she said.

"Yeah, I see you were...distracted," he said.

Andrea laughed outright and it felt good. "I'm sorry, Rowan. It's my fault. I hope we didn't shock you."

He shook his head. "No. No, I...I had assumed you two were, well...you know."

"Yes, well, we are...*you know*," Andrea teased. She walked past him, playfully patting his arm. Oh, it felt good to lighten the mood, even if he did interrupt a major make-out session.

Cameron seemed at a loss for words as she wordlessly handed him a bottle of water. He took it without comment and hurried back to his computers.

Andrea followed him, leaning against the door, watching him as he scanned through what looked like gibberish on the screen.

"How long did you know them?"

He didn't seem surprised that she was there and he didn't turn around. "Carina and Jack? Only a couple of days longer than you. I was the last to join the team." He turned to her then, pausing to shove his glasses more securely on his nose. "Carina called me a nerdy geek, which is obviously redundant," he said with a shake of his head. "She didn't like me. Jack, well, he didn't say much. I can't think of a time where we had a real conversation."

"Yes, he was rather quiet," she said.

Rowan looked at her intently, as if he had more to say and she raised her eyebrows questioningly at him.

"Do you love her?"

Andrea nodded. "Yes. Very much."

"She was crying, you know," he said quietly. "When I told her I didn't know if you were...alive or not. I don't think I've ever heard such pain in someone's voice before." He met her eyes. "She must really love you."

"Yes. She does."

He turned back to the monitor. "I like her," he said. "She treats me like an adult."

"She relies on you," Andrea said. "And she trusts you. She must. She's letting you play in here," she said with a smile. "She doesn't even let *me* in here."

Conversation was sparse as the four of them shared pizza and beer. Well, Rowan shared pizza. He was still sipping on water and trying to keep Lola from stealing off of his plate. Cameron relaxed in her recliner, her eyes roaming over Andrea who sat cross-legged on the floor. Reynolds, although he'd changed from his suit, was still impeccably dressed in pressed pants and a crisp, starched shirt. She and Andrea were both in shorts and bare feet, Andrea having kicked off the borrowed flip-flops earlier.

"Murdock is sending in an explosives team," Reynolds said. "The C4 setup that we found was pretty rudimentary compared to this."

"They're going to look for a signature?"

He nodded. "They haven't even found the trigger yet."

"Well, simple or not, there's not a doubt in my mind that Baskin is behind the bomb," she said.

"He said he worked in the infirmary while in prison," Andrea said. "That's where he learned about...drugs and stuff." She glanced at Cameron. "Maybe he also learned about explosives there as well. Might see who his cell mate was," she suggested.

"But how does a guy fresh out of prison get his hands on C4?"

"Maybe he made some contacts while inside," Rowan said.

"Or maybe the safe house was wired all along. I mean, some

of the victims—the heads—were obviously more than a decade old. Maybe he's had the explosives all along," Reynolds said.

"That could be why it's considered *rudimentary*," she said. "He may have placed the C4 years ago when he first started killing. Maybe Andrea is right. Maybe he learned more about explosives while inside."

"Of course, all of this doesn't help us in trying to find him," Andrea said. "The so-called safe houses that he could use—we've hit them all, haven't we?"

Rowan nodded. "I haven't found anything else that we could link to him or the Burke family." He stood up. "I'll go play with the data some more."

After Rowan left, Reynolds turned to them, his voice low. "Is he okay?"

"This is probably his first experience with losing someone," Andrea said. "I talked to him about it earlier. I think maybe he's feeling a bit guilty." She turned to Cameron. "I can relate to that emotion."

"Why guilty?" Reynolds asked.

"Guilty because he's not emotionally affected by it. He didn't really know them. Carina never showed him anything other than disdain," she said. "Yet they were a part of his team."

"Maybe him being here so much while we've all been out has made him feel less a part of the team," Cameron said. "He might feel disconnected from everything."

"Everything but his computers," Reynolds said. He wiped his hands on a napkin, leaving his half-eaten piece of pizza on his plate. "Well, I know Carina didn't care for him and she didn't attempt to hide it. She was old school," he said. "You do the work out in the field, not on a computer."

Cameron laughed. "This whole rig is one giant computer. If I had only half of Rowan's smarts, I might be able to use it to its potential. If he wasn't here, I would be fumbling with the algorithms myself, taking time away from the field." She smiled at Andrea. "Or getting Jason to help me."

Reynolds stood. "It's late. I don't know about you two but I'm wiped out. It's been a terribly long, emotional day. I think we all could use some rest."

"Yes. I'll second that," Andrea said. "I'd like to be at the hospital early. I promised Eric."

He nodded. "Of course. How about I swing by here in the morning and drop Rowan off. We'll head to the hospital then. It's not that far from the police station."

Cameron motioned to the office. "I'll go get Rowan," she said.

Rowan was staring at the monitor when she walked in. He glanced at her, then back to the screen.

"Time to call it a night," she said.

"Yeah. Okay. I've got two programs running. Both with just a little different data. I hope you don't mind, but I emailed Jason earlier. He wrote me back with some suggestions." He smiled. "He's a genius. I still can't believe I'm getting to use these programs he wrote."

Cameron watched him as he fidgeted with his laptop. "You okay, kid?"

"Yes. I'm fine. Why?"

"It's just been a trying couple of days." She touched his shoulder. "I need to thank you. I...well, I went a little nuts earlier today, when I didn't know if...well, if Andrea—"

"I understand. I'm really glad she's okay."

"Yeah." She stepped back. "So we'll see you in the morning?"

"I'll be here." He pointed to the computers. "Don't touch them."

She held up her hands. "I wouldn't dream of it."

CHAPTER TWENTY-NINE

Andrea turned the small bedside lamp on, then pulled the covers back on the bed. Despite the long, stressful day, she was surprised at the early hour—half past nine. It felt like it should be nearing midnight, not ten. She stepped out of her shorts and tossed them aside, then pulled her T-shirt over her head, leaving her in nothing but her panties. She was about to slip out of them too when she felt Cameron's eyes on her. She turned, finding Cameron leaning in the doorway.

"You're so beautiful," Cameron said quietly.

Andrea stood there, exposed, the lamp casting a soft glow on her body. She waited as Cameron came to her, feeling her heart flutter in her chest. Cameron's gaze was smoky hot, leaving her eyes and drifting down to her breasts. A light touch and her nipples hardened immediately. She closed her eyes as Cameron lowered her head, her lips moving slowly across her skin, her tongue bathing a nipple, making it harden even more.

She moaned when Cameron's lips closed over her, suckling her nipple, her hands gliding lower, slipping inside her panties, kneading her flesh as she pulled Andrea closer to her. Her arms snaked around Cameron's shoulders as Cameron raised her head, her mouth finding her own, their quiet kiss turning passionate as Andrea let her tongue engage with Cameron's.

The need to breathe separated them and Andrea smiled as she tugged on Cameron's shirt. "Off."

Cameron obliged, lifting her arms as Andrea pulled it over her head. It was her turn to stare, her hand following her eyes, lightly brushing a fingertip across a nipple, hearing Cameron's quick intake of breath at her touch.

"I love you," she murmured, moving in for another kiss, her hands cupping both her breasts. The soft moan she heard fueled her desire and her hands moved across Cameron's body, her fingertips gently touching scars, the one marring her upper body still giving her chills.

She felt Cameron's hands pushing her panties down and she stood back, letting her remove them. She felt the dampness of her desire wetting her thighs and she had to stop herself from grabbing Cameron's hand and leading her there.

Cameron removed the rest of her clothing, leaving her as naked as Andrea. The sounds of their rapid breathing filled the room and Cameron guided her to the bed, urging her back.

Andrea parted her legs, welcoming Cameron between them, moaning as their bodies touched, skin on skin, both damp with perspiration and desire. Cameron kissed her slowly, their passion simmering, not boiling. Cameron's lips paused at her ear, her breath teasing her.

"I love you so much, Andi," Cameron murmured. "So much."

Andrea's head fell back, giving Cameron room. "Make love to me," she whispered. "I want you inside me tonight."

"Anything," Cameron said. "All night if you want."

Andrea smiled against her mouth. "If only I had the energy for all night."

"Then let's make it good." Cameron pulled away slightly. "Roll over."

She did, then groaned as Cameron covered her, her breasts pressing hard into her back, lips trailing kisses along the back of her neck. Andrea arched back, feeling Cameron thrust against her.

"Open your legs," Cameron whispered.

Andrea did, gasping as Cameron entered her from behind, her fingers sliding slowly through her wetness before going inside her.

"God, *yes*," she hissed as Cameron filled her.

Cameron rocked harder against her, each thrust shoving her fingers deeper inside. Andrea raised up, giving Cameron more room. Andrea was groaning, her face buried in the mattress, unable to contain her moans as Cameron slammed into her from behind. She felt Cameron's passion as it soaked her, the sound of wet skin slapping together with each stroke fueling her desire even more.

She tried to hold it, wanting to prolong her pleasure even longer, but Cameron pushed her over the edge with another deep stroke inside of her and Andrea bucked back against her, her orgasm taking the breath from her as she cried out. Cameron continued to pound against her, seeking her own release. It came quickly, her deep moan sending chills over Andrea's body as she climaxed, her weight resting on Andrea as they caught their breath.

"I love when you do that," Andrea murmured, her eyes still closed.

Cameron pulled her fingers out before rolling Andrea back over. "Maybe we should get a toy," she said before kissing her.

"A toy, huh? That could be fun."

"Yes. But I love being inside you."

Andrea pulled her close, their legs entwining. "You know what I love?" she teased, her tongue running along Cameron's lower lip.

"Tell me."

"I love my mouth on you, tasting you, making you come like that," she whispered. "I feel so close to you." She pushed

Cameron to her back, her mouth finding an erect nipple. "Let me love you like that."

Cameron moaned as she pushed Andrea down, urging her between her legs. "Yes," was all she said.

Andrea smiled against her breast, lifting her head enough to meet Cameron's eyes. They were filled with love and desire, want and need...for her. And at that moment, everything else faded away. There was nothing but the two of them, loving each other. And they had all night.

CHAPTER THIRTY

Cameron smiled at Andrea over her coffee cup, getting one in return, plus a wink. She laughed.

"Did you have a good time this morning?"

"Oh, yeah," Andrea said, nearly purring. "Last night, this morning. No complaints from me, sweetheart."

"Well good. I aim to please," she said, unable to keep the smile from her face.

Andrea got up, pausing to stretch out her back. "More coffee?"

"I'll take a mug along with us. Reynolds should be here any minute."

Andrea peered out the side window, nodding. "Right on time." She opened the door before they could knock, stepping aside to let them in. "Good morning, guys," she said.

Reynolds glanced between the two of them, his gaze finally landing on Cameron with a smirk. "I see you slept well."

"Yeah. Very well. You?"

"I've had better," he said.

Rowan pointed to the office. "Can I?"

"Of course. But wait a second. We need two new phones. For Andrea and Eric. I already called Murdock. I wrote down a purchase order number. Can you find a place in town?"

"Sure. I don't think it will be a problem."

"Great. Then do your thing."

"I'll call you and let you know where you can pick them up."

"What about what you were running last night?"

"I'll let you know as soon as I compile the results," he said as he hurried away.

"I'm sure he dreamed about those things last night," Cameron said. "You want some coffee, Reynolds?" she asked, shaking her head at his fancy black suit and crisp white shirt. A red tie today had him looking quite dapper.

He shook his head. "Got Starbucks."

"Okay then. Let's hit it," she said, nodding a thanks as Andrea filled a travel mug for her. "I guess after we spring Eric we should pay a visit to Chief Hudley and see if their lab found anything at the Burke house."

"Did you get a call from the county CSI yet?"

"No. But since we've got a forensics team and an explosives team here, I'm sure they'll go through them first. Murdock told me he would run interference."

"So we don't worry about anything?"

"Our job is to find Leonard Baskin, not worry about the details," she said. She leaned her head down the small hallway. "Rowan? We're out of here."

"Okay. I'll call when I have something."

"Lock up after us." Cameron smiled as Lola was slinking along the wall, heading into the office. "We'll need to watch so he doesn't steal our cat when he leaves," she said to Andrea.

"I'm sure Lola likes having company. We've left her alone so much on this case."

Once outside, Reynolds headed to the rental car while she eyed her truck. They had planned to all go together, but she thought now it might be better to have two vehicles.

"You know what? Why don't you go get Eric," she said to Andrea. "Reynolds and I can head over to see Chief Hudley, see if he has anything to share." She raised her eyebrows. "Okay with you?"

"Sure." Andrea turned to Reynolds. "You?"

"Yeah sure. I hate hospitals. And I'm sure he'd rather see your pretty face than mine."

Andrea laughed then deftly caught the keys Cameron tossed at her. "Meet back here later?" she asked.

Cameron nodded. "Be careful."

"You too."

Cameron crawled in beside Reynolds, feeling his eyes on her. "What?"

"You could have kissed her goodbye," he said. "I wouldn't have minded."

"Thanks, but we took care of that before you got here," she said with a laugh.

"I'm sure you did. You took care of a lot of things, by the look of it."

She laughed again. "You fishing for details?"

"I assure you, no." He pulled out of the RV park, going in the opposite direction of Andrea. "But it must be nice, having that closeness. How do you manage it?"

"You mean working together, living together, being able to separate it?"

"Yes. I would think that's a little too much togetherness."

She shrugged. "We love each other. When we're at home, at night, it's not about the job. We enjoy each other's company. It's hard to explain. Like now. We're working. We're partners now. Not lovers."

Reynolds looked away quickly, a light blush flushing his dark skin. She smiled but said nothing.

The lights in the hospital seemed inordinately bright, but the cool air was welcome after the oppressive heat from outside. One of the perks of the job—being able to flash her FBI credentials—granted her instant attention. She was led to Eric's room immediately.

"Still in the hospital gown? Aren't you the sexy one."

He quickly pulled the sheet over him, smiling. "You came."

"I told you I would." She pulled up a chair and scooted closer to him. "How's the head?"

He looked around suspiciously. "Don't tell anyone, but I still have a killer headache."

"You probably will for a few days." She took his hand, holding it lightly. "Ears?"

"Better."

"Really?" she asked skeptically.

"Well, some. Why?"

"You're talking really loud."

"Damn."

She brushed his hair away, revealing his neatly stitched wound. "When are they releasing you?"

"They're waiting on the doctor to come around. They won't even let me get dressed."

"I didn't even think to ask Reynolds to get you some clothes."

"Well I don't have any. Mine from yesterday were ruined."

"We'll find something for you. I'll take you by the hotel. Cameron and Reynolds went by Barstow PD to see if their lab turned up anything at the Burke residence," she said. She squeezed his hand briefly, then released him. "Did you call your parents or anything?"

"No, hell, I didn't want them to worry. They did enough of that when I was in Iraq." He leaned his head back. "I still can't believe what happened," he said. "It was so fast. I mean, if we had been just a few feet closer—"

"I know, sweetie. I don't want to think about it but it's all I *can* think about," she admitted. She didn't add that they had made love last night until she was too exhausted to keep her eyes opened. But still, it was the first thing on her mind this morning. That is, until Cameron's kisses had distracted her again.

"How is Reynolds? I didn't even get to talk to him. I thought maybe he'd come by last night..." he said, his voice drifting away.

"Reynolds was at the rig last night until about nine," she said. "I'm not sure how he is, really. He's acting okay, but Cameron said he and Jack had known each other for years. I'd like to say his death has affected him but I'm not sure I really understand," she said.

"Understand what?"

"The military life," she explained. "It's almost as if you are totally unaffected by it all."

He pulled his eyes away, staring at the ceiling. "We've all lost buddies in war, lost men we were close with. I guess in some ways you do get used to it. It's a part of this life. You don't ever take the time to grieve. You never know when there's a bullet—a bomb—with your name on it." He turned back to her. "Jack knew the risks. Carina too. It's almost like you're living on borrowed time as it is. You see a lot of shit when you're in Special Ops," he said. "You see a lot of shit, you do a lot of shit. After a while, nothing surprises you anymore. You stop *feeling*."

"You're still young enough to learn again," she said with a gentle smile. "Life is...life is precious. We should all enjoy it for what it is, not live each day in fear of dying. That's something Cameron has had to learn too," she said. "Mostly fear of *me* dying, but still."

He smiled. "I like you a lot, Andrea. I'm glad you have someone who loves you like that. Someone who you love equally as much." He sighed. "I will admit I'm jealous though."

She raised her eyebrows.

"Not like that," he said. "I'm jealous of the closeness you have with someone. At the end of the day, it would be nice to have that."

"Don't give up on finding it."

He nodded. "Maybe some day," he said wistfully. Then he sighed again. "God, how did we get off on that subject?"

She stood, then leaned over and kissed him lightly on the mouth, surprising him. "Let me go flash my badge around and see if I can rustle up a doctor."

"He's got a stick up his ass or something," Cameron said as she slammed the door behind her. Chief Hudley didn't know anything, didn't have anything for them, couldn't even offer a guess as to when lab results would be back. "That was a waste of an hour."

"It's a small department, Ross. They're all shook up over Burke," Reynolds said. "Cut him some slack."

"Slack? We're trying to find the goddamn bastard who did this," she said as she stormed out of the police station. "You'd think he'd bend over backward to help us."

"Maybe if you hadn't pissed him off by going over his head," he said.

"Maybe if he'd cooperated I wouldn't have had to go over his head. And it's not the fact that I'm FBI," she said. "It's because I'm a woman. I'm not stupid."

Reynolds laughed. "Little does he know you could kick his ass all over the place."

She glanced back at the door, shaking her head. "Well, we don't need him anyway. We've got Rowan," she said, following Reynolds to the car. She was about to call Andrea when she remembered Andrea's phone was damaged in the blast. She called Rowan instead.

"Sorry to interrupt, kid," she said, then paused. "Unless you have something?"

"Not yet."

"Okay. What about phones?"

"Oh. I forgot. Yes, you can pick them up. I'll send you the GPS location of the store."

"Good job. Thanks. I don't suppose you've heard from them," she said.

"No."

She got in beside Reynolds, adjusting the AC vents to hit her in the face. "Damn, how do people live out here," she murmured as she wiped the sweat from her brow.

"Where to?"

Within seconds Rowan had activated the GPS device on her phone, the bright red line indicating the route.

"How does he do this so fast?" She pointed up ahead. "Take a left up here on East Fredricks Street. We're going back to West Main."

"Rowan's good," Reynolds said as he followed her directions. "Although I believe he thinks he works for you and not me."

Cameron laughed. "Whatever gave you that idea?"

"I still don't like him hacking at will," he said. "It's not right. It's not *legal*."

"Get off your high horse, Reynolds. Why do you think Murdock assigned him?"

"I doubt it was to hack other law enforcement's systems, which I'm quite sure he's doing now to San Bernardino's lab."

"The quicker we get information, the better," she justified. No, Murdock hadn't given them carte blanche privileges, but she knew he'd back her if someone complained. Not that she expected Rowan to get caught snooping around. He was very good.

"Oh, my God. Will you quit complaining? You're worse than Cameron," Andrea said as she pulled into the hotel's parking lot.

"I'm in a hospital gown, for God's sake," he said, pulling it tightly around his legs.

"And I'm going to get you some clothes." She grinned. "You've got nice legs. You should show them off more often."

He glared at her. "I hate you."

She patted his leg. "You told me you loved me earlier."

"Yeah, well, I was having a weak moment."

She laughed as she got out. "That's because you were planning your escape and you needed my help." She leaned on the door, a smile still on her face. "So, just bring you some jeans or what? I'm guessing you want to go up for a shower," she said.

"Definitely. Just bring down some shorts and a T-shirt."

"Okay. Be right back."

She didn't anticipate having a problem getting a keycard and she didn't. The hotel staff knew the FBI had the string of five rooms on the third floor. She rode the elevator alone, her thoughts going to Cameron more often than not. Mentally, she was feeling much better today. Last night had been nearly magical and Cameron had loved her to the point of exhaustion. So despite having to function on only a few hours sleep, she felt sharp and alert today. More focused, at least. Like the others, she was trying to put yesterday's blast behind her. They'd lost two agents. Whether it was negligence or just bad luck, that was to be determined.

Eric's room was tidy and it was evident that no one had slept there last night. She rummaged through the drawers, finding a pair of running shorts and a plain white T-shirt. She ignored the underwear there, knowing he would be coming up for a shower anyway. His running shoes were in the closet and she grabbed them as well.

Out in the hallway, she glanced at the door to Carina's room, wondering if Reynolds had already packed her belongings, shipping them off to her family as if that would make a difference to them. Surprisingly, her mother's face flashed through her mind. Maybe it was time to call her, let her know where she was, how she was.

Then she shook her head. No. Her mother wouldn't want to know what she was doing. The last time they spoke, she seemed almost relieved that Andrea was in Sedona, away from the city and its crime. Their relationship would never get back to the way it was before her father was killed, but at least they had talked. Now, if she knew Andrea was with the FBI, doing these types of cases...well, that would probably sever their ties completely.

Back outside, the desert heat attacked quickly and she hurried to the truck, finding Eric anxiously waiting for her.

"Turn around," he said as he took the shorts from her.

"Trust me, you have nothing I'm interested in seeing," she said.

He grinned mischievously. "You never know. One look and I might steal you away."

"Don't think so, big guy."

He laughed. "*Big* being the operative word," he said as he lifted his hips to slip on the shorts.

She dutifully turned her head away as his hospital gown slipped open, causing him to laugh again.

"You're evil," she said.

"Oh, just having a little fun."

She watched as he tossed the gown aside, his chest hairless and well defined. He was a very handsome man. She couldn't believe some woman hadn't latched on to him yet.

"What?"

"Just admiring your physique."

"Told you so."

It was her turn to laugh. "Not like that. But it does make me wonder why you don't have women falling all over you."

"Who says I don't?"

She only smiled. "Come on, stud. Let's go in. You need a shower."

CHAPTER THIRTY-ONE

"I refuse to eat pizza again," Reynolds said. He glanced at Andrea. "How do you put up with her?"

"Hey," Cameron said. "I was just offering a quick solution to an early dinner. That bag of chips you fed me for lunch just didn't cut it."

"I could go for some Mexican food," Eric said.

"Chinese," Reynolds countered.

"Pizza," she said with a smirk. "Andi?"

Andrea laughed. "You're insane if you think I'm voting with you." She walked beside Eric, rubbing his back. "I'd vote with Reynolds because Chinese would be a quick take out, but I'll have to go with Eric on this one."

"How did I guess that?" Cameron said with a smile. "Your fondness for Mexican food nearly matches my love of pizza."

"Hardly. I can actually go a week without it. You, on the other hand, get very, very cranky if you don't get your pizza fix."

"That's because—"

"I got it!" Rowan said excitedly as he rushed into the room. "I know where he is."

They all stared at him, waiting. His hands were shaking as he tried to hold up his laptop.

"Slow down, Rowan," she said. "Take your time."

He visibly took several deep breaths, then grinned. "Jason is a genius," he said.

"Yes, you've mentioned that several times." She pointed at his laptop. "What do you have?"

"Well, you know I've already run every program with the hot spots—his grandparents' place, and the other property—and we got our hits. But now, there's no new data really. So I started a list of abandoned properties and included data like how long they'd been vacant, what structures were on the property, access to a major highway, that sort of thing." He took another deep breath. "Nothing stood out. They all registered about the same. Then Jason suggested—"

"Wait a minute," she said. "How often do you talk to him?"

Rowan's face turned red. "We email a couple...well, several times a day. He's very nice."

She raised her eyebrows.

"I'm not bothering him. I promise."

"Okay. Continue."

"Jason suggested I put in another variable. Distance between occupied dwellings."

"Meaning?" Reynolds asked.

"Meaning an abandoned building in town is less likely to be used since there would be occupied buildings in close proximity. Same as a vacant house might have a close neighbor. That would also be less likely to be used. In other words, I started looking for abandoned properties that were also isolated from occupied properties."

"And?"

"The abandoned water park," he said with a grin. "Eighty-nine percent."

"The water park," she stated skeptically. "I didn't get a good look at it, but didn't it have a fence around it? Everything locked up?"

"It's got a fence but it's not secure. Years ago, they used to have guard dogs patrolling it but not any longer. It's got a multitude of buildings, good for hiding," he said.

"But if there is a fence, secure or not, he stands the chance of getting cornered," Andrea said. "Would he take that chance?"

"Only if he's got an escape route," Reynolds said. "Like at the shack, he had the tunnel."

"That's where it's interesting," Rowan said, bringing his laptop closer for them to see. He had a satellite image up. "Here, behind the park, is a desert road. This," he said, pointing to a couple of smaller structures, "is private property, but there is no residence. Outbuildings only. This is Cherokee Road. If he's on a motorcycle or a dirt bike—like you suspect—then all he has to do is hop over this little hill here and he's on the road. Then he's got options. Swing around and head back to I-15 or go north farther into the desert."

She felt everyone looking at her. "It's worth checking out. It's not like we have a lot of options."

Reynolds stood. "We can be there in what? Twenty minutes?"

"No, no, no," Cameron said. "We wait for nightfall. We're not going to just show up there. We'd be sitting ducks. We know he's got Burke's gun and he knows how to use it, obviously." She motioned to the loveseat. "Sit. Let's go over our options."

"What kind of equipment do you have?" Eric asked.

"One pair of night vision goggles," she said. "And a new toy that we used in Utah. I've got a thermal infrared imaging camera. Not quite as high-tech as the military, but it should serve us well here. I have a couple of assault rifles but I'd like to think we could manage this without using the big guns."

"We could always do long range," Reynolds said quietly, his eyes questioning.

She shook her head, surprised at Reynolds's subtle suggestion. "I'm not a sniper any longer," she said. "Besides, we need to at least make this appear to be a police mission and not military."

"In looking at the images," Rowan said, "my suggestion would be to come in from the back on Cherokee Road. You won't have a vehicle that can cross the desert without a road, but the hike in wouldn't be very far."

"I don't want us with only one option. We'll go in with two teams, one from the front and one in the back," she said. "We'll have open communication again." She glanced at Rowan. "Right?"

"Yes. Not a problem."

"Eric? Are you up for it?"

"Got a little headache, nothing more."

He looked a little pale but she said nothing. They needed him to go. Hell, if she thought Rowan could pull it off, she'd put him out in the field too.

"What about the locals?" Andrea asked. "Do we want backup again?"

"No. We do it alone. This bastard is ours."

"I'll be prepared to call them on a moment's notice," Rowan said. "What would you like my role to be in this?"

Cameron knew he was speaking to her and not Reynolds, confirming Reynolds's assertion that Rowan thought *she* was his boss. She glanced at Reynolds and couldn't keep the smirk off her face.

"Get us a good satellite image of the place, the back road you want us to take, the escape routes. A layout of the buildings and names of each, if you can find that. Make sure Andrea's and Eric's new phones are up to speed so we can all link up again."

"Will do." He turned to leave, then stopped, glancing at Reynolds. "Anything else?"

Reynolds actually laughed. "Oh, let's don't pretend I have any say in this Rowan. You're doing fine."

Rowan nodded then fled back to the office, leaving the four of them alone again.

"So? Dinner?" Eric asked.

"I think Mexican food is out, buddy," Andrea said.

Cameron nodded. "No time for a sit-down meal. You two,"

she said, pointing at Reynolds and Eric, "need some proper clothes for this mission. No damn suit, Reynolds. And wear your vests. On your way back, why don't you pick up something."

"Chinese it is then," he said. "And I don't have military fatigues, so don't expect that."

"It would shock me if you did."

CHAPTER THIRTY-TWO

They sat around the small living area much like the night before, Chinese food cartons replacing the pizza boxes. Andrea and Cameron shared an amused smile as Reynolds looked completely uncomfortable in jeans, even though they were starched so heavily they probably would have stood up on their own. Eric looked every bit the military operative he used to be with his dark fatigues and boots, a weapon secured to each thigh. His bulletproof vest was military issued—a tactical vest, Cameron called it. Her own vest was run-of-the-mill police standard. She and Cameron were dressed much the same in jeans and dark T-shirts under their vests.

"I think Andi and I will take the back road," Cameron said. "No offense, Eric, but I don't think you need to be hiking across the desert. You and Reynolds can take the easy route from the road."

"My head feels fine," he said, "but I won't fight you for it. You guys have fun out there."

Andrea knew he was lying. She could see the pain in his eyes. No doubt Cameron and Reynolds saw it too, but he couldn't sit this one out. They needed him.

"We'll take the night vision goggles. We'll need them to cross the desert in the dark," Cameron said. "There's no moon so we should have good cover. You get the thermal imaging camera. Your job will be to locate him. We'll come in from the north," she said, pointing to the satellite image. "These are the offices. Here are the restrooms and the locker rooms. Around the side is the old arcade. There is no power or water," she said. "Unless, of course, he's got something rigged up."

Andrea watched Cameron as she spoke, watched her hands and fingers as they pointed and gestured. Her hands were strong, yet elegant. Sure hands. Andrea knew that from their touch. She brought her gaze to Cameron's face, loving the strength Cameron showed as she took them through the steps they would take in a few hours.

"And you're sure you don't want backup?" Reynolds asked.

"No. This has to be precise. It has to be quick and quiet. Less chance for a mishap if it's just us," Cameron said.

"Okay," Reynolds said with a nod. "I agree."

Cameron leaned back, her eyes moving from one to the other. "Questions? Concerns?"

"I'm good," Eric said.

Andrea nodded. "Me too."

"Great. We all stay in constant contact. And we stay in pairs. No unnecessary chances." She paused, glancing at Reynolds. "We shoot to kill."

Andrea expected a protest from him, but he gave no indication that he thought otherwise. Unlike Patrick Doe, where Cameron had wanted to bring him in alive, Leonard Baskin would not be given the same choice. A part of Andrea still clung to the police training she'd received. A police officer is only that. Not judge and jury as well. But she agreed wholeheartedly with Cameron. And not because she had looked into his eyes, not because she had been touched by him. Not just because it was personal. She suffered only briefly at his hands. She hadn't been exposed to the horrors the other women had endured, the horrors the Burke family had to bear before he ended their lives. Leonard Baskin didn't deserve to take another breath let alone the privilege of a judge and jury. Yes, it went against all of her training, all of the morals, laws and ethics she believed in. Maybe that's why Murdock's teams were made up of the ex-military elite. Morals, laws and ethics were something for everyday life, not something to be weighed and measured while staring into the eyes of a serial killer, your weapon pointing at his chest, ready to pull the trigger.

Rowan interrupted the quiet moment as their glances bounced off each other, looking for confirmation.

"I've got your phones all set," Rowan said, handing Andrea and Eric the new devices. "I have everything loaded so I can track you all by your phones. I'll have the satellite image up, and I'll be able to help you coordinate that way."

"Good job, Rowan," Cameron said, giving him a quick smile.

Andrea knew Cameron had developed a soft spot for him. He blushed slightly at the praise, then escaped back into the office. She glanced at Reynolds, seeing his amused expression as he expertly used chopsticks to grab a shrimp from his carton. She set her own food aside, her appetite vanishing with each tick of the clock.

She crouched behind Cameron, her eyes adjusting to the darkness. Cameron scanned the desert with her night vision goggles, trying to find the best way to hike into the complex. Above them, millions of stars twinkled in a cloudless, moonless sky. The sound of their boots on the rocks, the cool night air replacing the staggering heat of the day, the smell of the desert, all teasing her senses, making her long for the quiet nights in Sedona. She hadn't realized just how much she'd grown to love Sedona. It was where she fled to, where she healed, where she became a person again, where she met and fell in love with

Cameron. No matter where they traveled, she would always think of Sedona as the magical place it was. But the high desert there in Arizona was nothing like this barren land they crossed now.

"Should be smooth hiking," Cameron said quietly. She took off the goggles, her hands reaching for Andrea. "You okay?"

"Yes. Ready for it to be over with. I'm tired of this desert."

"I second that," Eric's voice sounded in her ear. She squeezed Cameron's hand. She'd already forgotten the microphone she had attached to her wrist.

"Quit eavesdropping," Cameron said. "We were having a moment."

"How's it look?" Reynolds asked.

"Clear. We're moving now."

"We're parked about a half-mile away," he said.

"Give us about ten minutes, then head out." Cameron pulled her up as she slipped on the goggles again. "Can you see well enough?" she asked.

"Yes. You'll guide me around thorns, right? I have no desire to tangle with an ocotillo cactus."

"Yeah? What about this barrel cactus thing here?"

Andrea followed Cameron's lead, sidestepping the round, low-growing cactus. "Thanks."

They moved quickly, heading south, neither speaking. The sky had an eerie glow to it as the lights of LA illuminated the horizon. Andrea's eyes adjusted to the near total darkness, able to follow Cameron now without keeping a steady grip on her shirt. They crested a small hill and Cameron stopped, squatting down again. Andrea did the same, her hand resting on Cameron's back.

"We have a visual on the buildings," Cameron said.

"We're just heading out," Reynolds said. "We're following the road, right up to the gate."

"Copy that. Don't move in until we're in position."

"We copy."

Cameron glanced at her. "Ready?"

Andrea smiled. "You look incredibly sexy in those goggles." Eric and Reynolds laughed in her ear. "Sorry," she whispered.

"Careful there, Agent Sullivan. Next time I may forget to warn you when we're near a cactus."

"*Special* Agent Ross, I'll try to control myself then."

Walking faster now, she could just make out the bulky shapes of the abandoned buildings. Cameron paused again as she scanned the area around them.

"Creosote bush to the right," she said, pointing. "Reynolds? What's your position?"

"We have a visual on the gate. Eric is setting up the camera now."

"Do you see a way in?"

"Yes. The fence has gaps in it. There is nothing secure about this place."

"Okay. We're about two hundred yards out." Cameron held the earpiece tighter. "Rowan? You copy?"

"Yes, I'm here."

"Can you bring up the satellite and our locations?" She turned. "Andi? Get your phone out."

"Sending it to you now," Rowan said.

"Got it," Andrea said, holding it up to Cameron.

Cameron took her goggles off, shoving them on top of her head. "Rowan, the building directly in front of us, that's the office, right?"

"Yes. The long, rectangular building to the left of that houses the old locker rooms. The arcade is closer to the main entrance."

Cameron studied the satellite image on Andrea's phone, then slipped her goggles back on, scanning the area again.

"There's a group of creosote bushes and something else. Can't quite make it out. Could be old trash barrels or something. Let's head for that. It'll give us cover. It looks like it's maybe a hundred feet from the back of the office."

"Lead the way," Andrea said, her hand again touching Cameron's back as she followed.

"We're slipping through the fence now," Reynolds said, his voice quiet. "A lot of palm trees around but not much for cover."

"Slow and easy," Cameron murmured.

"Holy shit," Eric said, his voice excited.

Cameron stopped, a hand held to her ear. "What is it?"

"Got something."

"On the camera?" Andrea asked.

"Yeah. Two images. One is moving. The other appears to be prone."

Andrea's hand squeezed tightly against Cameron's arm. "You think it's him? You think he's got another victim?"

"The one moving appears to be pacing. No movement from the other."

"Location?" Cameron asked.

"I think it's the old locker room," he said. "I've got a visual on the arcade and it's past that. Rowan?"

"Yes. Behind the arcade and to your right is the locker room. Cameron, the locker room is to your left."

"That's it then. We're going to try to get closer and get a better read on it."

His voice tinged with excitement and Andrea felt her own heart race as Cameron started to move again. Her pace had slowed, her steps sure, deliberate now.

"I'm sure I don't need to remind you to look for trip wires," Cameron said quietly.

"Copy," Reynolds whispered.

Cameron took Andrea's hand, guiding her behind her as she crouched low. Andrea squinted, seeing the trash barrels and creosote bushes. They hurried now, taking cover behind the bushes. Cameron again removed the goggles, her gaze landing on Andrea. She reached out and touched her face gently, reassuringly.

"We're at the trash barrels. We have cover," Cameron said.

"We're at the edge of the arcade," Eric said. "I'm picking you up now on the camera. He's on your side of the locker room."

"Rowan? Windows?" Cameron asked.

"I wasn't able to ascertain that in my research. But I would assume not. Locker rooms are for changing and showering. They are adjacent to the restrooms. I wouldn't think there would be windows."

"We can speculate but we can't assume," she said. "Let's proceed with caution and assume there *are* windows."

"Copy that," Reynolds said. "We're moving behind the arcade now."

"Remember, we don't know for sure if this is Baskin," Cameron said. "Be sure of your target."

"It better not be a couple of goddamn kids," Eric murmured. "They're about to get the shit scared out of them if it is."

"No. It's him," Andrea said. She couldn't have told them how she knew but she did. She could feel it in her gut. She felt her adrenaline kick in and suddenly it was hard to breathe. He had another victim. What was he doing to her? Had he drugged her? Was he waiting now? Waiting for her to wake up so he could play with her?

Cameron leaned closer, her lips to Andrea's ear, the words for her alone. "It's okay, Andi," she whispered. "We'll get the bastard this time."

Andrea nodded, giving Cameron's hand a squeeze. "I'm okay."

Still crouching down, Cameron moved quickly against the wall of the old office building, then motioned for Andrea to follow.

"Eric?"

"I'm picking you up fine. Hang on. He's moving."

Andrea's heart raced. Had he heard them? Did he have a trip wire to signal him? She followed Cameron's lead as they both grabbed their weapons. She took even, deep breaths, trying to still her racing heart.

CHAPTER THIRTY-THREE

"Eric? Talk to me," Cameron said. She impatiently pulled the goggles off her head, not needing them any longer. She could see the alarm on Andrea's face, and she took a moment to squeeze her hand.

"It's hard to tell where he is," Eric nearly whispered. "He could be at the door looking out. He could be on the outside of the room."

"We're still behind the office building," she said. "He's still on the south side?"

"Affirmative."

"We're moving to the back of his building." She glanced at Andrea, trepidation flowing off of her in waves. She wasn't concerned that Andrea couldn't do the job. She'd seen how Andrea reacted firsthand when Patrick Doe had been a threat.

Andrea hadn't hesitated in taking the shot. This time though, it was personal. Leonard Baskin had stripped her naked, had drugged her, had chained her to a bloody table. If Andrea was forced to take the shot again, would she do it? Would she feel she was doing it because it was her job to? Or would she feel like she was exacting revenge? She knew Andrea's character. If the latter were the case, she doubted Andrea's conscience would allow her to pull the trigger.

"I know what you're thinking," Andrea said, her eyes finding Cameron's.

"Do you now?"

"I'm fine. Don't worry about me. I can handle it."

Cameron nodded. "Okay. As long as you have my back."

"I'll always have your back."

"Okay. Stay here. Wait for my signal," she said. She peeked around the corner, seeing no movement, then ran quickly but silently between the two buildings, pressing herself close to the weathered bricks. "Eric?"

"Hang on. He's moving around again."

"Where is he?"

"He must know we're here. He's made us. Somehow he's made us."

"What the fuck? How?"

"He's running. He's outside the building. Running north."

"Which building?"

"I fucking can't tell," he said, his voice loud in her ear.

"Goddamn it." She whirled around, hearing the crunching of footsteps across the sand and rocks as he headed for the desert. "Andi?"

"I don't see anything."

Cameron fumbled for the night vision goggles, slipping them on her head. She took off, around the old office building, finally seeing him as he ran barely a hundred feet from them.

"Andrea, stay here," she said, not bothering to look back.

"The hell I will."

"Agent Sullivan, that's an order."

"Goddamn it, Cameron. No!"

"You can't see shit out here, you know it. Check on the victim."

She ran on, wondering where the hell the bastard thought he was going. If he had a motorcycle or dirt bike stashed, no doubt Reynolds and Eric had cut him off from it. It appeared he was simply fleeing into the desert.

At night. With no moon.

"Son of a bitch," she said. "He must have night vision goggles too," she said to anyone listening, her breath labored as she tried to keep up with him. "He's running too fast, too easily."

Andrea met Eric and Reynolds at the door to the locker rooms. She was furious with Cameron but she tempered it down, nodding when Eric held up two fingers, then one. Reynolds flipped on his flashlight, going in first, Eric behind him. The main room was empty except for a row of rusted lockers along one wall. Eric motioned to the hallway and proceeded slowly, his weapon out, his flashlight's beam bouncing off the walls.

They found her tied to one of the benches, naked. Rope this time, not chains. Andrea stared, her eyes locked on the needle lying beside her head. Is this how she appeared when Cameron and Reynolds had found her? Had they stared like this, wondering if she was dead or alive?

Reynolds moved first, placing a hand at her neck. He nodded quickly.

"Still alive."

Andrea let out her breath, finally rushing forward, trying to untie her. They all jumped, heads turning to the door when they heard gunfire. Two quick bursts, followed by a third.

Andrea dropped the rope, intending to go after Cameron when Reynolds stopped her.

"I'll go. You stay with the girl."

"No. I need to—"

"Agent Sullivan, you need to stay here." He looked at Eric. "Both of you stay here." Andrea was about to protest when Reynolds grabbed her arms, holding her still. "Eric has a goddamn concussion and that woman needs an ambulance. Call it in."

Another two shots were heard and he didn't wait for an answer. He spun on his heels, running quickly outside and back into the desert.

She ran her hands nervously through her hair, glancing at Eric, then at the woman. "Okay, so I don't have her back on this one."

"She told you to stay behind. She was right," Eric said.

"If it were the other way around, would she have stayed behind?"

"Of course not."

"Exactly. But she's so goddamn stubborn...and arrogant," she said. "We're supposed to stay together. Her words. Let's stay in pairs. Let's don't take unnecessary risks." Andrea went back to the woman, touching her face, seeing her shallow breathing. "And then what the hell does she do? She takes off by herself, at night, running after a crazy man." She paused. "Rowan? Ambulance?"

"Already called it in."

She jumped again when another two shots were heard. Her eyes flew to Eric's.

"She is highly trained," Eric said. "Jack said she was the best. You have to trust her."

"I trust her with my life. I'm just not so sure I trust her with *her* life."

"I'm kinda busy right now, Andi, but you do know I can still hear you, right?"

"Oh, shit," she murmured as Cameron's voice sounded in her ear.

"I can't see anything, Cameron. Where the hell are you?"

"There's an old rusted-out car," she said. "I've got him pinned."

"That's not helping me find you," Reynolds said.

She turned and adjusted the goggles, seeing Reynolds some fifty yards away.

"Christ, Reynolds, you're in plain view. He's got a—" But a bullet cut off her words and Reynolds dropped like a rock. "Reynolds?" she yelled. "Goddamn it! Reynolds?"

"I...I took it in the vest. I'm okay."

"Jesus, man." She let out a shaky breath. "Stay down, will you? I was trying to say he's got a rifle."

"No shit, Sherlock."

She chuckled. "Glad you haven't lost your sense of humor, Reynolds."

"I wasn't aware I had any."

"You two are pissing me off," Andrea said.

"Sorry," they said in unison.

"Want to tell us what's going on?"

"He took cover behind an old car," she said. "Unfortunately for him, I have a plain view of all sides. He has nowhere to run."

"And what are you using for cover?"

"A pile of rocks."

"And does he have a plain view of you?" Andrea asked.

"No. Hard to explain but there's a space between the rocks." She instinctively ducked when another shot was fired from the car. She fired back. "You got nowhere to go, Baskin," she yelled. His response was two quick bursts, one hitting the rock above her head, shattering fragments onto her face. "Bastard," she murmured.

"Do we have a plan?" Reynolds asked.

"I'm hoping one comes to me pretty quick," she said. "I'm thirsty as hell, I know that."

"So what? You're just winging it?"

"Pretty much."

"Agent Ross, you can't just make this up as you go. For God's sake—"

"*Special* Agent Ross," she corrected. "And I had a plan. It was to shoot the fucker in the locker room. That kinda fell through," she said. "You got any ideas?"

"Yeah. Have Rowan call in our location and send in a helicopter with a sniper."

"You want to trust a county SWAT team sniper with this guy? Besides, by the time they get a bird in the air, he'll be dead."

"How so?"

"Because I'm going in behind him."

"How do you plan to manage that?"

"You're going to distract him."

"God, I hate when she does this," Andrea said. "At least there aren't any cliffs around."

"Cliffs?"

"She tends to fall off them."

"I heard that," Cameron said. "How's the girl?"

"Still out."

"Rowan? You call for backup?" Cameron asked.

"No, ma'am. Not until you give the word."

"Ma'am? Haven't we been over that?"

"Sorry."

"Andi, if an ambulance has been dispatched, chances are a unit or two will follow. You and Eric keep them there. I don't want a bunch of deputies with guns running out here."

"Copy that," Eric said.

"Will you please not do anything stupid?" Andrea asked.

"Like you said, there aren't any cliffs around." Andrea heard the sound of gravel and assumed Cameron's wrist microphone was dragging along the desert floor. "Reynolds? Can you see anything?"

"I can see stars."

Andrea smiled at Cameron's heavy sigh.

"Yeah? Try lying on your stomach and looking this way."

Again, rustling sounds and Andrea found she was gripping Eric's arm tightly.

"I think I can make out the car. There's a dark spot to my left, about seventy-five yards or so."

"That's it," Cameron said. "I'm southeast of the car, only about twenty-five yards from him."

Andrea's eyes widened. *Twenty-five yards?* "She's an idiot," she whispered to Eric.

"I can't make out anything that looks like rocks," Reynolds said. "Everything is just dark."

Cameron sighed again. "When we get out of this, would someone remind me to buy another set of goggles? This is fucking ridiculous to be blind out here. Baskin has a pair of goggles, Reynolds. Why the hell don't you?"

"Is now the time to be discussing this?"

"This isn't really a discussion. I'm just pointing out the obvious."

"Is she always like this?" Eric asked.

Andrea nodded. "Pretty much, yeah."

"Okay, here's the plan," she said.

"Great. You have one. That's progress," Reynolds said.

"It involves you getting shot at."

"Of course it does."

"I'm going to fire four rounds at him. When he starts to return fire, you get up and run to your left—west—and start firing. You'll need to do a fast tuck and roll. There's enough of an incline there that he won't have a good angle on you. When he returns your fire, I'm going up around him from the back."

"You'll be out in the open."

"Yes. But hopefully he'll think I'm still behind the rocks. You have to keep him occupied."

"I'm not crazy about this plan," he said.

"It's all I got." She put a new clip in her gun and slammed it in. "You ready?"

There was only a slight pause. "Yeah. Go."

"God, I hope this works," she murmured before raising her hand above the rocks and firing four quick shots at the car. Baskin returned her fire as expected.

Within seconds, Reynolds was shooting. She watched as he ran west then when Baskin took aim at Reynolds, she sprinted away from the cover of the rock pile, her eyes glued to the car and Baskin. It seemed to unfold in slow motion—Reynolds shooting while he ran before falling from her view, Baskin taking aim at Reynolds then firing haphazardly at the rock pile again, she dodging a barrel cactus and a small creosote bush while she circled behind him.

She could see him crouched low against the driver's side door but she didn't have a clean shot. Her chest heaved from her sprint and her breath sounded loud in her ears. She slowly took her flashlight out, intending to use it to blind him, anything to give her a few more seconds. As if sensing her presence, he tilted his head, listening. Then he jerked around, a handgun replacing the rifle she expected.

She shot once, doing her own tuck and roll as he returned fire, feeling the whir of the bullet as it passed close to her head. The flashlight fell uselessly from her grip as she landed on the desert floor. Blindly, she fired again, four, five quick bursts, her shots ricocheting off the metal with loud clanks before one finally found her target.

He fell face down, the gun still clutched in his hand, his fingers loosening and tightening reflexively. She got up, her eyes trained on him, gun aimed at his head.

"Reynolds? You okay?"

"Yeah. You?"

"I think so."

"Baskin?"

"He's down. I'm moving in."

Andrea was afraid Eric would have a bruise on his arm where she'd been clutching him for the last several minutes. She sighed with relief at the sound of Cameron's voice, finally releasing her hold on him.

"I'm sorry."

"No problem. We need to go show them the way."

"Huh?"

"The ambulance."

Only then did she hear the wail of sirens, her focus had been solely on Cameron. She nodded. "You go. I'll stay with her."

The woman was still out and they had not tried to wake her. They'd found her clothes in a bag and had debated whether to cover her or not. They finally decided evidence wouldn't be needed and they'd covered her the best they could.

Eric was just leading the EMTs in when more gunfire was heard. They both instinctively touched their earbuds, their eyes flying together.

"What the hell?"

Andrea took off in a fast run, Eric on her heels.

She kicked the gun from his hand, then nudged him. When there was no movement, she almost let her guard down. Almost. But Patrick Doe's face came to mind, the knife he'd hidden from her. So she took a step back, adjusting the goggles as she looked for Reynolds. She felt sweat trickling down her face and she raised her hand to wipe it away. In that instant, he rolled over, a bright flashlight flooding her goggles, rendering her blind.

She ripped at the goggles, her eyes feeling like they were on fire. She heard him scrambling, knew he was looking for the gun she'd kicked away. She fired—once, twice, a third time.

"Goddamn it. Reynolds?" she yelled. "I need backup."

She hit the ground, rolling away, not knowing where she was...or more importantly, where he was. As shots rang out around her, she curled into a ball, covering herself, blinking feverishly, trying to clear her vision.

"Cameron? Where are you?"

"Reynolds?"

"I'm here."

She squinted in the darkness, her vision finally clearing. "Where is he?" She shielded her eyes as he flashed his light around them.

"He's not here." Reynolds bent down. "Blood. Not much."

"Goddamn bastard had a vest on. Burke's vest." She followed his light, a few blood drops splattered on the sand, farther apart now. "He's running," she said, pointing to a smeared footprint. She looked up, following the direction of the footprint. "He's heading back to the water park." She looked at her wristband, gritty with sand. She tapped it, not getting any feedback in her ear. "Mine's dead. Find out where they are."

"Eric? Andrea? You copy?"

Cameron listened, hearing nothing. Then, finally, the sound of heavy breathing. Her eyes met Reynolds's, recognition dawning on them both. "Son of a bitch," she murmured, turning and running back toward the water park.

CHAPTER THIRTY-FOUR

It happened so fast. One minute they were running, being swallowed by the darkness, Eric passing her with his long strides. The next—Eric lay sprawled on the ground, the blow to the head knocking him unconscious. She instinctively grabbed her gun but it was too late. Leonard Baskin grabbed her from behind, knocking the gun from her grip, a dirty hand covering her mouth, silencing her scream.

"I told you I was going to fuck you, remember? Fuck you until you bleed," he whispered, his voice thick, uneven.

She struggled against him, kicking his legs, his shin, but he lifted her off the ground and slammed her down hard. She landed next to Eric, her vision swimming as she tried to clear her head. Focus...*focus*, her mind screamed at her. Blindly, she reached for Eric, trying to find his gun. She found his combat knife instead, grabbing it only seconds before she was jerked up again, face to face with Baskin, his foul breath heavy, a calloused hand squeezing painfully against her neck, cutting off her oxygen.

She blinked several times, trying to draw breath...trying to find the strength to finish this. She tightened her grip on the knife, bringing it up low, under the vest she knew he wore. With one quick burst, she sliced through him, his hands loosening on her throat immediately. Sucking down greats gulps of air, she pulled the knife out, only to plunge it in again, harder. She felt his blood on her hands, the warm liquid flowing freely from his gut.

She pushed him away, enough light for her to see disbelief in his eyes.

"You bitch," he gasped. "How dare you?" He coughed, the sound garbled. "How...how dare you?"

He stumbled forward, taking one last lunge at her. Then a sound pierced the night—gunfire. He was knocked sideways from the shot, his head nearly exploding from the direct hit. Andrea fell backwards to the ground, landing again next to Eric, her eyes searching the darkness, seeing two shadows moving toward her.

"Andi?"

She squeezed her eyes, letting out a relieved breath. "Took you long enough," she said.

"Had a little equipment malfunction," Cameron said, dangling her night vision goggles from her fingers. She squatted down beside her. "Are you injured?"

"No. But Eric took a blow to the head," she said, reaching for him now. She felt the wet stickiness of blood on his face. "Flashlight?"

Reynolds shone his light on Eric, his previously stitched wound open again and bleeding freely. His pulse was strong, his breathing even.

"Knocked out cold," Cameron murmured.

Reynolds held his wrist to his mouth. "Rowan? You copy?"

"Yes. Your communication has been spotty. Is everyone okay?"

"Cameron's mic bit the dust. It didn't work out exactly as planned," he said, his glance landing on Cameron. "But the end result is the same. Call it in, Rowan. Leonard Baskin is dead."

CHAPTER THIRTY-FIVE

"I could sleep another hour or three," Andrea said as she stretched under the covers, her hands coming to rest on Cameron's stomach.

Cameron turned, faced her and twined their legs together as she pulled Andrea closer. "I'm just ready to get the hell out of here," she said. "I want to see some trees. Something green. I want some cool air, not this damn desert heat."

"Will you settle for junipers and cottonwood trees around Sedona?"

"Yes. At least it'll be cooler there."

Andrea leaned closer and kissed her. "Murdock is really giving us a week?"

"At least a week, maybe more. Depends on what comes up."

"Let's hope our next case does not involve a serial killer. They suck."

Cameron brushed her fingertips across Andrea's nipple, watching in fascination as it hardened. She let her hand drift higher, lightly touching the bruising around her neck, feeling angry all over again that that monster had his hands on Andrea like that.

"Don't," Andrea murmured. "I'm fine."

Cameron pulled her eyes from the bruising, finding Andrea's instead. "I realize that no matter how hard I try, I can't always protect you," she said in a near whisper. "I also realize that I don't always have to. You're strong. You're smart. You can take care of yourself," she admitted.

"You say that as if it's a bad thing," Andrea said.

"It's because I *want* to protect you. I want to be the strong one."

"Are you afraid I won't need you then?" Andrea guessed. "That I won't need you as much?"

Cameron sighed. "I was always so...so empty," she said. "I always felt that way. Even when I was younger, it was like something was missing, something I couldn't put my finger on. When I met Laurie, she was so full of life, so happy, I thought I'd found it." She rolled to her back, staring at the ceiling, letting in memories of the woman she'd loved so long ago. "I know now that I hadn't. She was a pleasant distraction from my life. I loved her." Cameron turned to Andrea. "But it wasn't like this. She didn't completely fill that empty spot. You do." She reached over, tracing Andrea's lips lightly. "I need you. And it scares me sometimes to think that you don't need me like that."

"Sweetheart, I *do* need you like that. You equate it to feeling empty. For me, it was more like I was drifting, never finding a place to land, never feeling that pull from someone." Andrea moved closer, her lips brushing against Cameron's mouth. "*You* pulled me, Cameron. You are the one who grabbed my heart and I let you take it and run. I need you for so many things, not just emotionally and physically. I need your presence—I need to see you, to be near you, to touch you. I need you as much as I need air to breathe." She smiled slightly, hers eyes locking with Cameron's. "And sometimes I need you to shoot bad guys."

They stood in the hotel lobby, the five of them sharing glances and smiles. It had been a hell of a case and they'd grown close in a short period of time. Eric sported a white bandage on his head, his wound stitched for the second time. The rock Baskin had hit him with had nearly cracked his skull.

Cameron smiled as Andrea touched his cheek lovingly, then stared in shock as Andrea kissed him full on the mouth.

"Excuse me?" she said with raised eyebrows. "Something I should know?"

"Oh, hush," Andrea said as she pulled Eric into a hug. "You," she said to him, "take care of yourself. I won't be around to watch your back."

"Maybe I should say the same to you." He pointed at his head. "I seem to take the brunt of it."

"Yes. I like it that way."

Cameron turned to Rowan, squeezing his shoulder. "If I had more room in the rig, I'd steal you away from Reynolds. You did a great job. We couldn't have done this without you."

He blushed freely and shoved his glasses up higher on his nose. "Thank you. I enjoyed working with you. Thanks for letting me play with your computers."

"You're welcome. And maybe the next time I get stuck on something, I'll call you instead of Jason." Her phone buzzed and she glanced at it, grinning. "Speaking of," she said. "I'm pretty sure this is for you." She handed him the phone which he stared at like it was a foreign object.

"Jason? For me? *The* Jason?"

"Take the damn phone," she said, watching as he turned away in embarrassment, the phone held tightly to his ear.

"Yes. I'm Rowan," he said as he walked farther away from them. "Oh...*wow*."

"I think he has a crush," she said.

"I thought he was straight," Eric said.

"So is Jason."

"Ah," he said. "It's a computer thing."

"Well," Reynolds said with a sigh. "No rest for the weary."

"Where are you off to?" Andrea asked.

"Portland. There's been a kidnapping that's gotten ugly."

"Just the three of you?" Cameron asked.

He nodded. "Gonna keep the team small, I think. For a while."

Cameron touched his arm. "I'm sorry about Jack and Carina," she said. "It's tough."

"Yeah. But it's something we face every day with this job. We all know that."

Cameron took a step away from him before she did something stupid, like hugged him. "Well, I guess this is it. You guys—" She frowned, finally looking them over. "What the hell, Reynolds? You're in jeans? Real jeans? Not even super starched?" She laughed. "You loosening up your rules?"

He smiled. "You were right, Agent Ross. We're not typical FBI agents, with our suits and ties and expensive shoes. This case taught me that. *You* taught me that. Sometimes you have to get down and dirty. Sometimes you have to break the rules."

She finally gave in, giving him a quick but tight hug. "*Special* Agent Ross," she corrected.

"Of course."

He turned to Andrea who did not hesitate in giving him a hug, hers much longer than Cameron's.

"Thank you for everything, Reynolds. It was a pleasure working with you," Andrea said. "I hope we meet again."

"Thank you. I wish you the best of luck." He glanced at Cameron and smiled. "You'll need it."

Cameron laughed with the others, and then stood by Andrea as they left. Rowan, after returning her phone, gave Andrea a hug but held his hand out to Cameron. She took it, squeezing tightly, then pulled him in close, causing the young man to blush again before hurrying after the others.

"I'm going to miss them," Andrea said, almost wistfully.

"Surprisingly, I am too," she said. She nudged Andrea's shoulder. "Come on. Let's get the hell out of here."

Andrea linked their arms together as they headed out into the desert heat. The rig was parked illegally on the curb, the generator running, keeping it cool. Her truck was hitched behind it, all ready to hit the road. She glanced up into the endless blue sky, not a single cloud in sight. As a drop of sweat trickled down her face she wiped it away with a smile.

"Can't say I'm going to miss this place."

"Me either. Come on, Sedona is calling."

Her phone buzzed again and she stood at the door to the rig, grabbing it from her pocket as Andrea went in ahead of her. *Murdock*. She sighed, then answered after letting out a deep breath.

"This better be good."

"Cameron? Say, just how set are you on this Sedona trip?"

"Are you kidding me? Whatever it is, no."

"It won't take long, I promise. Just a quick trip into Nevada."

"Nevada? Do you know how hot it is in Nevada?"

**Publications from
Bella Books, Inc.
Women. Books. Even Better Together.
P.O. Box 10543
Tallahassee, FL 32302
Phone: 800-729-4992
www.bellabooks.com**

CALM BEFORE THE STORM by Peggy J. Herring. Colonel Marcel Robicheaux doesn't tell and so far no one official has asked, but the amorous pursuit by Jordan McGowen has her worried for both her career and her honor.
978-0-9677753-1-9

THE WILD ONE by Lyn Denison. Rachel Weston is busy keeping home and head together after the death of her husband. Her kids need her and what she doesn't need is the confusion that Quinn Farrelly creates in her body and heart.
978-0-9677753-4-0

LESSONS IN MURDER by Claire McNab. There's a corpse in the school with a neat hole in the head and a Black & Decker drill alongside. Which teacher should Inspector Carol Ashton suspect? Unfortunately, the alluring Sybil Quade is at the top of the list. First in this highly lauded series.
978-1-931513-65-4

WHEN AN ECHO RETURNS by Linda Kay Silva. The bayou where Echo Branson found her sanity has been swept clean by a hurricane—or at least they thought. Then an evil washed up by the storm comes looking for them all, one-by-one. Second in series.
978-1-59493-225-0

DEADLY INTERSECTIONS by Ann Roberts. Everyone is lying, including her own father and her girlfriend. Leaving matters to the professionals is supposed to be easier! Third in series with *Paid In Full* and *White Offerings*.
978-1-59493-224-3

SUBSTITUTE FOR LOVE by Karin Kallmaker. No substitutes, ever again! But then Holly's heart, body and soul are captured by Reyna... Reyna with no last name and a secret life that hides a terrible bargain, one written in family blood.
978-1-931513-62-3

MAKING UP FOR LOST TIME by Karin Kallmaker. Take one Next Home Network Star and add one Little White Lie to equal mayhem in little Mendocino and a recipe for sizzling romance. This lighthearted, steamy story is a feast for the senses in a kitchen that is way too hot.
978-1-931513-61-6

2ND FIDDLE by Kate Calloway. Cassidy James's first case left her with a broken heart. At least this new case is fighting the good fight, and she can throw all her passion and energy into it.
978-1-59493-200-7

HUNTING THE WITCH by Ellen Hart. The woman she loves — used to love — offers her help, and Jane Lawless finds it hard to say no. She needs TLC for recent injuries and who better than a doctor? But Julia's jittery demeanor awakens Jane's curiosity. And Jane has never been able to resist a mystery. #9 in series and Lammy-winner.
978-1-59493-206-9

FAÇADES by Alex Marcoux. Everything Anastasia ever wanted — she has it. Sidney is the woman who helped her get it. But keeping it will require a price — the unnamed passion that simmers between them.
978-1-59493-239-7

ELENA UNDONE by Nicole Conn. The risks. The passion. The devastating choices. The ultimate rewards. Nicole Conn rocked the lesbian cinema world with *Claire of the Moon* and has rocked it again with *Elena Undone*. This is the book that tells it all...
978-1-59493-254-0

WHISPERS IN THE WIND by Frankie J. Jones. It began as a camping trip, then a simple hike. Dixon Hayes and Elizabeth Colter uncover an intriguing cave on their hike, changing their world, perhaps irrevocably.
978-1-59493-037-9

WEDDING BELL BLUES by Julia Watts. She'll do anything to save what's left of her family. Anything. It didn't seem like a bad plan...at first. Hailed by readers as Lammy-winner Julia Watts' funniest novel.
978-1-59493-199-4

WILDFIRE by Lynn James. From the moment botanist Devon McKinney meets ranger Elaine Thomas the chemistry is undeniable. Sharing—and protecting—a mountain for the length of their short assignments leads to unexpected passion in this sizzling romance by newcomer Lynn James.
978-1-59493-191-8

LEAVING L.A. by Kate Christie. Eleanor Chapin is on the way to the rest of her life when Tessa Flanagan offers her a lucrative summer job caring for Tessa's daughter Laya. It's only temporary and everyone expects Eleanor to be leaving L.A...
978-1-59493-221-2

SOMETHING TO BELIEVE by Robbi McCoy. When Lauren and Cassie meet on a once-in-a-lifetime river journey through China their feelings are innocent...at first. Ten years later, nothing—and everything—has changed. From Golden Crown winner Robbi McCoy.
978-1-59493-214-4

DEVIL'S ROCK by Gerri Hill. Deputy Andrea Sullivan and Agent Cameron Ross vow to bring a killer to justice. The killer has other plans. Gerri Hill pens another intriguing blend of mystery and romance in this page-turning thriller.
978-1-59493-218-2

SHADOW POINT by Amy Briant. Madison McPeake has just been not-quite fired, told her brother is dead and discovered she has to pick up a five-year old niece she's never met. After she makes it to Shadow Point it seems like someone—or something—doesn't want her to leave. Romance sizzles in this ghost story from Amy Briant.
978-1-59493-216-8

JUKEBOX by Gina Daggett. Debutantes in love. With each other. Two young women chafe at the constraints of parents and society with a friendship that could be more, if they can break free. Gina Daggett is best known as "Lipstick" of the columnist duo Lipstick & Dipstick.
978-1-59493-212-0

BLIND BET by Tracey Richardson. The stakes are high when Ellen Turcotte and Courtney Langford meet at the blackjack tables. Lady Luck has been smiling on Courtney but Ellen is a wild card she may not be able to handle.
978-1-59493-211-3